tHat's WHat brotHers do...

Redux

by

Derekica Snake

Self-Published by Derekica Snake

Cover art by kiha-ki.deviant.com
ISBN: 978-0-9811802-8-1

Acknowledgements

Grateful thanks are extended to my fans, those I call the Loyal and True, for sticking with me and being patient through the trials of the past few years. I was motivated to write the kind of books I wanted to read and I have. I haven't found a publisher that fits but the Loyal and True showed me that there are other likeminded individuals out there. If there are readers who want "Dark Romance" I will keep on working to keep us entertained.
I hope you enjoy this revisit.

Table of Contents

Chapter One: Six Months to Go

Hmmm… seven hundred and fifty-seven holes in the piece of acoustical tile just above my head. I was about to start counting another tile when the door to my assigned chamber opened: my eyes slid almost closed against the sudden difference in illumination to see the outline of a figure standing there. I had hoped that I was done for the night. It seemed that Wilber was bent on getting a good return on his investment at this event. So far, the clients who had been visiting were higher end and no doubt wanted exceptional service for their given favors. This is a business after all.

The spa quality robe covered client hesitated. "He looks rather used."

It was hard to block out the man's censure but I'd been doing this for years and could at least fake my performance. However, the simple timber of the answering voice could shred that façade all to hell. My heart clenched as another man stepped into my room.

Wilber dropped a hand on the Robe's shoulder. "Despite appearances, Brant has proven quiet adept at this line of work. I'll have you know that his initial training was cut short by seven weeks and after working a mere six months in the salons, he was promoted to the rank of 'Exclusivity'."

My eyes closed as I listened to Wilber extol my virtue… or lack thereof.

"He's that good?" The client's voice trembled with anticipation.

This meant that this was going to be fast and more than likely nothing more than stinging pain.

Once again that low voice wound its way into my chest. "Only you can make that decision, but I will have you know that Brant does have an outstanding clientele list and is fully booked at private events. It is only due to age and health concerns of a certain gentleman that a spot has opened up in Brant's schedule."

Wilber was never that free with his praise so this little enticement told me that this man was an important client that needed to be taken care of. I would have to endure and give an Oscar winning performance that would leave the client salivating to get at me another time for an exorbitant fee.

One more bed bounce to clearing up the family debt and gaining my freedom.

Pulling on my artfully maintained client face, I opened my eyes I gave him a smile even though I was physically exhausted and wanted nothing more than to take a shower and fall asleep. Robe regarded me with the eyes of a collector. It wasn't an expression that I encountered often but it sent a chill through me. My tender nipples that had taken enough abuse this evening hardened into nubs. Robe took it as a willingness to be fucked. His hand shook as he reached out, gathered up a handful of my hair then leaned in and inhaled deeply.

"You smell absolutely divine, my little dumpling."

For some reason, when Wilber offers me wrapped in black leather straps people can't wait to get into my ass. People, ha! *Men* can't wait to be in me.

Robe's eyes that gobbled me up as if I were a piece of candy in front of a fat kid at Halloween. Wilber had told me that the eyes were the windows to the soul and if I couldn't hide my misery from the client, then I was better offer burying my face into the mattress or closing them completely. I shut my eyes. The pads of his fingers were soft and his nails were manicured to a fault as he rubbed the sensitive skin around my budded nipple. He twisted. I gasped at the sensation. Unfortunately, the client was right; he would be number seven tonight which was more than beyond my norm and this reaction as more the lingering effect of the previous man who had a nipple fetish. Robe's soft hand released at my moan but he didn't pull away.

This was going to be hard and fast.

His palm flattened on my chest then slowly caressed its way down to my sweat slicked stomach. I could feel the trembling in his fingers as he stroked my pubic hair. I was startled as he combed my groin.

Apparently, he had never bought a whore before…or at least a male one.

"I can do whatever I want?" The client licked the bottom lip that stuck out from a carefully groomed moustache.

"Within reason. Brant is rated Exclusive but not Private. There can be no scars, burns, tattoos or piercings. If blood is drawn, no matter if it is accidental, membership and protection will be immediately withdrawn."

Robe's voice was filled with disbelief. "The company would forfeit our mutually beneficial enterprise for a piece of ass?"

Wilber continued in his businesslike tone. "Brant is paying off debt with the only currency he has and when it is closed on the books, he will be just an ordinary citizen free to go his own way."

The client's voice grew angry. "Are you telling me, he'll walk out of here someday knowing names and faces?"

Wilber tsked the man.

That was not the way to get on his good side.

"Brant does more than entertain clients on his backside for us. This type of party is lucrative and you can rest assured, Mr. M. the Organization values the services you provide. I can blindfold him if that is what you wish."

"I think that would be best."

The client backed off quickly as Wilber approached the bed. The whole of the mattress sank as he sat the edge of it. One hand in the strap of the leather harness pulled me forward as he moved behind me then urged me back against him. I was still dirty from the last client. When I tried to move away from keep my filth from staining his suit, a massive hand, thick, scarred and calloused closed around my neck.

He was touching me.

That voice whispered in my ear. "I've told Mr. M that you were obedient. Are you trying to make me out to be a liar, Brant?" Wilber's words sapped what little will I had left.

9

"I don't want to get your clothes dirty." My voice was rough from the earlier workouts.

"Clothes are clothes. They are made to get dirty." The rough hand left my neck then swept my hair back over my head. A soft black leather blindfold was held over my eyes and fingers lingered in my sweat slicked hair as it was buckled into place. The outline of Wilber's erection pressed up against my spine.

"Headquarters needs to keep this one satisfied, so do your best."

He didn't need to say that. I would because that was what was expected of me. It would make Wilber proud of me and then he would give me what I wanted. I'd done this enough times that I could make the client believe that he was the best lover I had ever known because when I did, they paid more to get back into me, and when they paid more, my family's debt lessened, which meant one less client to service in the long run.

Wilber pulled my hair at the nape of my neck, forcing my face up towards the ceiling. "Can you see anything?"

"No, Wilber."

"Are you lying to me?"

"No, Wilber."

There was a slight brush of the back of a finger against my skin on my neck then the bed shifted as he moved away. The massive warm hands were replaced with soft cool ones. Those buttery soft fingertips traced the seam of my lips. I opened my mouth and let my tongue lap at them. The taste of some sort of strong gourmet cheese clung to his flesh.

Didn't he even wash his hands before coming in here?

Those cheese tainted hands lingered at my mouth for a moment before running down my throat. His finger paused and stroked the hollow at the base of my neck then moved towards my right nipple.

"You are more beautiful that most women I've fucked." Robe was panting.

I gasped as he rolled my abused nipple between his fingers.

"That sounds sexy. Is this side just as sensitive?"

It was more a cry of pain but I tried to cover it by pushing my chest up towards him, which was difficult because the leather straps around my upper arms and the forearm binders restricted most movement. It must have looked enticing because his mouth started suckling me as if he were going to get milk.

"Your skin is so pale...you bruise so easily." The client continued with his running commentary so I only had to writhe beneath him and moan.

He liked that, I could tell by the sudden thrust of a hard cock against my own. The heat of his body intensified as he stretched his torso against me. Warm sloppy wet kisses slipped back up my neck pausing near my ear.

Warm breath made my ear flare with heat. "God has not granted me a face that attracts the ladies but he has made up that with this." The feel of the client's huge cock as he rubbed against my groin sent a shiver of dread through me. "I am average in length but my width is more than most women can handle. I am always the anchor man because everything has to be loosened and well lubricated. I dislike giving my partners pain."

I twitched in surprise as cold lube was poured on my groin until it began to slide down between my ass cheeks. Soft pads of his fingers pushed the lube inside me. Those fingers reached deep but not deep enough to hit that spot. Quickly the client twined his fingers then coned them, stretching my asshole wider. I grunted as the fingers worked me.

"Relax my dark beauty. It's better this way, that you can't see it. You'd just get scared and tighten up."

Wilber had told me to make the effort but...the heat of the cock head as it prodded at my ass was as if it were a branding iron. There was no way it was going in. My heart was starting to throb of a drum.

It wasn't going to fit!

Soft hands seemed to know it. He whispered as his cock shifted and slid down the crack of my ass. "Think of who you want...call out his name. I don't want you to just endure...Go ahead."

"…Wilber…" It was more of a gasp as the client tried to push forward again.

"I think he's calling for you. I don't mind if you want to take his mind off things. I'm not a brutal fuck but it will be hard for him if he doesn't relax."

Warm calloused fingers gripped my jaw and turned my head back and away from the client.

Wilber was touching me.

His thick finger ran along my skin under my jaw, leaving a tingle of excitement, until it reached my mouth. The pad painted back and forth across my lower lip, getting it wet with my salvia. The client slowly pushed forward. When I gasped Wilber stuck his thumb deeper into my mouth.

"Suck it, Goth boy."

I bit Wilber's thumb as Robe began to push his way inside. It wasn't going to fit.

"Mr. M. If you don't mind, I think a change in position would help Brant here."

Robe must have nodded because the next thing I knew was that Wilber was back climbing on the bed behind me. The scratchy feel of his suit against my sweaty back then I twitched as his hands ran up my inner thighs then slid over to my outer thighs and back down to my knees. "Open up wider."

Wilber's hands cupped the back of my thighs, lifting my legs up until knees hit my chest. "Arch your hips forward, Goth." It was almost impossible to do as he asked, bound as I was but the little I could move was enough to satisfy him.

"If you would, Mr. M." Wilber urged.

The client breeched me. He wasn't long, but he was thick, bordering on brutal. Soft hands replaced those rough strong ones on my thighs. When I turned my face away, Wilber's palm caught under my chin turning my face back towards the client. When I opened my mouth to cry out, that rough hand slipped across my lips.

Wilber's voice began to trickle into my ear, words of praise and encouragement. "That's my Goth boy. You look so desirable right now. Your entire body is flushed pink. I love it when you're that shade of pink."

The client buried himself to the hilt as my legs weakly protested the strain.

I was caught between the pain of penetration and the liquid honey streaming into my ear. I would always choose Wilber's pride over any client. I would wrap myself in his words and endure just like I've done for the past nine and a half years. Fucking is fleeting but pride could last for days. Wilber's words swept over me, wrapped around me like a comforting blanket while physical sensation was disengaged.

It was another night of debt repayment.

The warmth of the water with the scent of mandarin orange bath salts roused me. Blinking everything into focus showed me that I was now in the elegant en suite master bath. Wilber's hand splayed across my chest holding me upright as well as pinning me against him. My head rested on his shoulder and my forehead was against his neck.

"The client..." My voice came out weaker than I felt.

"He's come and gone, Goth Boy." There was a brief pause then a rumble of laughter shook my forehead.

"I didn't..."

"Mr. M. is more than satisfied with your performance. As a matter of fact, Goth, he has made a more than generous commission for your services once a month until the end of your contract."

Shifting slightly sent off a riot of pain down my spine where it turned to searing lightning at my ass then burned down into my thighs and calves.

"I've had the club doctor attend you. This is strain of over use. You'll be sore for a few days." Wilber's hand came up and cupped the back of my head to his shoulder. "You did what I needed you to do and we have secured Mr. M. for the Organization. I am very proud of you, Brant."

Those simple words were a balm to my wounds than any amount of painkiller could ever be.

"Are you ready to go home?" My whole aching body shivered as Wilber's chest rumbled with his words.

"Yes, Wilber."

It was always a secret amazement that I kept in my heart when Wilber would pick me up in his arms as if I still weighed nothing at all. There wasn't a movement of hesitation as he carried me into the room that housekeeping had re-sanitized. The feather soft pillow top mattress was still too much pressure as he laid me on it. There wasn't going to be any way of ignoring the after effects of repayment this time. I felt abused.

Wilber swept my hair back off my face. "Just relax, Brant. I'll get you ready when it's time to go."

The light blanket folded on the bench at the foot of the bed was draped over me then Wilber walked naked back into the bathroom. I was never going to look like that. I might have grown taller and filled out a bit but I was never going to have that kind of physic. Wilber was broad at the shoulder and chest but narrowed down to the hip and thighs. He wasn't a bodybuilder but he had the solid muscle of a fighter, of someone who had done hard labor to get to where he was now. Light hit the scars on his back that proved it; long jagged cuts on the back of his bicep, diamond shaped raised lumps of knife thrust and a silvery pucker of a small volcano left by a bullet. I found it fascinating that all of Wilber's injuries were on his back, as if his enemies didn't have the guts to meet him head on. Wilber could be scary face to face.

When I started as a prostitute, I would lay still and offer up my ass because that was what I was there to do. I was a whore-hole. I wasn't going to enjoy it. I wasn't going to participate. I was here to get fucked because of the outstanding debt my father had accumulated and I wasn't going to resist no matter how much it hurt or how filthy it made me feel. I thought that simple non-resistance would be enough to pay back what was owed.

I was such a child.

Inaction has consequences.

Wilber put a stop to my defiance and laid it out to me in terms that a young man, hell, a boy could understand. Clients had paid money for my companionship. Client complaints cut into my share that went toward the debt and Wilber made it clear that he had to offer other young men at a discount to make amends. Since those men were also in a debt contract debt this meant that I was forcing more to their repayment schedule, the number of clients they had to service, to increase.

I could recall the disappointment in Wilber's voice even now it cut deep in my heart. "You came to me and made an offer which I accepted it because I judged you to be a man of your word regardless of your age. Are you a man of your word, Brant, or are you not?"

"I am." I tried to smile thinking of how my adolescent voice had cracked with earnestness but even my face ached right now.

"Then prove it." Wilber's tone was pure challenge.

This was the challenge I had been meeting since I had offered myself up as a sacrifice for my family.

Laying was too much effort to shift my weight, so I relaxed, taking slow deep breaths to handle the pain and find my center. When my eyes closed the story of how I came to be a sought after male prostitute played in my memory. It wasn't a unique story. It wasn't as tragic as others but it was the reason why I would continue to endure customers like Mr. M.

Dad had five kids, with me being the oldest and the only boy. I had just entered grade ten when our lives fell apart. Mom got cancer. When she got sick, I dropped out of school and took over running the household to keep the family together. For a while we'd all thought she was going to pull through. She came home for Thanksgiving and we all had a big meal even if it was a little too quiet from my sisters; but then, Mom was gone by Christmas. I was secretly happy when she died; her suffering was finally over.

Little did I know that ours was beginning.

We had barely come back home from the funeral when the hospital bills came in. Other bills began arriving daily; harassing calls to anyone who picked up the phone; our furniture was repossessed; the phone was disconnected. The water and electricity were cut off. When Children's Aid came to take us kids to different foster homes. I managed to get the girls to run and hide out in a neighbor's backyard shed until they left. We had just lost our mother. I wasn't going to allow anyone to break up this family.

Not long after that someone came to kick us out of the only house we had ever known.

Suddenly, Dad had money.

Enough money to pay off everything. Enough money to make bill collectors go away and leave us in peace.

Peace lasted six months but then one night, Dad came home later than usual; drunk, beaten and crying.

I thought I was an adult because I'd had to grow up quickly when Mom got sick; I'd taken over the house, made sure everyone ate, got dressed then made it to school on time. That night, I realized I was just a punk-assed, still growing kid. I was so helpless. I didn't know what the hell to do.

Dad was crying about how "they" were coming to take Emily. She had been the collateral for the loan he had taken out to get the house back, get the utilities on and pay off the hospital, but he hadn't taken them seriously.

I didn't need him to spell it out for me. Dad had gone to a loan shark and now they wanted their money back so my baby sister would start paying off the interest on the loan, and if she got good enough, she would start paying back the capital.

They were going to make her a whore.

I wanted to run. I remember the feeling of urging Dad to grab what we needed and take off in the night.

Dad dropped his head into his hands and whispered in no uncertain terms that every one of his girls, my little sisters, would end up in a brothel if we even looked like we were running. We were being watched.

I couldn't allow Emily become a prostitute. Mom had dreams for her girls and hooking wasn't one of them.

Getting Dad the rest of the scotch out of the china cabinet I kept pouring him glass after glass until he passed out then I stole Mom's locket from her jewelry box on her dresser. It was one of those 14 K gold fold-out things that had family pictures in it from happier and more innocent times. I kissed each of my sisters goodbye before I draped Mom's knitted peach afghan over Dad's crumbling shoulders.

Pulling my black windbreaker from the hook by the door, I stepped outside and found the watchers. With all the resolve of a sixteen-year-old, I asked them to take me to the man Dad owed money to.

Mr. Wilber Brawden.

****

I could feel myself starting to fall asleep as I waited there on the bed. The shower turned on in the distance so I knew it was going to be a while. I let my thoughts drift.

Wilber.

When I first met this man, I thought he was a monster size wise. I was tall for my age; I looked like I was a couple of years older even though I was excessively skinny. It didn't matter how much I ate, I just burnt the calories up and grew taller so I was sure I was going to be massive when I got older. If I got older; that option really wasn't a given. I remember straightening my shoulders and looking up at him with all the courage that I could muster as I offered up my terms –me for all my sisters. I honestly thought I was going to piss myself while this man looked me over as if I were an expensive purchase. I guess I was. The debt was now up into the hundreds of thousands. I clutched at my windbreaker, but made myself stand still.

Wilber wasn't impressed.

Then he explained in graphic detail what was expected from me if he took me up on my challenge. "I'm not the bad guy here, Goth Boy. Your father came to me for help and with just his promise of repayment I loaned him the money he needed. I kept my word. If your father had come to me saying he had difficulties, maybe we could have worked something out -- a different schedule; a trade of goods and services."

"I know the type of service you want and I'm here to tell you it's not going to happen." My voice squeaked with puberty and I made myself stand as tall and resolute as I could. Then I realized he had named me already. "Goth Boy?"

Wilber circled me slowly. "Hair as black as night, skin as white as snow. I could call you Snow White if you'd rather or another princess."

There seemed to be a teasing tone there, but I was a little too freaked to make anything of it. "My name is Brant."

Wilber's tone was far from that teasing tone when he spoke again. "Don't talk back to me, Goth Boy. You come to me hat in hand begging for forgiveness…"

I cut him off. "I'm not begging for anything. I'm here for a straight up trade. Me for my sisters."

"I'm not talking about money from your paper route."

I wanted to make a strong statement but my voice cracked in the middle of it. "You want a prostitute…so, make me one instead."

For a big man, he moved fast. His one hand encircled my neck and yanked me up to the tips of my sneakers. "I have killed men for daring to challenge me. Why are we even talking? I should be speaking to the man of the house."

I squeaked again. "I am…"

Wilber dropped me unceremoniously.

I staggered back on my heels, grabbed at my throat, and sucked in a lung full of air. "I am the man of the house." I was fully prepared to face down this demon and offer my body up for devouring, but what he said next always stuck with me.

The palm of his hand cupped the side of my face and it felt like I was engulfed with a catcher's mitt. Wilber made me feel small. I came up to his shoulder, but I was about as wide as his forearm. "Don't hate your father, Goth Boy. His world just collapsed and he's doing the best he can; only his best isn't enough. You think you can do better?"

I could feel my face blanch at his words. My knees got weak. Right then it was confirmed that I was way out of my league, but there was no turning back. The alternative…. there wasn't an alternative.

"I have to."

His hand traced the marks he'd left on my neck, fingers brushing over them lightly. I flinched, but managed to resist the urge to take a step back. He grabbed a handful of my black hair forcing my head back to look up at him. "Do you fully understand what you're agreeing to, Goth Boy?"

"Yes." I swayed with fear, but I stood my ground. That simple word sealed my fate. It saved my sisters and sent me down a road there was no turning back from.

The next moments in my memories are surreal.

My first time.

My first everything was a back interest payment.

After Wilber shook my hand sealing the business deal, I was taken off to a warehouse that doubled as a x-rated film studio. The lights were bright and hot. I couldn't see anything beyond the spotlights, but I heard voices talking about camera angles and scenes. Wilber's voice was rumbling off in that darkness then a young man came up and gestured for me to follow him.

The man grinned at me and slapped my shoulder. "Don't worry, this is a solo."

"Solo?" My hands were hanging onto my coat with a death grip.

"You've jacked off before, right?" The man gestured to the set that looked like a high school locker room.

My face blushed red.

The man snaked his fingers in my hair and pulled strands forward into the bright illumination. "I thought it was a dye job but this is going to look good on the camera. You have that natural blue black highlight. Makeup!" The man shifted me around into the light so I ended up squinting to see what was happening around me.

Another man shoved a hanger into my chest. "Here put this on."

I changed into a school uniform then stood hugging my arms around myself. I had used up all my bravado making that bargain with Wilber.

I was scared and I really didn't care who the hell knew it.

I jumped when someone yelled. "Kid!"

I ended up called further into the studio

An older man with his hair pulled back into a pony tail sat in front of a bank of monitors. "Don't look at the camera, but know where it is. We want to see everything without it looking like we have to tell you what to do. We are going to start with you digging through people's lockers and you find a skin mag. Start reading it. You get excited and start touching yourself over your clothes…"

I went numb. Saying I was going to do something and actually doing it was another thing. I was blinded by the bright lights.

"Remember why you're doing this, Goth Boy!" Wilber called out to me from beyond the lights.

Emily, Sarah, Tanya, and Erris. If I didn't do this…I had to do this.

The pony tail man called out again with his booming voice. "Make up! Still got too much shine on his forehead and nose."

"Quiet on the set!"

"Action!"

The skin mag I ended up finding in the locker was of large muscle bound men in tight black leather. I stood there rather stunned

20

and overwhelmed. There was murmuring behind the bright lights, but I couldn't make myself move.

Pony tail's voice boomed out again. "Do something!"

Blinded by the lights, overly warm in my woolen private school blazer as the blood pulsated in my ears and to my horror my cock was began to stir. My lips were dry and when I licked them I thought I heard someone moan off camera. Suddenly, a hand closed around my arm and jerked me back against a wide chest. I gasped as a hand closed around my throat and the other one grabbed me through my pants. The magazine fell to the floor.

"You're talking too long and the director's getting pissed." My attacker's voice hissed lowly into my ear. "We'll all pay for it."

I was lifted off my feet and plastered against this man's body.

"Well I finally caught the locker thief read handed." His hand snaked down into the waistband and squeezed my cock hard.

I squeaked.

"Oh yeah, that sound was fucking adorable. Doesn't mean I can let you get away with stealing. You shouldn't be benefiting from robbery."

His hand began stroking my cock and when I tried to resist I found myself slammed hard against the locker face first with his knee rammed up between my legs forcing me up on my tip toes.

Lips brushed against my ear low, his breath hot against my neck, and the man whispered. "I know you're scared, but don't fight me. I'll open you up right and make you feel good before the others get here…"

Others?

I closed my eyes and kept my hands plastered on the cool metal. I was going to be raped, right here, right now. Tears burned my eyes and rolled down the side of my face. My body turned cold as I trembled, but I fought the urge to bolt. If I didn't do this, it would be Emily. It wasn't going to be her. I couldn't let it be her.

The director's voice called out from beyond the bright lights. "If you can't stop crying turn your face to the camera…perverts lap that shit up."

I didn't feel good by the time the rest of the basketball team showed up in the locker room. The one who caught me wasn't a man, he was a punk ass kid just like me. The rest of the team looked underage as well.

Then it started…

I was out of it when I heard a distant shout of "Cut!"

Cum dripped off my body. My ass was stinging and even my jaw hurt from having cocks shoved down my throat. I wouldn't say I'd stopped crying, but my tears were dry.

The first boy who stuck his cock in me knelt beside me and offered up a robe. Before I could even gather enough strength to reach for it Wilber was there.

"I've got him, Kenny. Get yourself cleaned up." Wilber's massive mitt brushed my hair back from my face.

"You bruise easily." His hand lightly traced where Kenny first had gotten a hold of my neck. "So, Goth Boy, the back interest has been paid. Can you see yourself doing this for the next five years?"

My voice was raw. "Yeah."

"Yes, not yeah." Wilber's tone was quiet correction.

"Yes." I gave him the response he wanted.

A thug in a suit came up behind Wilber. "I'll take him to the brothel."

There was a long pause and Wilber turned my face from right to left, then lifted my chin up to face him. If I wasn't so overwhelmed I might had cringed as those huge hands wiped cum off my cheek and the side of my mouth. "I'll take personal charge of this one."

"Sir?" There was true puzzlement in the thug's comment.

"Not too many men stand up to me and this one isn't even a man yet. It'll be interesting to see where this will go. Take the others back…no clients for them. They did a good job here." A rough thumb ran back and forth over my lower lip as I stared up into that unexpressive face. Those eyes weren't showing any thoughts I could read behind that façade.

When I blinked it felt like it took an eternity to open my eyes again.

"This was business, Goth Boy. What happened on camera a bit ago was a business transaction between you and I. You do what I tell you when I tell you, with who I want you to and I will see that you get what you need to survive when you walk out of this place. If you understand, nod."

I nodded myself out of existence.

Wilber was true to his word. Instead of being in a stable of men, a brothel, who took on johns nightly; Wilber turned me into a higher class of prostitute. Instead of being broken in mind, body and spirit but fully repaid in less than five years, I was given an education and lessons in refinement. Less clients meant a longer tenure but I considered worth it and quickly rose in demand by the clientele. Eye Candy. Arm Candy. If they paid well enough and were up to Wilber's standards, I was Bed Candy as well.

When the DVD it hit the underground markets labeled as "Cinderella's First Time" it became a runaway sensation leading up to a catalogue of performances with other underage boys until I turned legal then I became a visual feast, an adult performer, for my burgeoning fandom.

After Wilber's lecture on performance, I became "a good boy" with my training that eventually I earned 1% of the profits. Instead of keeping the money for myself, I paid the mortgage to the house off in six years and left the remainder in a trust in my sisters' names so my father had no right to it whatsoever. He never was that good with money before he married Mom and he had proven he was worse now that she was gone.

****

Wilber's fingers skimmed my still sensitive skin yanking me back to the present.

It took a moment for my eyes to focus as he took hold of my jaw, tipped my head back and began lightly kissing my mouth.

I twined my tongue with his.

Finally he rewarded me with a deep kiss.

Even though my body was exhausted I moaned into his mouth.

"Turn over." Wilber helped me when he saw that I really couldn't do it. My nipples ached from the pressure from the comforter. Wilber's hands gathered my hair and he began drying it with a towel.

When our bargain had been first struck, Wilbur had ordered me to let my hair grow. Now when it wasn't pulled back out of my face, it reached pass mid-thigh like a straight black curtain.

"Brant." Wilber carefully began sliding the comb through my hair. "You are aware that your time of service is coming to an end."

I murmured into the bed. "Only six more months."

"With tonights' new patron, it is more like four. I wasn't prepared to broach the subject today but now seems to be the best time after all." Wilber set the comb down then the mattress shifted as he headed to the suit jacket that was draped across the side chair.

He reached into his inner pocket and pulled out an envelope.

An opened envelope.

"News for you, Brant." Wilber pulled the paper free from its package.

I never got mail.

"This is from your Father." Wilber handed it over.

Updates on life outside of the world of whoring. Emily had graduated college and was now working in a vet clinic in a larger city. She was pregnant and was to be married in this fall. Sarah had graduated high school and had been accepted into Dartmouth University. She didn't get a scholarship and didn't want to take out a student loan, so she was going to put her dreams away and get a job at the local donut shop to save up money. She could go next year.

My sisters had grown up with normal worries. This proved that what I had done was worth it.

Wilber adjusted his tie as he stared into the mirror's reflection of me naked on the bed. "The Scholarship of Brant is available."

I caught his gaze in the mirror. I frowned not really understanding what he meant.

"I am offering a four-year ticket to each of them to continue on to higher education. The price would be a year of personal service to me for each year of schooling for each of your sisters: Sarah, Tanya and Erris." Wilber pressed the salt and pepper hair at the side of his temples back from his face.

"Since you insisted on that clause for the original agreement about the William house never being used as collateral for future loans, you have hobbled your sisters' ambitions."

What?

My mind fought through a blanket of physical fatigue into mental gymnastics. They'd all be finished with college in twelve years.

Twelve years?

The letter fell from my fingers. I was free from the initial loan in four months. Everything I endured was based on that fact, that I would be free. I could go home. Wilber caught my shoulder and pushed me onto my back. A slight hiss of pain was swallowed but I knew he had heard it. His touch gentled as he urged my chin to face him.

"This new contract would start after the original loan is paid. However, I will flow the funds immediately, so Sarah can start this semester. All of this is based on your verbal agreement. I only need your word for this to start, Brant."

"But..." My voice was grated and hoarse.

His fingers curled around the back of my neck. "Once we enter this new agreement, you are for my eyes only. You are my accessory, my bauble to display and play with. No one else will be allowed to touch you. You are mine alone."

I was stunned and knew I wasn't thinking clearly. I was never able to think clearly when Wilber had his hands on me. Even when I was nothing but a punk-ass kid Wilber's comforting touch befuddled me.

My words stammered out. "Why... why would you think I'd do this? I'm going to be free...."

Wilber spread his fingers and cupped my cheek. "You have grown so beautiful, Goth Boy. This business between us is based on how much you can make with this face and body. I also see this brilliant mind of yours and I would like to nurture it."

Warm tongue slipped up the side of my neck followed by a lingering suck on my ear lobe. I shivered.

I'd been fucked over all night yet, I wanted him.

"What makes you think I want to stay here?" I was surprised that I could make a coherent sentence.

Wilber's lips brushed the curve of my ear as he whispered. "I remember a skinny brat with straggly black hair and big grey eyes standing in front of me with balls bigger than my own, offering his body up for whatever use I wished to make of it in exchange for his little sisters."

Catching his wrist, I meant to push his hand away but somehow, I ended up caressing his forearm instead.

Suddenly the bed shifted and my world canted upright as Wilber pulled me up against his chest. I could feel the rumble of his voice against my skin.

"You know what captured my attention most from that initial meeting? I asked you a simple question 'why?', and your answer floored me. Do you remember your answer, Goth Boy?"

"I... said that's what brothers do." I'd be lying to myself if I said that this position was comfortable. My hips and ass were in agony. The sting of a tear in my eye made me turn my face into his chest.

"Your little sisters still need you." Wilber whispered into my ear. "When you become mine, you would be private stock, Brant. Others could look, but they couldn't touch."

26

Wilber retrieved the letter. "Finish it."

There was more on the other side. Tears filled my eyes as I blinked over the words. Dad apologized for being a horrible father. For being less than a man, unable to protect his children… all his children. Then the writing changed. Emily.

"When Dad first told me that you didn't run away and that he knew where you were, I was so angry with him for not going after you. Then he told me why you did what you did. I could never thank you enough for the sacrifices you made for us, for me especially. I wish you well. You saved my life, Bran-flake."

I let out a hiccupping sob. I'd forgotten that she used to call me that.

"You saved us. We are your sisters. Please find happiness."

Wilber ran the back of his hand down my cheek. "Once the original debt is over, you can see them for a visit. So, Goth Boy, are you still their brother?"

Haven't I done enough for them?

I still remember the day each one of them came home from the hospital after being born. I stood by their crib and looked down into their chubby, red faces and introduced myself as their big brother. I explained how it was my job to look after them. It was my job to protect them. I broke down and started crying.

Wilber's voice whispered in my ear. "Only four more months as a slave, Brant then you can become something different."

I looked down at the crumpled paper. It could be worse.

I knew life in a brothel was harsh and short. You could die there from any number of STDs or clients. I got fucked because I was paying a debt. I got beaten only because I was disobedient. Punishment was never without a cause, and a verbal correction was always given first. Wilber fed me, he gave me a roof over my head, I had clothes, and I was educated. I wanted for nothing of the necessities of life. Yet…

"Brant, your answer?" Wilber's warmth faded as he pulled his hand back from my skin.

The paper crinkled between my fingers. I had said that I would look after them. I made a vow when I lay my hand over their tiny little hearts. Bowing my head and closing my eyes it was plain to see that I wasn't done with the world of whoring.

"We will need to negotiate this new contract, Wilber."

"You would have disappointed me if you hadn't said that. And your reason?" Wilber's warmth returned to my chilled body as his chin rested in the shallow hollow of my shoulder and neck.

"That's what brothers do."

"Good boy. We are out of this place." A kiss pressed against my neck.

I folded the letter up and I brushed my tears from my eyes. I knew what was expected for these last four months. I would be perfection. After that... we'd just have to see what would become of me.

Chapter Two: Homecoming

I couldn't believe it. I kept expecting to wake up from this dream and find myself waiting in another cold, non-descript bedroom for the next client.

Finally, I was dressed like a normal person toasty warm all the way down to my toes. It's been ten years since I remember being this covered up and cozy. Wilber kept his house on the cool side even in winter. Today, Wilber had presented me the full length black wool top coat with matching leather gloves along with the dove gray cashmere scarf. He had even given me handmade Italian shoes protected with rubber galoshes so the leather didn't get wrecked in the snow. Huddling in my new clothes I was glad that from the tips of my toes to the top of my head, I was toasty cozy. Even my nose was warm.

Staring out the side window of the limo watching the scenery pass made me realize how odd it was to be alone. Three months ago, I was still in debt and Wilber treated me like the collateral I was. He protected his investment by having me watched by bodyguards, which I called Shadows. Even traveling with Wilber there were Shadows set up especially for me - one to open doors, two to watch my back and make sure I didn't run away. Technically, I wasn't alone even now because I was being chauffeured. Since the debt was now paid it was just me and Guy, a transplanted French Canadian, and he was more than just a chauffeur; but unlike the others who watched me with stoic features and closed mouths, Guy talked to me.

I've moved from being the campus slut to an exclusive frat house piece of ass.

I watched the Christmas lights of the houses pass by giving the night a rather festive appeal.

No, that's not right. I am the frat house president's piece of ass.

Wilber explained that point in detail that I was his and his alone and nobody touched his things. Fingers would go missing if they strayed where they shouldn't. Truthfully, I found that oddly comforting. I knew that this new situation wasn't the norm, but it made me feel safe. Compared to how I spent my formative years as every man's whore, this was a giant step up.

Wilber and I had worked out an agreement for my exclusivity and for the most part I got all my demands except for one point that he was not going to budge -- my hair. He wanted my hair left long so there would be no drastic haircut in my future. It still hung pass my waist but at least I could pull it back into a ponytail off my face when we got back to the mansion at the end of the day.

I wasn't kidding myself about my situation. I knew I had just risen from satin sheets of a call escort to the silk sheets of a concubine. It still meant I got fucked. The only differences were that I was fucked in better surroundings. I was trotted about in a tailored suit and tie during the day, I could wear blue jeans and a sweater at home but at night was expected to be ready and willing in bed.

This change in status was appreciated; but it didn't mean I wanted it. It was still a slap in the face to remind me of what I was.

My cell phone rang interrupting my thoughts. A missed call from Wilber meant another Shadow was added to my entourage unless I could prove that I was in an emergency or in lecture at university where I was upgrading my degree to get into graduate school. The phone rang again. It was easier to answer every ring. I wasn't giving up this little bit of freedom. I had worked hard for it.

"Yes, Wilber?"

Memories of his low voice whispering along the nape of my neck had the ability to send shivers through me even when it was coming through a smart phone.

"Lovely voice, Goth." His tone had a warm growl in it.

"Thank you, Wilber." I touched my throat lightly.

"Are you nervous?" There was a hint of concern in his voice.

"Kind of."

As far as I knew, Erris might not even remember me.

The limo turned up a familiar, tree-lined street. Like the rest of the world around me, Christmas lights sent the shadows I now lived in further behind me. It was almost like a Hallmark moment.

I heard Wilber grunt slightly. He did that when he thought I was belittling myself. "Nonsense. I can't see David erasing your existence from the family. Not after what you did for him, for them. We will be traveling over the Christmas holidays, so I provided presents for your family since you will not be there. They're in the trunk. If my meetings all go well, we will be in Paris for the New Year. I want to show you the sights."

Uh... what do I say to that?

My pause was too long.

I heard a heavy sigh through the phone. "I don't need you to pretend to be happy with everything I do, my Goth Boy. I prefer honesty from you."

I slumped into the corner of the seat. "Your anger is scary, Wilber."

"Honesty. There it is. That is all I have ever asked of you since our new arrangement. Have I scared you, Brant?" It didn't take much imagination to see Wilber in my mind's eye. He was working tonight so that meant he was in a tailored suit. I couldn't hear any background noise so he was probably in his office back at the club. The width of his massive hand would make that cell phone look small.

I felt a burning at the back of my eyes before I whispered through a tight throat, "You did a long time ago and then when...my throat..."

"Don't cry. Tears do not become you and you're stronger than this Goth." His statement was just that, full of fact and expectation.

I wiped at my eyes and sniffed.

"I would much rather have your eyes glazed over with pleasure than with sorrow, Goth. Enjoy your day with your family. I will be waiting for you to come back to me."

The line went silent. He had hung up. Hearing those words warmed the chill of the fear of rejection that was making me wary.

I tucked the cell phone back into my coat.

The anguish of returning home, with all of them knowing what I had been doing for the past ten years, formed a hard lump of ice in my stomach that grew larger as we got closer and closer to my destination.

Physically I had changed so much, and the change wasn't just from the sex trade. I had been in the middle of a growth spurt when I left. Back then, I was all arms and legs and about as wide as a No. 2 pencil and no matter how much I scarfed down I couldn't put on any weight. Now I was still a lean, but toned six-foot-two man with the same unnaturally pale skin I'd had ever since Mom got sick and I took over the household. Wilber preferred me like that, like the Goth look he'd named me after. My naturally black hair, pale grey eyes and almost porcelain skin tone made his hands look so dark against my flesh when he stripped me naked. He could also tell when sex had been too rough when I was working. I bruised easily and the discoloration lingered for days.

I leaned back against the leather seat and closed my eyes. My fingers brushed my throat which was hidden under a turtle neck and scarf. I'd ended the debt service the way I'd entered it— videotaped for mass market consumption.

That last day of service was almost the last day of my life. The black and blue handprints around my throat had faded, but the stoma where the tube had to be inserted so I could breathe was still noticeably visible against my pale flesh as it continued to heal. Wilber's comments about my speech assured me that my voice had finally returned to normal.

The client who did this wouldn't be doing anything ever again. After having sex with me several times, he'd wrapped his hands around my throat placing his thumbs against my windpipe and used his body weight to press hard. I had started choking right there on the sound stage.

Later, I was told Wilber had killed him with his bare hands to get him off me. I really don't remember anything of the murder, because I was trying to breathe through a mangled windpipe.

When you can't get enough air, nothing else matters.

I woke up in the hospital. The staff knew I had been raped. My tell-tale skin told a story I couldn't lie about. My windpipe was bruised in the place where his thumbs had been. I was scared that I would never speak again when my grasping hands found a piece of plastic cut into the base of my throat. The EMS had to do an onsite tracheotomy to make sure that I arrived alive at the hospital. The police came and pestered me. I couldn't talk to them even if I had wanted to.

Sometime later, a rape counselor came and sat by my bedside telling me that this wasn't my fault and that I should absolve myself of the guilt and shame. I sat there staring out the window of my private room as he nattered on about how our therapy should progress.

Guilt and Shame? What if I didn't have those feelings? Idiot, I came to Wilber to do this – I knew I would become a sex slave, but that was better than Emily's doing the same thing at the age of ten. I did this for my sisters because not doing it was something I couldn't live with.

Two weeks into the hospital stay, I awoke to the tender touch on my forehead and when I opened my eyes I saw Wilber's face with his guard down and emotions exposed. He looked stricken. When he saw me watching him, I expected that cold expressionless mask to drop down, but instead his eyes gentled further.

"Be well, Brant." He leaned over and kissed my forehead. "The debt is paid. You're mine now. I won't ask you to do something like this ever again. No one else will touch you."

Gentleness was something I'd never anticipated coming from Wilber. It threw my known world off its axis, so I couldn't stop the shaking nor the tears. Maybe it was a long time coming, but I had some sort of breakdown and the monitors went a bit wild. Nurses rushed in and, after talking to me failed, the doctors sedated me. Medication was the only thing that had a chance of calming me. Afterwards, I lay curled in bed waiting for everything horrible to start up again, only it didn't.

34

While I was hospitalized, I didn't speak to anyone. I just listened to the rented television, gazing out the window at fall's dazzling display of colors or staring ahead at the beige wall at nothing as I waited, and waited, and waited. Finally, the police left me alone when they realized that they were going to get nothing from me.

I heard the nurses whispering about the beautiful, but silent young man in room 523. I guess that was me. I didn't feel beautiful. My bruises were taking longer than usual to heal… or maybe they were just that deeply imprinted into my flesh.

Finally, Wilber came for me and I recall looking at him, feeling as fragile as a spun glass unicorn. He brought me clothes that I could tell were tailored. Wilber never settled for second best in anything. After he placed the clothes on the bed, his large hand cupped the side of my neck and I flinched.

Softly, so as to not allow anyone else to hear, "No one will ever hurt you again, Brant. I *will not* allow it. You're mine."

Once I was dressed he fussed over my pants then straightened my sweater before he pushed me out of the hospital in the mandatory wheelchair. Wilber's protective presence made it intimidating for the hospital staff to interfere with us.

He confused me. I'd gone from coveted frequently used sex toy to cherished, fragile keepsake. Wilber changed my status almost overnight, and even though I hated whoring, being a sex toy was familiar at this point. After all I'd been through this tearing away of everything I knew left me floundering more than before that client had tried to kill me.

I didn't know how to handle this change and I kept glancing at Wilber trying to figure out what he was trying to do on the drive home.

After the driver opened the car door, I was stunned when Wilber carried me into the house and up to a separate room which was apparently now mine. I had been expecting to sleep beside Wilber this first night home. I liked listening to his breathing as he slept with me wrapped in his arms. Instead, I was left alone in my new room to rest.

This was the start of a new routine that did nothing, but throw me further off kilter.

Wilber didn't call me to him for service. I didn't have to try to navigate the stairs to the dining room; my meals were delivered to me. No one came to visit me; even my former Shadows didn't so much as peek into the room to check on me.

I didn't have perfect emotional control except when with clients, so when I started crying after I'd lost the normality of being a whore, it went on for hours. I cried for so many days that I scared myself.

I know I frightened Wilbur, because suddenly the door to my bedroom flew open and I found myself in his arms. Once Wilber was with me, everything was fine again. That, I didn't understand. After all, this was the man who had changed me to a whore. I should have tried to beat the crap of him, not cling to him for comfort, but I did just that. I needed to. Wilber Brawden, loan shark and pimp, was my world and everything was alright once I was back in his arms.

I am so fucked up.

****

The limo edged to a halt. I blinked and looked out the window. I was outside of the house - the same house I'd bought for my sisters with the proceeds of the DVD that showed me losing my virginity in a locker room gangbang. I sat there, staring at the familiar structure as the Christmas lights blinked warmly from the windows out into the night, and it didn't feel real.

"Hey, *petite bonbon*, you get out now, eh? You surprise your family while I bring in the gifts." Guy turned and hung his arm over the driver's seat to look at me.

I couldn't make myself reach for the door.

I can't see them. Not after all this. Not after all the things I've done over the years.

"Ah, look! Another *tres petite bonbon*." Guy gestured to the house. I glanced out of the tinted window of the limo and saw a slender girl standing there backlit by the hallway light.

Guy let loose a small chuckle. "I would have thought that you'd all have the tallness, *non*?"

I watched mortified as she called back into the house. Soon the whole doorway filled with a crowd of petite blonde women staring out at the black limo idling at the curbside.

Guy turned off the engine. "*Petite Bonbon,* you get out now."

"Drive." My voice cracked.

Guy turned around in the front seat to catch my eye squarely. "*Monsieur* Brawden said you are to see your family and I know he didn't mean from the window of the car."

I pleaded. "I can't let them see me... not after... not..."

"Look, one of those girls has a baby." Guy turned back to the front and caught my gaze in the rearview mirror. "If you didn't do what you did, there would be no babies for that one. Of all the gifts in this car, you are the most precious, *Petite Bonbon*. Put on your client face if you can't be happy to be here."

Guy opened his door. "*Monsieur* Brawden said that you will see your family. You don't want to make him angry. Your neck is still nasty to look at."

"Wilber didn't do this." My hand covered my neck protectively.

"*C'est vrai, Petite Bonbon*. You survived being a whore. You survived being strangled. You will also survive Thanksgiving dinner. Get out. I think that is your Father coming to the door."

I started as the limo door was wrenched open. The cold air of November swept into the confines of my haven. I stilled like a rabbit in the middle of the interstate that finally realized the danger it was in. I thought my heart was going to beat out of my chest.

"Oh, my God. Brant!" Dad climbed into the car and hugged me hard to him. "Brant... my baby boy..."

"Daddy." My voice was tight and gravelly.

I guess the effect of the near strangulation is still evident.

"I'm so sorry. I'm sorry. I should have found another way…should have done something…" He pushed me away and held my face in his hands. Staring up at him he looked older than his fifty-five years. Life had treated him harshly.

I couldn't say anything.

"My Brant… my boy…"

"Does everyone know?" I whispered, mortified and still ready to flee.

"Just Emily…"

"Don't let them know," I begged, holding on to his sleeve, "I don't want anyone to know."

Dad pulled me back into a tight embrace and hung on to me. His hand came around and buried itself in my hair.

Instinctively, I jerked back out of his hold, wide eyed.

Dad's face took on a look of horror. "I'm sorry…I couldn't find a way to pay back the money I owed and then they were coming for…. I thought you ran away then Mr. Brawden came and said that you had offered yourself as collateral and that he had taken you up on that offer." Dad's hands curled into fists on his legs as he lowered his head.

"Mr. Brawden assured me that he would watch out for you. It still didn't mean…I'm sorry… I'm sorry… the hell you've been through because of me." Dad's voice broke.

"It's okay…" I hesitated a breath then added, "Dad… can I stay for dinner?"

He jerked himself upright, "Is it over?"

"The debt's paid," I confirmed in a whisper, still not wanting anyone to overhear.

Guy came to the back door and gestured at me. "Get out now."

He gestured back toward the house and Emily's baby, "That *bebe precieux* does not need to be out in this cold air. I will bring in your things."

Dad's eyes welled up. "It's over? It's finally over."

Dad pulled on my arm, dragging me out of the back of the limo.

I towered over him. I don't remember him being such a small man.

Emily turned and handed her baby to her husband and bolted out the door in slippers and without a coat. She caught me under my arms and latched on with a hug worthy of Wilber. She squeezed me hard, "Bran-flake, I am so happy to see you. You're so damn tall and good looking. What's that?" She pulled down the front of my turtleneck before I could stop her.

"What the hell?" She grabbed my hand pulled me toward the house. "What the hell did that man do to you?"

"Emily…"

She stopped and looked back at me then dropped my hand and covered her face. "I'd forgotten what your voice sounded like, Brant." Tears sprang to her eyes. "After all you did for us I forgot what your voice sounded like."

I couldn't help, but laugh aloud at her comment. My voice had bounced between a castrato's soprano and a solid baritone sometimes in the same sentence when I made the choice to leave. "I sounded more like a squeaky mouse back then."

Emily turned around and shooed everybody back into the house as she dragged me inside behind her. Dad followed us then took my coat and scarf, but I kept my leather gloves on because my hands were like ice. Since getting out of the hospital I was always cold. The thermostat could be up in the house, but this was a deep-seated chill that clung to me. It only went away when Wilber touched me. I didn't tell Wilber because he would start looking at me with that pitying expression again. He could tell when I pulled my client face on, but these past few weeks he allowed it. I'd get warm again, eventually. According to him, coming home was the first step in making that happen.

How could my thoughts linger in the dark places when the house was filled with the scent of roast turkey, voices filled with laughter and pure joy?

My stomach growled in sharp response to the homey smell.

Emily patted my belly.

I was barely able to keep from flinching but covered it up with a smile.

Emily grinned back at me. "The same as always. Girls! This is your brother, Brant. Brant this is Tanya with her thumbs permanently attached to her cell phone. Sarah is upstairs, she just got off the train from university and this little minx is your baby sister, Erris."

Emily looked so much like Mom before she got cancer. They all did. Little cookie cutters in smaller step sizes on down the line. Erris looked up at me with wide cornflower blue eyes. She was all of four-feet-six.

"You're tall." She just made a statement.

Bending over slightly so I wasn't towering over her, I brought my face close to hers. "Well if you eat all your veggies, you'll get tall, too."

I had to smile as Erris wrinkled her nose. She crossed her arms in front of her chest and demanded. "Where have you been?"

Dad stepped up and gestured me forward to the dining room. "Brant was working, baby girl."

The door to the kitchen opened and a matronly woman stuck her head out. "David, I need your help in here."

I straightened up abruptly. *What? What is she doing here in Dad's kitchen? I can't be mistaken, can I?*

The woman pressed the door open wider then caught sight of me. "Happy Thanksgiving, Mr. Williams."

"Happy Thanksgiving, Helen." I returned.

Why is one of Wilber's comptrollers cooking turkey in my Dad's house?

I glanced over my shoulder to see where Guy was, but he hadn't come in yet. I wasn't mistaken. That woman was one of Wilber's financial advisers. I had met her a few times when he called meetings at the house.

"You know Helen, Brant?" Erris tilted her head back to look at me.

I glanced over Erris's head to see Helen disappear back into the kitchen. "Only in passing. When did she...what does she do here?"

Erris grabbed my hand. Startled, I stared down into wide innocent eyes.

"Daddy hired her as a housekeeper back when I was small. Mrs. Helen says that Daddy has a good heart, but he is like a sieve when it comes to money - that's a bowl with holes in it so water can drain out. So, Mrs. Helen takes care of all the bills and stuff."

"Really?" Wilber had to have sent her to Dad. As far as I knew Dad's hardware store was making a small profit, but not enough to pay for a housekeeper.

If there had been enough money coming in surely Wilber would have snatched it up. So, why did he send Helen in?

"Brant." Emily's voice called to me.

She stood beside a man who was holding a little, white bundle in his arms. Emily touched his arm softly. "This is Roger Carson, my husband of three months, and this is Madison, our little girl. You're an uncle, Brant. Would you like to hold her?"

"An uncle." I don't know what kind of expression was on my face, but when I took a single step forward Emily's husband backed away.

"I'm not letting that man touch our daughter." There was absolute venom in Roger's voice and it cut me deep because it came unexpected.

"Roger?" Emily stared at him, shocked and embarrassed.

Roger glared at me. "My brother is gay, Emily."

"I know that..."

Roger's jaw hardened as he stared down the stairwell at me. "I've seen his AV collection. Your brother is a featured star in the worst of them."

What little color I had drained out of my face. The warmth that had begun to thaw me drifted away.

"Roger!" Emily hissed at him. "Tanya and Erris go and help Dad set the table. Now!"

41

I heard the girls move off, but my eyes were locked on my attacker. I was bleeding inside. If I was at one of Wilber's mixers, I would have been prepared for the snide comments, but to have this hatred directed at me out of the blue. It wasn't ceasing.

"Em, I can't share a table with that kind of person." Roger shook his head.

My client face came down, hard. The emotional carnage ripping through me was hidden away. My voice was ice. "What kind of person? Gay?"

Roger lifted his daughter closer to his chest then laid a protective hand over her head. "No, I have no problems with gays. As I said my brother is gay and I love him with all my heart. What I can't stand are whores who sell themselves for money."

"Roger! You don't understand, Brant saved…" Emily reached out towards me as her husband turned away with their little girl.

"I'm taking Madison upstairs. Tell me when he's gone. I'll come down and eat then." Roger started up the stairs brushing past another girl, who looked so much like Mom, as she stood frozen on the stairs. Was that Sarah?

"Brant?" Sarah turned and looked at me with unhidden horror on her delicate features. "You made gay porn?"

With that, any hope for any warm and fuzzy feelings I had for this Thanksgiving died.

"Sarah, Brant had no choice…" Emily was torn between running up the stairs or coming down to me.

I took the decision out of her hands. "I made hardcore fetish DVDs. I'm a superstar oversees. They absolutely love me in Russia."

"Brant?" Sarah clutched at the banister so hard that her knuckles turned while from the strain.

My client face was on. Nothing could hurt me now. "I owed money. I couldn't pay it back so they made me work for it. Because of my looks, they decided I was suited for porn. Porn was more profitable for them than having me slave away on the docks loading cargo into ships for twelve hours a day."

Sarah took a couple of steps back up the stairs, "For ten years!!!"

"Interest was compounded every ten days. Every movie paid down the principal." My tone was almost like a bored high school teacher paying lip service to the curriculum.

I watched my younger sister pale even more and I thought she was going to faint. "How? How could you have done something like that?"

I couldn't deny the horror in her voice.

"Who else was going to do it?" I am frigid.

"There are always choices!" She was fire.

I felt my eyes grow hard. "That was the choice I made. It was the only option open to me at the time. Don't you dare stand there and judge me. You have no idea what I've been through."

"Brant." Emily moved down the last few steps to hug me. I pivoted and brought my shoulder between us effectively blocking her.

Tears glittered in Sarah's eyes, but they weren't of joy. "No, I don't. I don't know you. My brother ran away when he was sixteen. We stupidly hung flyers around the neighborhood offering up a reward of everything in our piggybanks for any information. We searched for you… and you were selling yourself!" she hissed angrily before shouting, "I don't want a gay porn star for a brother! Maybe it would have been better if you had just died."

"Sarah!" Emily tried to catch the second oldest sister as she turned and bolted up the stairs.

I turned back for the front door.

"What's all this shouting about?" Dad stood in the doorway his hands full of a perfectly cooked turkey with that familiar clueless look on his face that seemed to be his main expression.

"This was a mistake," I flatly admitted.

The sound of a bedroom door slamming shut floated down the stairwell. Dad looked up the stairs. "Sarah knows? She's so like her mother. I'll explain it to her. I don't want you to shoulder all the blame. What you…"

I snorted. "Blame? What blame? There are no lies between us. I *was* a whore. I bought you this house with my first DVD."

I was tempted to shove the client face off, but just thinking about the emotional aftermath brought stinging tears to my eyes. "I guess they're right, you can't go home."

"You are home, Brant." Emily moved forward to hug me. I held up my arm and stepped backwards.

My façade was breaking but I wasn't going to lose it here. The lump in my throat made it hard to talk. "I'm glad your life is good Emily. It looks like you have a lovely daughter. Your husband is a man of conviction – that's a good thing. He won't land you in this sort of predicament."

The front door opened, and Guy walked in carrying an armload of brightly wrapped presents. He could feel the tension in the air before he even stepped fully into the house. I grabbed my coat and slid into it, but my long hair got caught in the sleeve. Guy set the presents on the bench beside the door then took my coat from my hands. He waited until I pulled my hair up and out of the way then slid the coat up my arms and settled it on my shoulders. Just like he had been doing it for the past five years since he came into Wilber's employ.

"Brant, where are you going? I thought you said you were done." Dad's voice was pure anguish. He was still holding the platter of turkey. He looked absurd.

My eyes traced the path upstairs that my little sister had stormed off on. "The original loan is paid. I took out another one and repayment begins immediately."

Emily grabbed at my wool lapels and shook me with her fury. "What? Why did you do that?"

Closing my hands around her fists, I pried her grip free. "So, Sarah doesn't end up selling donuts as her only career option. Mom wanted more for everyone."

Emily's face was pure anguish. "What about you? She wanted something better than this for you, too."

I reached out and almost touched her face. *I was tainted. I had no right to spread it to my sisters I had protected these past ten years.* "You don't remember how Mom treated me, do you? She couldn't be bothered to give me the time of day, even before she got sick. I'm probably living the life she wished on me."

I reached down into my pants pocket, felt the familiar lump then pulled it out -- the locket. Mom's fold-out locket that had everyone's picture, but mine. "I stole this."

I handed it to Emily; small, but delicately featured Emily, with golden blonde hair and cornflower blue eyes. Sarah had that those tones of gold and blue and so did the smaller ones. Tanya and Erris watched the tableau, not truly understanding, but fully aware that something bad was going on.

"Come on, Guy." I turned on my heel.

I was tugged to a halt by my sleeve, "Brant."

I turned and looked down at Dad. His hair was starting to go grey. Brown peppered with grey. I can't get over his being so short or looking so old.

My throat was tight. "Don't go borrowing any more money, Dad. I can't help you. I'm tied up for the next twelve years."

I opened the door and stepped outside, back into the winter night. "Son!"

"BRANT!" Emily's voice was cut off as my Shadow pulled the front door shut quietly behind me.

Guy brushed past me as he headed for the car, then halted when I remained on the front steps. "*Bonbon?*"

The cold night air sliced at my lungs. "Don't let Wilber hear you call me that. You might want to keep your tongue."

The phone inside my coat rang as if on cue. "Yes, Wilber?"

"Homecoming was short." There wasn't a hint of joy in Wilber's tone. He never was a man to wallow in someone's misfortune even if it turned out to be for his benefit.

I scanned the road and sure enough, further down the block the lights to a car came on. Wilber's limo idled in the darkness. "You're nearby. Come and get me."

I could hear screaming voices and sobs behind the door. Mom was blonde, azure eyed and very petite. Dad was brunette, brown eyed and all of five foot eight. I was six foot two with jet black hair and pale gray eyes. I was a cuckoo's egg. I didn't belong in that nest on the other side of the door. I suffered all that sexual abuse for so long, because that's what brothers were supposed to do. Now, I find out that I'm not even their full brother.

I can't even pretend. Tears stung my eyes.

Wilber's driver double parked.

I wrapped my coat around me and trudged toward it as Guy moved to open the limo's rear door. I climbed in and settled myself beside Wilber. His arm came up and wrapped around my shoulders. "So now you know the truth, Goth Boy. Those who have fallen to the darkness, no matter how well meaning, remained touched by it. Is your decision the same?"

I leaned into his warmth as my client face began to craze like ice cracking as it's load was reached. "What do you want to hear from me, Wilber?"

He pulled me closer. "That I am a better Father to you than that poor excuse in that house."

"You're both rating about the same right now with keeping secrets. What is Helen doing in there playing housekeeper?" I braced myself for a strike for my sass. I opened my eyes to find Wilber watching me intently, but his expression was unreadable.

"I shouldn't have called David a poor excuse for a man. He's just naïve about the ways of the world, even after all of this. I sent Helen to keep him on track and keep the rest of your inheritance intact. She came up with the housekeeper ploy on her own. She was close to retirement and thought that this was a way to keep herself busy."

Wilber wrapped a hand in my hair pulling my face up to look at him directly. "Honesty is something I expect from you. Now, think

46

about this next question. I will gift you this first semester. Does your sister Sarah continue her education?"

"Of course." I didn't have to think about it. The way she ran from me was probably the best thing she could ever do.

I'm tainted after all.

"This is the only option you will get from me to back out of this deal." Wilber's hold softened in my hair and a rough thumb smeared the single tear that escaped my eye.

"I am yours for as long as they need me, Wilber."

Did I say that out loud?

There was a sudden stillness about him, but was then gone as he let go of my hair. He ruffled the top of my head sending strands everywhere. The touch was light and teasing but
I don't think I gave him the words he wanted to hear.

 His voice returned to its usual gruffness. "Even though they are not who you thought they were?"

I felt the burn start behind my eyes. I let the mask drop, and my face screwed up with my emotional trauma. I wiped at my eyes. "It doesn't matter if we are not full blood relations. I met each of them when they came home from the hospital, and I made them a promise that I would protect them. I *will* protect them."

"They despise you."

"Not all of them. If living with Sarah's disgust is the price I have to pay, so be it."

Wilber tightened his arm and pulled me closer until I was plastered to his side. I breathed deep to fill my nostrils with the scent of his cologne.

"And why do you offer up so much of yourself, Goth Boy?"

Taking a deep breath I slowly let it out. "I made a promise and I will keep it. My sisters need me so I will do what brothers do, Wilber."

I felt a kiss on my temple, and his hand slipped inside my coat.

The shield that protected me those long dark years was shattered, barely in place. "Please, not tonight, Wilber. I don't think I'd survive if we fucked tonight. I'm barely hanging on by a thread right now."

Wilber maneuvered me until my head was lying on his lap. His fingers stroked my hair like he was petting a cat. "You're mine now, Brant. No one will dare threaten you; no one will harm you. I will show you sights and sounds you haven't seen and give you experiences from around this world that will make your heart heal and rejoice."

"Why?" My voice came out like a sob.

I never got an answer. His fingers worked through my hair, and I was lulled.

"Anderson, turn up the heat; my Brant is cold."

I closed my eyes and gave a weak smile, as a blast of warm air hit my face. Maybe I did get my answer.

Chapter Three: Life...or something like it

The winter months passed by in a blur.

Wilber took his vow to show me the world seriously. We spent New Year's Eve in Paris watching the Eiffel Tower's light show dance up and down the steel structure. We were on the terrace of the hotel mixed with the crowd who were loud and they kept knocking into us until Wilber wrapped his arms around me and dragged me tight to him. Here in a cosmopolitan city in the middle of good natured mayhem, I admitted to myself that I would rather have been standing in Wilber's backyard looking up at the stars.

"You're not enjoying yourself, are you?"

"If you are..." He gave my waist a squeeze but we stayed on the terrace until the fireworks fizzled out.

I thought we were supposed to stay in Paris for the week and explore the museums and go shopping. Instead Wilber booked us on a flight back home the next day. I didn't know what I had done, but it was something to stop our overseas adventure. Once we got home Wilber immersed himself back into work. Aside from breakfast and some dinners, I never got to see him. The dinner conversations I looked forward to having with Wilber before New Year's dwindled to a few days during the week and Sunday only.

I was free to do what I wanted; only, I didn't know what I wanted.

Spring came slowly creeping in.

I'd been getting migraines continuously for the past five days. They were strong enough that by mid-afternoon I had to retreat to my darkened room. No matter how bad the pain was I got up when Wilber came back from the office to have dinner even though the thought of food made me nauseous. I should have known that trying to play it off as nothing more than a headache resulted in me getting hauled off to a backroom doctor whose specialty was patching up bullet holes, stitching up knife cuts and dealing with unwanted pregnancies and STDs.

So, here I sat in a backless gown in an old, but surprisingly clean, examining room getting felt up more than examined by this Doctor. I had my doubts about his qualifications when fingers slipped a little more south of the border than was necessary for checking for a headache. I could have done something about it, but I was nauseous and dizzy right then so I did what had become second nature - I dropped my client face. Wilber noticed immediately because the next thing I knew, the doctor was yanked away from me and was feeling the bottom of Wilber's size elevens on his face.

"We're leaving, Brant. Get your clothes on." The words were even, but I could feel the violence thinly coated behind them.

I got dressed and kept my face adverted as Wilber explained in graphic detail what would happen if the doctor so as much looked at me with perceived lust in his eyes.

I don't want to hear this.

I already had a headache before we came and this show of machismo was just enough stress to make it throb worse than the afternoon before. The light of the day was stabbing into my eyes. I felt clammy and I couldn't walk a straight line. Holding my head and feeling as though it would split apart, I staggered into the door frame.

I didn't make it another step before Wilber was there at my side. I found myself plastered against his warmth.

The doctor had red smudges on his cheeks as he climbed back to his feet. I could barely make him out through the shades of pain stabbing into my skull. He didn't try and bluff his way back into Wilber's good graces, but he had the good sense not to challenge him either. I cringed at the loud pop of him cracking his jaw back into alignment as if it wasn't so much of an effort. Still he stood upright and gave Wilber his professional opinion.

His diagnosis; get a haircut. These weren't migraines but stress headaches and the first thing I needed to get a haircut.

I was close enough to Wilber's face to see his eyes narrow before he guided me out ahead of him. He told the doctor that he'd get a second opinion. Now that we were on our way out the door the doctor felt safe enough to call out, "You really might want to try a hairdresser first."

Wilber pulled out his pistol and shot back into the examining room without even looking. I jumped and slapped my hands over my ears as the sound of it threatened to deafen me. Sharp, stabbing daggers of light pierced my skull, weakening my knees. I dropped down hard on the cement steps leading up to his door. Hands picked me up. I wanted to throw up. I glanced back to see the doctor cowering on the floor with a bullet hole in the wall just above his head. Wilber grabbed at my arm, and I jerked away, only to stumble down the five steps that led down to the street I would have fallen again, but another pair of hands caught me. The pain in my skull intensified tenfold. I shoved myself away from my helper, even thought I could barely open one eye, and I stalked back toward the waiting sedan.

It's always my way or the highway with him.

I wanted to hang on to the anger that I felt right then. Aside from the agonizing pain in my head, something else was going wrong inside me. I would rather have to deal with anger than blinding panic and fear. I didn't want to go back to the hospital. I didn't want to smell that antiseptic odor again. It brought back the feel of those hands around my neck choking the life out of me... I bolted for the car.

I didn't make it. Wilber never had much patience for drama; he caught me and easily slammed my backside across the cool metal of the trunk. My thick wool overcoat was still on the back seat so the only thing between my flesh and the metal was a white Egyptian cotton dress shirt and a suit jacket. I looked snazzy, but I wasn't warm and it wasn't the temperature that made me shiver. Wilber's huge hand was at my throat, using enough force to pin me there. I stilled, breathing short and sharp, heart beating hard like a rabbit's and my blood's roar drowned out my hearing. I must have turned as pale as a ghost, with tears streaming from my eyes. This was all done in silence because I was too scared to even sob. The last time a hand was around my throat...

The anger that transformed his face vanished like a passing shadow of a cloud and his eyes softened. The tight grip loosened, but he kept his hand pressing down on my chest.

"Ssshhhhhhh. I'm not angry at you, Goth Boy. Relax. I can feel your pulse racing."

Wilber trying to be comforting confused me.

That was what these last months have been – bewildering. The family debt was paid. My term of service to the Organization was over and I now was Wilber's private...what? I didn't know. I'd had a small closet like single bedroom when I was working, but after our Christmas in Paris I got a vacant room on the top floor that Wilber filled even more with clothes, shoes, books, movies, video games and music. Emily would have said, "you could really swing a cat in this place", but it might has well have never existed because I felt more comfortable sleeping in his king-size bed every night.

I didn't understand what he wanted.

Wilber had said that I would be able to do what I wanted yet I was told that I was going with him to his business meetings. Instead of Arm Candy clothing, I was decked out in fitted three piece suits and ties. His business associates knew what I had been and dressing me as one of Wilber's associates didn't make my presence welcome. The Organization catered to all sorts of sexual peccadilloes and I had even been the star attraction one time or another with a few of the men. I was still called Wilber's "Goth Boy."

Aside from the business meetings, I was brought along on the darker dealings that went on in the Organization. I knew Wilber hurt people. There were times when he'd come back to the house and be splattered with blood. I had just been worried that it was his.

I'd tell myself that whoever's blood was washing down the drain in the shower had deserved it. I'd been on the wrong end of Wilber's hand a number of times, but that was simple correction for minor disobedience. Despite Wilber's punishments and even despite the initial fear I'd felt meeting him, I've felt safe with him. He could be cold and cruel but it was done with resolve. He had never raised a hand against me in anger.

If anything, his anger was focused on his job.

That time...

That time, I was there to see what he was capable of was burned into my memory. Knowing and seeing is something else entirely, especially when you are physically there, up close, and personal.

****

The man, a large burly guy with a gut that hung over his belt even though his suit was high class, had done something unforgiveable. Whatever value the man once had to the Organization was now nil. A request had come down from Wilber's superiors that he handle the situation, personally. I was brought along in revealing whore boy clothes as a diversion and had to endure that man's painful gropes during the car ride. My job was to keep his attention on me and away from where the car was going. When the car came to a stop, it was in the middle of nowhere.

Wilber got of car and held his hand out to me. "Goth, come here."

Burly gripped my inner thigh and pinched hard as he pulled me back against him. "Not yet, Brawden, I'm just getting acquainted with his tender morsel. You usually flaunt your piece of fillet mignon in front..."

I ended up getting jerked across the seat out of the car while Mikey and Rick hauled Burly out on his ass in the opposite direction. Wilber kept me from dragging my knees through the gravel but I watched his eyes. Some men get angry their eyes burn in an inner fire.

Wilber's eyes get cold - frigid. That numbed fury was even more terrifying than an explosive outburst.

Burly rolled in the dirt reaching behind his back for a weapon. Wilber shoved me toward the car then stepped over and kneed Burly hard in the chin. The man's head snapped back and he landed hard sending up a cloud of dust.

"In, Goth." Wilber commanded without looking back. He reached down and pulled a gun from the back of Burly's pants.

Mikey grabbed my upper arm and pulled me to feet then steadied me as I swayed. This man who held me with such tender embrace had turned into a beast. The sound of fists slamming into the bloody mess that had been Burly's face were overly loud.

I'm not sure if I was afraid for Wilber or afraid of what he'd do, but I must have lunged towards him because Mikey and Rick both grabbed me and held me back. I stood there, held in place as Wilber pulled a long knife from his sleeve. I watched in silent horror as Wilber slid the knife up the man's cheek.

I don't know what was worse; the screams, the punches, or the brief moments of silence before the cycle started again. The fast rush of blood deafened my ears.

Wilber hooked the knife tip into the flesh of the man's lower eyelid, words that I could no longer hear slipping from his lips. The knife slid into the skin deeper and with such ease that it recalls the term of '*hot knife in butter*.'

I knew then what he was going to do as I fought against the hold the guys had on me, screaming words I don't remember now.

Wilber slammed the knife up into the man's eyeball and yanked. Blood and bits of flesh sprayed out from the wound and Wilber turned towards me. Specks of it clung to his face and blood dripped down on his chest and arms.

Burly was writhing on the ground behind him. Wilber said something then Burly rushed at him from behind. Mikey shoved me towards the car as he reached for his gun. I ended up sprawled on the ground frantically trying to turn over when I felt the ground shake.

Burly lay face down on the ground, his mangled eyeless socket staring at me and the hilt of Wilber's knife buried in the temple of his skull. The fingers of Burly's hand curled in death spasm. I could only think of those filthy nails digging into my flesh less than a few moments ago, and now he's dead.

I couldn't draw my eyes away from that twitching hand.

Wilber touched my face; something hot and sticky clung to my skin where his fingers brushed. Eyeball goo was plastered to my cheek. I threw up.

That sticky palm closed over my eyes blocking that bloody twitching mess from my sight. The stench of blood was everywhere. I'd been curled up in those same arms this morning; these hands had held me tenderly. I'd felt so protected and safe there.

I kept retching until I passed out.

When I woke, I was in the master bath at the mansion leaning up against his warm bare chest. Bathing with Wilber wasn't a chore it was a reward. It was something I always looked forward to and now he had put a different spin on it changing its meaning.

What did I do to deserve a reward?

I had thrown up on his shoes.

Wilber was gentle and…well, kind when we took a soak together. It was a treasured experience that I horded it in my heart when it happened, but at that time I hadn't felt anything, but weak and frightened. I'd witnessed a murder. I witnessed him committing a murder. This was a part of him that I had glimpsed on occasion, but he kept it so secretly hidden from me. I had made bold statements, big plans and bold gestures when I negotiated the scholarship loans. I told him that I was going to walk by his side. I started crying. How could I stand by him when I couldn't even keep from shrieking like a little girl? Then to make things worse his next words cut my legs out from under me.

"Sssssh, it was too much to expect from you, Brant. I should be glad that you can't follow me everywhere. I won't ask this of you again. I saw the world you came from, Goth Boy, and I should have

55

known you couldn't handle it. I know what you've done for the sake of your family. In my world, family fucks you over the first chance it gets. I won't bring you on Collections again. In a sick way, I am gratified that you cannot stomach what I have to do. It means that you aren't as tainted as you could be."

I didn't say anything. What could I say? I was considered to be nothing more than a bed warmer; a piece of eye candy, a coveted accessory.

After that incident, Wilber stopped touching me.

He didn't tell me to do sexual things for him or to him. It was like he'd given me a test and I'd failed miserably. I slept in my own big, king size bed all alone, barely breaking meals with him until this endless migraine forced us to this backstreet doctor.

****

Now, after three awkward months of deprivation, the first time he made skin to skin contact with me he'd wrapped his hand around my throat, but it wasn't his hand I was feeling; it was that hot demonic hand that tried to kill me.

I started to hyperventilate.

I can't take eleven years and four months more of this.

Wilber's fingers loosened slightly. "Ssssshhhh, Goth Boy. Calm down. I'll take my hand away when you relax."

Rick had jumped out of the car when it rocked from the force of my body hitting it. He stood and watched as his boss held his favorite toy on the trunk.

Wilber's palm began to lightly stroke up and down my neck. "Relax, Brant. You're going to have a heart attack if you keep this up."

"I want to go home." My voice was barely a whisper. I was surprised I could talk at all.

"I'll take you home after we see a real doctor."

"I want to go to MY home." Tears blurred my vision.

His hand tightened up on me. I closed my eyes.

He can kill me here; right at this moment. I don't care if he does. Sarah doesn't give a fuck that it was hard for me to do what I was doing or that I was doing it for her sake. I'm just a brother who should have died.

Tears poured out of the corners of my eyes, streaming back to my ears.

Wilber's words were clipped. "Goth, you don't mean that."

I kept my eyes closed. It was hard enough to say it once. My heart was beating so hard in my chest. He could kill me - I've seen him do it and he'd done it so easily then.

"You don't mean that. Say it." Wilber's voice sounded right against my ear.

That tone of voice meant that I pissed him off and the only way to avoid punishment was to cave. The sounds of the street surrounded us, but I could only hear my labored breathing and my quickened pulse pounding in my head.

"No, Wilber. I don't mean that."

He jerked me up off the trunk and pulled me right up to his face, "You're lying to me."

I turned my eyes to the pavement. "You told me to."

He let go of my shoulder with a little shove.

I staggered back until I hit the side of the car. I could feel his eyes on me, but I couldn't bring myself to meet his gaze. There was a sharp inhale as if Wilber was going to say something, but then he brushed past me and climbed into the back of the car, shutting the door behind him. I turned and looked at the blacked-out window back window.

Rick just shrugged then checked the rear door to make sure it was closed. "Maybe it's for the best, kid."

He returned to the driver's seat, and the sleek black sedan pulled away from the curb.

Wilber left me standing where I was in the street.

Now, I think I know what a family dog feels like when it gets dumped off on the side of the road. I watched the taillights come on and the car stopped at a red light. I wondered for a moment if he would come back, but when the traffic light turned green, the sedan traveled through the intersection and kept on going. I wrapped my arms around myself.

He really isn't leaving me here, right? He can't leave me here.

I watched until I couldn't see his car anymore.

He's left me here.

I blinked at the tears still in my eyes unable to block the sound of my heart still beating hard in my ears. I swallowed a couple of times and then used the white handkerchief that was tucked into my suit jacket pocket to wipe my face. He didn't like tears staining my cheeks.

What am I supposed to do now? I don't have any money. I don't have any ID. My woolen coat was in the car and while it's spring it's still a little cold.

I took a couple of steps after the car. It was going to be a long walk back to Wilber's house then staggered to a stop, a memory catching up with my pained numb brain. Wherever Wilber put me, I had to stay. It was a rule and punishment would be severe if I broke it.

This time the "spot" was on the sidewalk in a less than savory neighborhood. I moved off the road and slid my back down the nearest lamppost until my knees were tucked against my chest. I took a few deep breaths to help get my emotions under control while I thought.

I haven't seen him this angry in a long time. I shouldn't have talked back to him.

I rubbed at my aching throat and shivered from something other than the cold. The pain still throbbed from the migraine to the point it felt like a vise around my forehead.

The warmth of the early spring day dropped off quickly when the sun disappeared behind the height of the buildings, but still, I waited patiently. By the time the streetlights clicked on, I was shivering in my suit, with my hands tucked under my armpits, my torso hunched over. I pulled my knees even tighter to my chest to try to conserve heat.

Every breath I took produced a white cotton candy puff in front of my mouth. My hands were freezing, my ears were numb, my ass was cold, and my teeth were beginning to chatter, but the worst part was that my head still hurt and the cold was making it worse. I would have loved to burrow in my warm bed right about now and pull the covers up to keep the light from stabbing into my skull.

Where is Wilber? It's been more than three hours. What does he expect me to do?

I huddled miserably in the street, time crawling by. The sun went down and the street light above me came on. Lights from the apartment building across the street glowed and I watched a woman carry a bag of take-out inside. The reminder that it was way past dinner drew a growl from my stomach, but I was still more nauseous than hungry. I pressed my eyes against the top of my knees and hoped the sickness would fade.

"Lookie, lookie. Boys, I think we got us a stray."

Oh, shit.

I raised my face from my knees and saw three pairs of legs surrounding me.

"Look at that faggoty hair." From the corner of my eye, I saw a hand reach out and grab a handful of my long, black hair at the nape of my neck. He gave a hard yank that sent searing agony shooting from my head, to my teeth, and down my spine. I reached up and tried to pull my hair out of his grasp with numb and shaking fingers.

Another man tapped my foot with his dirty sneaker. "I think you're in the wrong part of town, pretty boy."

A hand from the other side grabbed another handful of hair and they yanked my head back, dragging me awkwardly from my sitting position with my face staring up towards the street light.

I scrambled, awkwardly attempting to get my feet under me.

"Or are you here waiting here hoping for a good fuck?" Spittle landed on my shirt as the hood snarled at me.

I yanked my hair out of his touch not caring that it hurt. I wanted to throw up. My head was pounding and I felt shaky.

"I'm n-not w-work-king any m-more." I knew I was cold and shivering, but I hadn't known that it would make it so hard to speak. It felt like my chest and my back muscles were contracting and conspiring against me to make me sound like an idiot. A second later, a large warm hand worked itself into my hair and jerked me onto my knees.

"So you ARE a working boy! We don't take kindly to faggots down here. Your kind usually end up stuck in a landfill somewhere. This is *our* street, fag. You pay *us* to work here. Give me your wallet."

"I d-d-don't h-h-have o-one." I couldn't stop shivering.

"You've been warming up our lamppost for hours. You owe us rent."

"Y-you d-d-don't ow-own the st-street." The knee to my kidneys, knocked me forward onto my hands and demonstrated his dislike of my truthful response. The hand, still tangled in my hair, yanked my head back up, straightening my body from its attempt at a defensive curl.

If I wasn't feeling so shitty I would be able to fight back against these punks.

Wilber had the boys at the mansion show me how to defend myself once my service was over. Everything they taught me was dirty fighting and Wilber said to avoid fighting, but if it couldn't be avoided, end it fast and end it hard. I couldn't see straight thanks to my migraine.

Where is he?

"Looks like you're going to have to pay up one way or the other." The thug behind me hoisted me to my feet, but my legs were in a different time zone. Combined with the stabbing pain in my head, my body didn't want to move the way I commanded it.

Boy number three grabbed at his crotch jerking it in my direction. "Lift his leg."

"I s-said I'm n-n-not w-wo-work-king. L-leave me al-lone." I grabbed at my hair trying to free it from the street punk's grasp.

This one had a scraggly patch of hair on his chin. His voice was mocking and cruel as he tightened his grip. "Leave me alone'? Who the *fuck* do you think you are? You think you're *better* than us just because you got fancy threads?"

Someone grabbed the collar of my jacket then pulled it off my back. The punk let go of my hair so I spun, grabbed wildly at the coat, and got a fist in the face instead. Blood filled my mouth. A knee caught me in the crotch and the next thing I knew, I was face down on the ground, cupping myself. I had nothing to empty out of my stomach, but I dry heaved anyway. I wasn't even sure which of the guys had done it.

"Manny, you need pants to go with that snazzy jacket." The fashion advice was given with a laugh.

Hands grabbed at me, yanking at my clothes, and before they'd left, they'd taken my pants and shoes. The pavement was freezing cold as I lay curled up on it in my boxers and thin cotton dress shirt with one sleeve ripped off. It was likely the only reason they'd left me that much.

Where is Wilber? He should have been back by now. Why isn't he here?

I gritted my teeth. My cock and balls were now throbbing in concert with my head. I had to get to someplace warm. I couldn't stay out here. I tried to stand and dry heaved again. Blood poured out my cut lip and mouth: everything ached and I had no doubt I'd have more than a few bruises where I'd been kicked and punched.

The only place to go was the only place I knew. I crawled back toward the doctor's door. It took more effort than I thought it would, but once I got there, I banged on it as hard as I could.

He wasn't in or he wasn't answering. Then again, why should he? Wilber shot at him. I slammed at the door again, but got no response.

I laid my back against it cradling my aching balls. In too much pain to do anything else, I slid to the stoop and leaned there. I don't know if I passed out or fell asleep, but when the door jerked open, I toppled over inside on the floor.

"What the hell? Shit." The Doctor swore as I sprawled on his floor. "Brawden beat the crap out of you?"

I couldn't talk. My teeth were chattering too much. The doctor grabbed me by my armpits and dragged my almost naked self into his hallway. "That fucker…"

I shook my head negatively.

The Doc paused for a moment. "Not Brawden?"

I heard him walk back and shut the door. The heat of his office was heavenly. I heard the beeping of cell phone buttons.

"This is Doc. I need to talk to *him*…. No, I can't leave a message…. Fine. I have his toy. Somebody broke it and left it naked in the street." I heard the cell phone snap shut. "Well, that should get us either a call back or a very pissed off loan shark at my front door. Come on, my dearie, you need some patching up."

I'm sure the cold must have frozen my brain cells but the warmth of the room thawed them.

Wilber wasn't coming back for me.

He was warm at his house probably eating dinner or reviewing loan files while I had sat and waited for him just like an abandoned puppy.

He's washed his hands of me, and it's no wonder why. I wasn't providing much service for the tuition and living expenses that Sarah was ripping through.

Irritably I couldn't help being slightly resentful of her.

Someone should have taught that girl that money doesn't grow on trees.

As soon as that thought zipped through my head, I felt ashamed of myself. I lived this lifestyle so my sisters wouldn't know hardship. It didn't make my balls ache any less, but I held onto the thought anyway. It was, after all, what had kept me going all these years.

The doctor finished poking and prodding, and pressed an icepack wrapped in a towel into my groin, then laid a warm heavy quilt over me. That felt good. It's been a while since anything had felt good.

"Thank you." At least my inner core was no longer cramping with cold.

"I don't work for free, Goth." the Doc glanced at me with a raised eyebrow. He tied two stitches in my inner lip before he stripped blood smeared gloves off and tossed them in the trash.

"Brant. My name is Brant."

Doc turned back to me. He was middle aged, well on his way to paunch and grey hair. In Wilber's world, you didn't ask anyone about their past for which I should be grateful. I've found that few want to talk to someone who's been a whore for the past eleven years.

Doc folded his arms across his chest. "Brant... I don't work for free."

"And I only know how to fuck," I retorted with a rueful, half-hearted laugh, lying back under the warm quilt, staring up at the ceiling.

"You don't need to tell me that." Doc started cleaning up as he continued, "You probably don't remember me, but I used to look after you when you were just a scrawny kid half as tall and half as wide and I was fifty pounds lighter. Once you got to the age of majority, Brawden took you to better clinics and better doctors. Don't know why he brought you back to me. You've gotten big and tall, but you ain't got anything in that the noggin of yours aside from fucking. You're still that skinny kid Brawden pimped out."

He turned toward me, scowling. "If he took you in that damn young, it was his responsibility to teach you how to survive," he snarled, throwing the bloody towel he'd used along with the one he'd just dried his hands off on into a big bin. "I need a drink. You want one?"

My tongue probed the stitches inside my lip. A drink would sting and I hadn't eaten anything since breakfast. I shook my head and snuggled down under the warmth of the quilt. There had been days when I thought I would never get warm.

Wilber isn't coming back. He's tossed me away. What am I going to do? What can I do?

Even though I'd been to "on-line university" and gotten top grades, I wasn't going to kid myself. The truth was as obvious as a pig in a tutu: my only wage earning accomplishment was fucking. For some reason, that unfortunate fact struck me and my lips curled into something that didn't quite qualify as a smile.

Look at me. If I had any survival skills, I could have hustled those three punks like most other "hardened" whores. I could have negotiated a price. I could have earned some money instead of being beaten and stripped. Inside, I laughed. *Who am I trying to kid? Without Wilber's protection, I'd be dead in some alley because someone didn't want to pay $20 bucks for a blow job.*

Tears began to burn in my eyes. I couldn't go home. Not to that place that held people like Emily and beautiful, innocent Madison.

I don't belong in that world anymore. I don't think I ever did. Tears leaked from the corner of my eyes.

Wilber was my home... and he doesn't want me anymore.

I started sobbing as I held the ice pack between my legs. I hurt everywhere. I was just one big bruise.

I must have cried myself to sleep, because the next thing I heard was the crash of the doctor's front door getting kicked in. I blinked and turned my head slightly to look over the edge of the blanket only to see Wilber's stone cold visage as he stood in the entryway scanning the room. The last time I'd seen that killer expression was when he pried the client, who was trying to make my final performance as an adult entertainer into a snuff film.

Before my brain could flip it's on switch, the blanket was ripped from its tucked, warmth conserving, position around my body, causing me to shiver.

"Who did this?" Wilber asked softly, his eyes scanning my body's injuries.

I just blinked, unable to believe that Wilber was here.

Mikey dragged the doctor into the examination room and shoved him in front of Wilber.

"Who did this?" Wilber's voice was calm and cool. His face was almost expressionless, but it was his eyes that told me just how enraged he was.

"I don't know," the doctor quickly replied, jerking his arm from Mickey's grip. "I thought I heard someone at the door and when I opened it, he fell in looking like this."

"Was he raped?" His words were softly spoken, but I could feel the energy vibrating within his massive body. I shuddered as Wilber's hand brushed strands of hair back off my face.

The Doc tried for nonchalance. "Is that the lesson you were trying to teach him?"

Wilber's arm snaked out and grabbed the doctor by the throat. "I asked you a question. Making me repeat it is not beneficial to your continued good health."

"No. There is no evidence of sexual..." Wilber shoved the doctor away.

"Oomph!" The doctor crashed backwards into Mikey.

"You were supposed to go home, boy." Wilber's hand gripping my chin. He turned my face firmly toward him and seeing the huge bruise that I knew had to have already started to form, he hissed.

His thumb pressed into my mouth opening it. He looked at the row of stitches on the inside of my lower lip and asked, "Why didn't you go home? That's where you said you wanted to go."

I couldn't meet his eyes. "I don't have a home."

"Your Dad would have come for you."

"He's not my Dad." I turned my head away from his touch. "I don't look like any of them."

"She was your mother, though."

Blinking, I turned back to look at him with slightly drawn together eyebrows. I honestly hadn't thought of that.

His eyes weren't that angry, flat-dull brown anymore. Wilber reached out and tucked another long black strand of hair behind my right ear.

I just lay there, cradling my bruised genitals with the ice pack looking anywhere but at him.

There was a slight pause before Wilber started talking again. "I checked into your background not long after you started working for me. Marion Jane Anderson Williams was your mother. She got pregnant when she was fifteen. Her father was a strict man. From what I gathered, he basically told her that if she could go out and have fun making a baby, she would be taking the responsibility of raising that baby as well. Once you were born, she stopped attending any after school activities because she had to come home and take care of you.

"Police reports stated that you only four and were alone with your grandfather when he had a heart attack and died so it's really no wonder why you really do not remember much of your childhood."

"If you were wondering, your biological father was a high school jock." Wilber's fingertips ran over my eyebrow then the back of his finger stroked down my cheek. "He was a fifteen year old punk in a panic when your mother told him about her situation. He denied you, but you look exactly like him. He was killed in a car wreck the same year your grandfather died. Your dad, David, married your mom even though she had a four-year-old kid but he took you in and gave you his name. There are few men who would do that, Brant. You could call him your stepfather however he IS your dad of his own free will."

"I'm not welcome there." I ached. I just ached everywhere, especially in the middle of my chest. *I'm not going to cry.*

"It's your house. You bought it."

"It's my sisters' house." Swallowing hard, I looked down at my ice pack, "Why…why did you leave me out there?"

"You lied to me."

"I'm sorry." I could feel the tears pooling in my eyes.

I need know. I can't live like this anymore. I don't know what I want I just know that I don't want…whatever this was. These past six months have been hell.

"I just…I just can't take it anymore. When you put your hand around my throat…it wasn't you. It was that guy again and I couldn't do anything to stop it. What did I do? I've been thinking and thinking, but I can't come up with a reason you stopped sleeping with me. Tell me. Tell me, what I did that was so wrong?"

"Goth?"

"You don't want me in your bed anymore?" I heard feet shuffling and the clearing of a throat.

I don't care if it's awkward for everyone here. I'm the one who must deal with this.

"I do want you in my bed." Wilber caught my chin and raised my head so I had to look him directly in the face. "I want you."

My heart was bruised enough for today. I couldn't bear to hear this on top of everything else. I knew better than to try and turn away from him as my tears poured over my cheeks and onto his fingers.

"Brant, you're *not* a sex slave. You've paid your debt to the Organization so that part of your life is behind you now. Our agreement is a partnership. If you want to share my bed, you'll have to decide to climb into it. I won't order you to join me. I want you to do it because you want to of your own free will and desire."

Wilber's voice was soft and low almost a deep rumble that vibrated through my chest.

For a moment he paused then he added, "I've been waiting for you to come to me, Brant."

"A sex slave is all I know how to be." My words were barely a whisper, but I knew he heard them because his face got still again.

"Boss?" Mikey called from the front door of the office.

"What'd you find out?"

"Brant just sat in the street and waited. When it got dark, three punks came up and kicked him around and stole his suit. The old man across the street said he just let them beat him. He never even tried to defend himself."

"Brant?"

My voice was low almost a whisper of shame. Wilber's fingers tightened on my jaw. "I have to stay where you put me."

The doctor rubbed at his reddened neck then gave a half-hearted chuff of a laugh. "You taught him well, Brawden. You taught him how to be anybody's fuck toy and doormat. If you're done treating him like a sex toy, you need to teach him how not to be. He came to you so young, he doesn't know anything else. He's got the body of a man but up here..." The doctor tapped his temple, "is the kid who entered this business."

Warm arms came around me shoulders and I was pulled gently up against his chest. The scent of his aftershave was mixed with cigar smoke.

Wilber was smoking? The only time he smokes is when he's wrestling with a decision. Was it over me?

The quilt was wrapped back around my shoulders then Wilber's hand settled on the back of my head.

"What do you want for fixing him up?"

The Doc cleared his throat. "One skipped payment. Not enough people getting shot lately. Well they're getting shot; they just ain't getting off the street to get patched up."

"Done."

Wilber's arms scooped under my back and legs before lifting my body, cradling me like I was nothing more than a child, swaddled up in the warm quilt. I was so damned tall, but Wilber could still sling me around as if I were a child half my age. "Those hoods are going to be coming to you..."

"Drop another payment, and it's as good as amputated."

"Done."

I leaned into him, thinking. *He was waiting for me to come to him while I waited for him to call for me. He was giving me a choice. The choice. So does this mean that I'm not a whore anymore? It's my decision?*

I pressed my good cheek up against his chest, savoring the warmth coming through his dress shirt. I finally felt safe.

Wilber climbed into the car. He sat back on the seat, slipped me down and cradled me against him. He'd been careful not to jostle me, but it didn't matter since I was just happy to be in his arms. I'd have put up with anything right then.

"We're quite a pair, Goth Boy, both of us acting like schoolboys with a secret crush on each other and being too damned stupid to do anything about it."

He pressed his lips lightly against the top of my head in a kiss. "First things first." Shifting me on his lap, he reached into his pocket and pulled out a switch blade. He grabbed a handful of hair at the back of my neck and moved to slice it off.

"Wait." I shifted so I was bent over and pulled handfuls my hair forward exposing my nape and the heaviest part. "Under cut it; that way the top would still make it look long."

Wilber pulled me back upright. "I think we will get you to a hairdresser."

He shook his head, pressing his lips together tightly. "The doctor is right. I taught you to submit to my commands. I need to teach you how to stand up again. The agreement between us is just that, an agreement. We are in an agreement for a specified amount of time for a specified amount of money. If there is something that you do not want to do, you have that option of not doing it. You are not a slave. You are not working off a debt. Your life is your own and you need to live it, but none of this would have happened if you weren't hiding things from me."

He leaned forward and gently pressed a kiss to my mouth. It was a short kiss and, when he pulled back, he ran his thumb over my bottom lip. "Don't keep things from me again, Goth Boy."

It'd probably have hurt more if he kissed me normally so I was glad he didn't, but I was also grateful for the affection after the terrible night I'd had. "Please keep me warm," I pleaded, still feeling the aftershocks of being cold. My black, wool coat was draped over the quilt and tucked around me. "I love you, Wilber."

"What did I tell you about lying?"

Immediately, I felt the rush of heat that undoubtedly colored my face at his quick censure. I didn't think I was lying, but I also wasn't going to talk back.

Wilber leaned closer and slipped an arm around my shoulders. "You don't know what love is, Brant. You know ownership. When you can stand on your own and hold your head up high, you can offer up those words and I'll believe you. Right now, you're not thinking clearly. We'll get you home, warmed up, and get you in my bed so we both can rest. Tomorrow, we'll see about getting you to a hairdresser for your headaches. I think you also need a job because you need to socialize more with people closer to your own age."

"Not collections."

"I'll find something, Goth. By the way, I've cut your sister's funding off." He pressed me back against his chest when I tried to sit up, "She needs to come to an understanding that there is no such thing as a free ride. She has grown up spoiled because you were on your back. Little Miss Sarah needs to have an attitude adjustment."

I was more than a little alarmed. "What are you going to do?"

"Nothing to harm her. I'm going to give her a budget. If she can't live within it, she gets herself a job."

"Wait. What about our agreement? You are supposed to be giving her money." I frowned and squirmed trying to sit up.

"You're paying her tuition, Brant, not financing her collegiate lifestyle. She's cut off until she calls the number at the bottom of the notice. A job, like something at the local copy shop will do her some good. Elbow grease goes a long way to building character. Humility will do wonders for young Sarah."

I couldn't help remembering when I used to change her diapers or that day I sewed the ear back on her favorite rabbit when she was so heartbroken that it'd fallen off. I taught her how to tie her shoes and how to skip rope. My most vivid memory of her though is of her screaming at me wishing me dead… He said that humility would do wonders for her and I hoped he was right.

"What are you thinking, Goth Boy?"

I don't know if I could really hear it or if it was just wishful thinking, but I thought I could hear Wilber's heartbeat from where I leaned on him. "You weren't coming back, were you?"

He took a deep breath and gave a sigh.

My whole body moved with the motion.

"At the time I was a little angry that you honestly believed that I would hurt you. I thought it best to leave you to your family. I won't do that again. I am your family. You are mine. Get warm, Brant. When we get home, you will start your new life all over again. This time, I'll help you adjust." His hand came up under my chin and he gently urged my chin up. "I know how strong you are, but you don't have a clue do you? Doc was right. I taught you submission. I need to demonstrate to you just how strong you are and that there is a time to surrender and a time when not to."

The cell phone went off in his coat pocket right beside my cheek. I sat up slightly so he could retrieve it.

Wilber looked at the call display. "Well, well, that was quick. I only froze her accounts three hours ago."

I listened quietly while Wilber laid out the facts of life to my sister. "Money doesn't grow on trees, Miss Williams, but you seem to think so. Have you ever considered how much you spend? Did you ever stop to think where it comes from? You exhaust all avenues to pay for your higher education, yet when a check arrives in your name, you cash it without question. You get a registered letter informing you of a generous benefactor who chose you out of all the students clambering for student aid to pay for your entire tuition, board, and books. Did you even think to stop and question it? Where does that money come from, Miss Sarah?"

Wilber wrapped an arm over my shoulder and hugged me hard against him so I was close enough to the cell phone to hear Sarah spluttering for words.

"You're a spoiled child. You grab at everything you see because you want it - not that you deserve or need it. Someone is paying your bills, little girl, and it's the same person who has paid the Williams' family debt."

Sarah started to say something, but Wilber cut her off, "While you were spending the money he works very hard to earn, did you even stop and offer up a kind word for his sacrifices? He doesn't *have* to do this. I would rather he left you twisting in the wind, but I am also benefiting from his generosity."

"I got a scholarship." Sarah protested.

"To a foundation you never applied to. Did you wonder about that before you deposited the check?"

"Well... yes." Sarah's voice was hesitant. "It was Brant?"

"Yes, it is. Even though you denied him as your brother, he takes familial duties close to heart. He paid off all your mother's medical bills, bought the house you grew up in and now is sending you on to higher education. For all that he has done for your family, a single ruined turkey dinner doesn't balance out, does it?"

"...what?" She remained silent as Wilber ran down an accounting of Dad's debts as well as my original offer.

There was a long silence as Wilber allowed realization to sink in. "Right now, Brant is working to secure a future for his little sisters. Once again he has done this of his own free will." More silence hung in the air after Wilber finished speaking. "Is there something you would like to tell your big brother, Miss Sarah?"

"Oh, my God, he's there?" There was a long period of silence.

Wilber glanced down at the screen on the phone to check if they were still connected. "Are you still there? Do you have anything to say to your brother?"

Sarah's voice was very subdued. "Please...let me speak to him."

Wilber pressed the cell phone up to my ear. I took a deep breath. "Sarah."

Her voice was a little shrill the way it would get when she was a little girl and trying hard not to cry. Her tone wasn't as hard as it was when she wished me dead, but it was just as forceful with her anger. "Why didn't you tell me?"

"What could you have done?" I took the cell from Wilber's hand.

"Dad could have rescued you."

"Would you have wanted Emily doing what I had to do?" Wilber began pulling the strands of hair that hung in my face back behind my ears making sure not to interfere with the call.

"No! But...there had to be another way."

"Things happened the way they were supposed to be. You're an auntie."

"You're an uncle."

"Not if Emily's husband has any say in the matter."

Sarah sucked in air. "Oh shit, you don't know! You should have heard the drag out fight after you left. I've only seen sissy that angry once before...when...when Dad must have told her what you had done for us. She never raises her voice so it must have been something important." Sarah's voice trailed off.

I cut her off before she could start imagining the horror I had gone through. The sad thing - no, the good thing, was that she couldn't imagine what I had gone through. "I was fine. I had a guardian angel."

Her voice came out in the rush of words and repentance. "I'm sorry, Brant! I should never have said those things. I regretted it once I calmed down. You came home and I drove you away."

"Don't worry about it. I don't belong there anyway. Do good in school."

"I'll get a scholarship next year, Brant. You won't have to pay for me."

"Do what you can. I've got you covered, Sarah."

"Why did you do this for us?"

"That's what big brothers do. You're my little sisters. When I was doing this I was hoping that you and your sisters were playing with dolls and experimenting with makeup and thinking about whether some boy likes you. You shouldn't have to worry how many clients you would have that night. No girl needs to know that."

"Boys don't need to know that neither," she whispered, managing to snap her voice at me again but this time for a very different reason. "Thank you, Brant. I know why Emily was so furious at me now, but I think it was Roger who took most of the flak." There was a long pause. "Can you come home for Easter? You've got about ten chocolate Easter bunnies waiting for you." She suddenly coughed a bit, as if embarrassed, before amending her statement. "Well, the ears are missing…"

I glanced at Wilber. "You are not contracted property any longer, Brant," he whispered too softly for Sarah to hear. "You can come and go where you please. Guy is there for your protection not your supervision."

Nodding, I accepted the olive branch. "I'll be there as long as everyone is okay with it."

"I love you, Brant. Thank you for doing what you did. You're the best big brother ever." Just before the click, I heard a bit of a strangled sob.

Wilber shifted me slightly, took the cell phone back, and tucked it into his suit pocket. "Do you understand your strength yet, Brant? Do you even have an inkling of what you are capable of? I don't think you do. Lesser men wouldn't have survived the past ten years and no matter what anyone else says, I did not take it easy on you. Keeping you safe and providing higher end clientele resulted in higher fees. Business is business." He hugged me tighter.

"Don't worry; life begins again for you today. I will enjoy showing you the wonders you have forgotten, Brant. We will figure things out day by day until you realize just how strong you are. Then I want to see just how far you can go."

I closed my eyes and nuzzled closer to Wilber. The spicy scent that was his alone filled my head. I only wanted to go as far as his bed. I missed his touch. I didn't want much out of this world. I just wanted him –Wilber Brawden, extreme venture capitalist and guardian angel. Why a guardian angel? Nobody lets a whore drag out debt repayment over ten years. He could have taken my sisters and forced them to the brothels one at a time as one burned out to get the debt repaid sooner. I was a rags-to-riches story, a *Cinderella*. My clientele was a list of fortune 500 and famous celebrities. A brothel worker brought in hundreds a night. I brought in tens of thousands.

Inhaling Wilber's unique scent, I let my body relax against him. His arm wrapped around my shoulder. That felt so good.

I wasn't stupid maybe just a little naïve even after all I've done. I'd have to learn to be stronger if I wanted to stay with him and I wanted to.

Chapter Four: Niche

A couple of days following the mugging and suffering through another migraine, I was taken to a beauty salon and spa. I had expected a barber's chair not this high-end sort of place. When I finally climbed into the back of the limo about twelve inches, a full foot length, was taken off my hair by a professional stylist who very dramatically and very reluctantly coiffed my glorious do. Once I explained why I needed it cut, he clucked and multi-layered my hair -- he left the top a long length, while the hair underneath was cut shorter and thinned out. The headaches disappeared almost overnight.

I wanted to be in Wilber's bed the moment he drove us back to his house and I was, just not the way I intended. At first, Wilber said that I was too injured to hold and that we should wait until all bruises had healed. I was allowed into his room and into his bed only to the extent of snuggling. As the nights went on, if I pressed for more, I was sent back to my room. I preferred lying next to him, feeling the heat of his body close to mine, with the sound of his breathing breaking the silence rather than my solitary, cold and lonely bed.

My bruises were healed. My headaches were gone. I was gearing up my courage to insist that I spend my nights in Wilber's arms when he sprung another surprise on me. Most mornings I ate breakfast with him then waved him off for his day. This time he bundled me in his car and we drove to a new destination.

"I break people, Goth. I don't fix them," he stated abruptly, slipping his arm around my shoulders.

Taking that as a sign I shifted across the limo's bench seat so I could lean in and steal a kiss. He turned his head at the last moment and my lips pressed against his cheek.

"Wilber?" My voice was a little hoarse with my desire.

He kissed my forehead then settled back in the seat, but pulled me up to his side. We rode like that in silence for a few more minutes.

We pulled to up to an old brownstone that had been newly renovated into professional offices.

"Wilber?" I didn't keep the puzzlement from my tone.

"I can't fix you, Brant. I don't know the first step on how to do it. Those punks were nothing, yet you let them kick the crap out of you. I tell you you're smart. I tell you you're strong. I tell you all these things because I believe they're true but you don't believe me so maybe you need to hear it from someone else. Dr. Robert Kirkpatrick is waiting for you. What you two decide to talk about is your business. I won't ask, but I will listen if you want to tell me things. My door will always be open to you, Goth Boy." He pulled my face towards him and kissed my forehead.

My expression must have been one of confusion and disappointment.

"Doc was right. You're not a whore any longer, Brant. You did what you had to because that was the deal we made. Now it's time to put it behind you. It's sad to say it, but I don't know how to help you."

"It *is* behind me." *Didn't he know it was fine if I was beside him?*

Wilber played with my hair allowing the dark strands to slip through his fingers. "We'll leave it up to a professional. Call Guy when your session is over and he will come to pick you up. I'll be home for dinner."

This time when I climbed out of the car and watched it pull away from the curb, I didn't have the devastating heartache. He was coming home for dinner. I couldn't keep a smile off my face.

How stupid was that? I was happy because he was coming home for dinner...with me.

I guess it was partially because I'd started puttering in the kitchen again and had rediscovered the joys of baking. Wilber didn't have much of a sweet tooth, but he did like cupcakes. I could make some for him. I kept that grin on my face until I finally got to meet Dr. Kirkpatrick. I thought this doctor would be a step up from the backdoor doc, but he wasn't that type of doctor. Honestly, I didn't know what Wilber wanted. A quick physical then I could get back to the house to start baking; however, there wasn't going to be anything quick about this appointment.

Kirkpatrick was a shrink.

I wasn't going anywhere quickly anytime soon.

****

I had excellent control over denying or disbelieving that something had happened that I didn't like. Apparently, that was part of my coping mechanism. It was necessary in the past, but I didn't have to live there anymore. I didn't have to stay in that place, but it was my choice to move forward...or not. So, Dr. Kirkpatrick said when our time was up.

I found it hard to move on when my ribs ached with every breath.

That night Wilber took me back into his arms and I greedily fell into them. He never said anything about the doctor's appointment and I didn't offer details.

I laid back in his king size bed and gave him my best come hither look.

Wilber hithered.

Wilber was fucking me, but he was considerate and tender. He held his weight off me and kept a large hand spread wide on my lower back supporting my hips while he thrust deep. He took care to find and hit my prostate which never failed to make me cry out in passion. Laughing in my hair, he hit it again.

The only problem was... maybe it wasn't really a problem at all... but I didn't want him considerate and tender.

I wanted his weight driving me down into the mattress, pinning me there, forcing to me to accept his hard, huge cock. I wanted all his strength.

79

He hit the spot again with a firm thrust. Considerate yet restrained consideration.

His tender strokes only made me feel fragile in his arms. I needed that other feeling, that brutal attack, so I could show him that I was strong like he wanted me to be. I arched my back up off the bed, driving him deeper. My legs locked around his waist pressing my heels down hard enough to make dents in his ass cheeks.

He swallowed my cry. His tongue forced its way inside my lips, rubbing against mine. His hands slid from my lower back up to my shoulders, as his knees anchored on the bed, and jerked me upwards, changing the angle of penetration. My forehead now rested against his shoulder and the hot sweaty flesh of our stomachs rubbed against each other.

That's better, but it's still not quite what I want. I wrapped my arms around his shoulders while he pistoned down into me, rocking me hard on his body.

"Tell me what you want from me, Goth Boy." He hit that glory spot deep within me again.

I threw my head back, exposing my throat. My cry was pure joy.

"Tell me."

When my brain started to function again, I whispered, "Tie me up."

Wilber's muscles turned rigid, making him still as a stone, then without any warning, he pushed me off. The move was so unexpected that I landed on my back - stunned. By the time, I got my wits about me, Wilber had snagged his purple silk dressing gown and disappeared into the master bath. Panting, I stared up at the ceiling the entire scene raced through my mind. He asked: I answered – truthfully this time.

Apparently, he didn't like my answer.

With a rough voice, full of sexual desire, I stage whispered, "Wilber?"

"You need to go to your own room." His answer was muffled by the thick wooden door, but the meaning was clear. If he had hauled off and hit me, it couldn't have hurt worse. I bit my lower lip and crawled out of his bed then searched for my clothes which were scattered across the room. Numbly, I picked up my pants and started to dress.

What is with him? He asked what I liked and I told him. I've always gotten the most pleasure from him when he ties me to his bed and fucks me into near oblivion.

I knew that I liked it because it only happened when he was genuinely pleased with me after a night of client service. Quitting that side of his business ventures had entirely halted that reward and I missed it.

To be honest, what I really miss is Wilber being proud of me. His satisfaction with my work and a hard fucking went hand in hand. Since I'd become Wilber's exclusive property it seemed as if I could never do anything right.

I padded to the bedroom door and was reaching to twist the knob, but the sound of the master bath's door opening again made me pause.

"Why did you say that, Brant?"

He called me Brant.

Lately, he only called me that when he was annoyed. I swallowed hard, turned to face him, and was unpleasantly surprised to find him stalking toward me. I'd fully intended to stand my ground, but when he marched into my space, I was struck with the fact that he was built like a linebacker and I wasn't. When Wilber continued to advance, I backpedaled until my back hit the wall. He placed both hands flat on either side of my head wedging me firmly into the corner.

"Do not slouch." His voice was a little tight and sharp, but the tone was even.

I hated it when he used that tone with me. It just highlighted his disappointment with me. I'd rather he yelled at me, anger I could handle.

I straightened my shoulders back into a straight line, touching either side of the wall's corner, but kept my eyes down.

"Do not cower."

I lifted my head to stare at his left ear lobe because I couldn't stare at him in the eye. I hadn't built up enough courage to do that yet, not face to face. A firm grip locked his fingers to the sides of my jaw, tilting it so I had no choice, but to look into his cold, brown eyes.

His gaze narrowed. The crow's feet lines at the corner of his eyes grew deeper and his lips pressed into a firm frown, "Look at me and tell me why you asked for that?"

I tried to duck my head.

Instead of letting go, he bumped the back of my skull into the corner. "Brant."

"It's *what* I know. It's *all* I know." I hated the way my voice cowered. This wasn't the way to show him that I was strong.

Less than a half breath later, I was on my knees, covering my head with my arms as Wilber punched a hole in the wall where my face had been.

Roughly, he grabbed my wrist then yanked me back to my feet.

It felt like he ground my bones together in his grip then a hard-sharp stab travelled up my arm. Panicking I swung instinctively with the other arm, somehow hitting Wilber right in the face.

There was a moment of stunned silence between the both of us.

His grip wavered.

I immediately took the chance to jerk my hand free and fled.

Oh, my God. I punched Wilber!

"BRANT!" His roar followed after me.

I bolted down the stairs absolutely convinced that he was going to kill me. I scurried down the risers away from Wilber's voice that chased after me and at that time, it didn't matter that all I had on were unbuttoned jeans.

Wilber's yelling brought Mikey, who had a spoon dangling out of his mouth and ice cream in a bowl, out the entertainment room off the second landing.

He attempted to grab me, but I dodged him, knocking the ice cream out of his hand. I didn't waste time, I jumped over the side railing to land in the foyer. Sharp agony ripped up my arm with the hard jolt. I yelped in pain.

Guy opened the door and began waving his arms like he was trying to corral a skittish colt.

I slipped to his right ducking through the nearest open door.

He turned, chasing me down the length of the dining room.

We emerged behind Mikey who had managed to get near the front door.

It took two seconds jerk the door open and get my feet working on escape, but luck was on Wilber's side: I ran right into Rick.

"HOLD HIM!" Wilber shouted from the landing.

Rick caught my upper arms.

I struggled, trying to kick at his shins, but my attempt to pull free was unable to get any force behind them. A sudden move on his part had me kissing the floor with my right arm angled up against my back. *Oh god, that hurts.* I continued to fight.

He just raised my arm further up my back and leaned his weight against the small of my back, effectively pinning me down to the floor.

Wilber came down the stairs at a slow and deliberate pace.

It drove my terror of the consequences of punching him to new heights. I'd never done this before, not even as a punk-assed kid. I just let him do what he wanted to my body without fighting him – physically.

"Stand him up."

Rick and Mikey both hauled me off the floor. Rick held me by my aching forearm and Mikey had his hand buried in my hair by the back of my neck.

The moment Wilber reached the foyer I tried to back through them. My whole body trembled and I broke in a cold clammy sweat. I screwed my eyes shut and tried my best to turn my head despite Mikey's hold.

"Open your eyes, Brant."

I hung my head forward staring down at the parquet floor.

Mikey wrenched my head back by jerking hard on my hair.

That hurt!

I gasped and opened my eyes, blinking a couple of times to clear my vision.

Wilber was right in front of me, blood slowly seeping out of his nose.

I could hear my heart beating faster than a hummingbird's as well as my shallow, panting breathing.

Wilber wiped at the blood trailing down his face.

"Goth…" he started as he looked down at the redness on his hand.

Whatever else he said, I didn't hear as I hyperventilated myself out of consciousness.

****

The next morning, I woke in my room, all toasty warm, still dressed in last night's clothes instead of my usual t-shirt and PJ bottoms, with a downy soft duvet tucked around me. I ached everywhere thanks to Rick who had not pulled his throw when he'd knocked me down. I slowly sat up and went to push the duvet off, but my wrist throbbed. A casual glance told me that it was discolored and swollen, but otherwise it seemed okay. I could open and close my hand, but it pulsed hot and felt weak. Other than that, nothing else seemed out of order which would mean I should consider myself damned lucky. I'd seen Wilber break people's hands and arms just for touching him and I'd drawn blood.

I eased into a sitting position to stare down at my feet dangling off the side of the bed. Someone had put socks on me. I slid off the bed and headed for the bedroom door, opening it.

Guy was standing there. He turned and looked at me. None of his French-Canadian *joie d'vivre* was in his expression today.

"*Bonbon*, take a shower then put on a suit. Try to hurry; *Monsieur* Brawden is not in a good mood. I am to bring you to

84

breakfast. Now, *mon Petite Bonbon. Tout suite*," he said then he pulled the door out of my hand.

The sound of him locking the door shook my hard-fought calm with the force of a pistol shot. I was still in trouble and I didn't need to compound it by being late. I glanced at the clock. Wilber left the house at 8:30 every morning so I had twenty minutes to get presentable and down to the kitchen table. I did a quick inventory in the mirror after I scrubbed up and washed my hair as best I could with only one hand. I had bruises on my chest and the front of my left shoulder. Although the shower's heat soothed the bruises, it stabbed at the agony already running through my purple tinted, swollen wrist causing it to pulse with pain. To give it some support, I carefully wrapped my hand and wrist in an elastic bandage from the medicine cabinet, then got into a dark grey suit with a pale green shirt and tie. I still had about five minutes to get downstairs. I knocked on the bedroom door with my good hand then waited for it to open.

Guy escorted me downstairs to Wilber. When we reached the kitchen door, Guy gestured for me to go before him.

My stomach clenched tight knowing that it was too late for food; it was already 8:28.

Wilber looked up from the morning paper as I walked in. His eyes flicked over me. Apparently, I passed inspection, because Wilber pointed to my regular spot beside him at the linen covered table, "Sit. Don't slouch." I winced at the hard-unforgiving tone he was still using from last night.

My long, but not so heavy, hair was still damp and was a little clammy against my neck. I sat up straight and leveled my shoulders. I dropped my bandaged wrist below the table so Wilber wouldn't notice.

"You didn't eat last night so you will eat breakfast." This command was followed by the snap of the morning newspaper. It sounded like a whip.

"But it's 8:30..." My voice trailed off at his sharp gaze that pinned me in my place.

"Arguing with me first thing in the morning is never a good thing. My first meeting isn't until 9:30." He set his newspaper aside and stared at me. "Brant."

"Yes, Wilber?" My voice was cracked and dry.

He reached out and caught my arm. Carefully, he lifted my bandaging job up to his line of vision. "This is broken?"

I shook my head negatively. "It just aches."

"I'm not surprised. The way you hit me you could have broken your thumb."

"I'm sorry. I got scared and I…" My words trailed off. There was no excuse for hitting him. If my arm was broken I deserved it. "I…"

"Sssh. Eat your pancakes," he soothed.

Guy set a big stack of pancakes and a warmed carafe of syrup were set in front of me along with cranberry juice and a cup of decaf.

I was hungry, but I was sure the food would get stuck in my throat.

"You do not want me to feed you, Goth Boy. You know how fun that can be." Which meant it wouldn't be.

Wilber's voice was still far from indulgent, so I took it as the warning it was meant to be. I had tried a hunger strike, once. Back when I was about nineteen when felt like I was losing the small sense of self that I still harbored. I had passed my home school secondary courses and had been accepted into the local university, but what was the point? Clients were still grunting away in me every other day. My stomach would ache some days so it was better to skip meals than deal with the burning pain for hours on end. That was when I realized that my life was regimented into hourly blocks. At this time, it was school, at that time it was a work out, at that other time I was working off my debt. I did what Wilber wanted because he said so and it didn't hurt, it was easier to cave than to make a fuss. The only time I had to myself was meal times. I wasn't trying to kill myself the way Wilber feared I was; I was trying to gain some control over my meager existence. I thought I could at least control my appearance. My body, my choice. I was proven woefully wrong. Being force fed was something I never wanted from Wilber again.

Guy picked up the carafe and handed it to me before slipping back to the door. Slowly I drenched everything on my plate in syrup thinking that it couldn't get stuck in my throat if it were slimy.

Apparently, I couldn't even eat right.

"Sit up. Chew slowly. You are not a barbarian. Keep your mouth closed. No one wants to see what you're eating. You have style and class; your eating habits should reflect that."

I was sick to my stomach, but I slowed down, cleaned up my manners, and ate like Wilber wanted me to eat. Finally, I scraped the bottom of the plate. This waiting for punishment was getting to me. "Wilber?"

"Yes?"

"Will you please just punish me and get it over with." I rubbed at my stomach. My windpipe felt like it was on fire from the moment food hit my stomach.

"Punishment? Last night, I asked you a question and you gave me an honest answer. I owe *you* an apology for overreacting to desires that I didn't want to hear. I deserve more from you than a punch in the nose." Wilber's voice was still clipped, but the ice I thought was directed at me was really reflected on himself.

My jaw dropped slightly As I gaped at him.

"I have asked you to be honest with me, Brant. I cannot punish you for being honest. It is true, that Client service is all that you have been exposed to, and that's my fault. So, I'm going to expose you to something else." He leaned over and picked a briefcase off the floor and set it on the table. "This is yours. Now, go brush your teeth. We're going to work."

What?

"Wilber, what are you talking about?!"

"You have a university education. You graduated with honors in business administration. You have book smarts, Goth Boy; Now I'm going to teach you life smarts. Today you'll start working for me as a low level executive entry in the Organization."

Hearing that made me swallow hard so Wilber added, "No one needs to know of our personal arrangement. My car leaves in five minutes. I can tell you right now, your boss does not like tardiness but I will make this one exception."

Uh...

At this point, I couldn't even think coherent words so I got up and brushed my teeth then headed out to the limo. I almost got to the door before I realized I left the briefcase on the kitchen table. I turned around and almost bounced off Rick. He handed me the briefcase and an icepack.

"Twenty minutes on your shoulder. You're moving rather stiff. There are aspirins in the front pocket of the case," He said before he turned and headed back into the house.

Rick took me down hard last night in less than a heartbeat. Now he gives me some painkillers with an ice pack and just walks away?

"Goth!"

I trotted back to the car and climbed into the limo, hugging the briefcase to my chest. "You said, work for you?" I hesitated, trying to get some information out of him before being thrown to the wolves in the Organization.

"I've taken you to meetings and asked your opinions in the past, while the other heads might have thought of you only as eye candy, I know better. Your insights on people's characters have always impressed me, Goth Boy." Wilber reached into his suit front and pulled out a calfskin wallet and handed it to me. I flipped it open. I had credit cards and my ID and about two grand in bills. I stared at the gift shocked. I'd never had this much money, ever.

"You remember about a month back you were checking some figures that weren't sitting right with me. You pointed out that there was consistent transposition of numbers in the books. Well I had an outside source check into it and it turns out that that someone has been doctoring the figures to cover up embezzlement. We recovered most of the money but if you didn't find him when you did, there would have been hell to pay at year end. So, your internship is over. You are starting as our point man at a small office on 56th."

I just sat there glued to the seat, slouched but rigid as an oak branch.

Point man?

"In your briefcase are six applications that came in last week. If you're wondering if this is a legitimate job, it is. However, you only have this day to prove yourself."

His gaze made tingles crawl up my skin.

"If you fail, you'll be following me around as eye candy for the next eleven and a half years."

The hint of a threat sank in and I straightened up on the seat. "Others wanted this job?"

"Of course, they did, Goth. I pushed hard to get you into a position where you could earn a shot at a job like this. I did it because I have faith in your abilities and not because of our relationship. Hopefully you can believe in yourself." The limo cruised to a halt.

"Brant, I cannot show you favoritism. Truthfully, you don't need it. I've always admired your force of will and your brilliant mind. It's time to put them both to good use." Wilber turned to me and brought his hand up to my face.

I tried not to flinch.

The skin around his eyes seemed to furrow a little deeper as he urged me closer. I felt a small spark of fear in my chest as I forced myself still. Somehow, he must have realized what I felt because he let out a sigh and the lines of his face relaxed a little.

"I didn't mean to scare you last night, Goth. It just makes me angry when you drop back into service mode because I see you as being so much more. I want you to stand tall on your own and I know that I often lack the patience necessary for you to learn. Honestly, that has always been one of my faults. I must keep telling myself that you have basically been a slave for almost half your life so I can't expect you to shake everything off in a few months. I hope Dr. Kirkpatrick will help you work things through." Wilber kissed me with his usual possessive force.

I got my happy on as my lips throbbed and swelled slightly.

"Hmmm, maple syrup. I would love to lick that off your pale soft skin. All of your pale, pale flesh."

I shivered with that imagery in my mind.

"You're late." His thumb ran over my bottom lip. "You will have a performance review tonight, Goth. All I ask is that you try. Guy is your shadow. Your secretary, Loretta, is at the door. She'll show you the ropes."

The door on my side opened and I stared out of the dark limo into the warm light of a bright, spring morning.

"Remember this, Brant. People come to us; we *do not* solicit them. We are not the final resort, but we are a safer one than some of the others who offer out a branch of hope then strip them of everything they value. I remember the desperation your dad was in when he came to me. If he could have kept to his payment schedule, or if he had made the effort to explain his situation, I would never have had to come after him in Collections. You would never have had to work to repay that money. That is the darker side of this business."

"I've been the business."

Wilber caught my chin and turned my face toward him. "No, Brant, you were my business. Prostitutes don't get beds, or clothes, or computers. Common prostitutes don't even get a name. They don't get the protection I gave you. The few times you were injured were because of a lapse in my concentration. The only reason your dad was given a loan was because he had collateral and I don't mean the house you bought for your sisters."

"He had daughters." There was bitterness in my voice that I normally kept hidden.

I had no right to be bitter because when it came down to it, the choice had been mine.

"This is a harsh world we live in, Brant. Only the strongest survive and only the strongest can stand as a protector. You've shown that you were that protector when you stood up and took over your dad's debt. You shouldered a heavy burden at fourteen years of age. Most grown men aren't that strong. Just remember what I told you before – The Organization will get its money back one way or the other."

I felt my face crow cold as anxiety crept into my heart.

"Don't worry. I agreed with your conclusions when you reviewed those papers I gave you." Wilber reached back into his pocket and pulled out a simple silver hair clip.

"Keep your hair down only for me." He gathered my layered hair into a single tail and locked the metal clip around it. He let his hand trace the tail to the end, which was now just above the small of my back. There was a soft rub on my shoulder and he sat back in the seat. That was my signal to get out.

"There are worse predators out there than me, Brant."

Guy took my briefcase.

I slid out of the cool recesses of the car and shut the door behind me. I watched as the limo pulled away from the curb and the memory of the last time I saw the limo from that angle caused a little hand to clench at my insides even after the taillights disappeared.

How long is that going to linger with me? The shrink would probably love to hear about this.

"This is not like last time, *Petite Bonbon*. Wilber will be back for you." Guy took off his sunglasses and gave them to me. "Not good to have employees see the new boss cry."

"I'm not crying," I sniffed.

"No… *Petite Bonbon*, I was mistaken. The *moutons de poussière* are bad this year, no?"

"Mute pus...what?" Guy was good at getting my mind off things.

"The bits that fly in your eyes and make them tear up so you look like you are crying, but you are not."

"Dust bunnies."

Pinching the bridge of my nose I brushed the threatening tear drops off my cheeks. "I'm a boss?"

91

"Wilber thinks so. I have not found him to be wrong very often."

I took a deep breath, putting the sunglasses over my eyes. "Can I keep these, until the …ah dust bunnies are gone?"

"They are yours. They do not suit your face, but we can get better ones at noon."

"Thank you."

"The employees…" he said, nodding slightly to the window, "they are watching. Buck up, *Bonbon*. Show the Organization that Wilber did not make a mistake. He has placed his reputation in your hands."

"No pressure," I snorted, dropped my client face down, and walked into my new place of business.

If I didn't fuck up, I'd get to more than simple eye candy and a fuck toy.

****

When I walked into the office, none of the faces that were peering at the windows were to be seen. I could only guess that they had been shepherded back to their desks. A woman stood up and walked over to greet me.

"Mr. Williams, I'm Loretta, your secretary. Please tell me if there's anything you need while you familiarize yourself with the office."

There was only one way to describe Loretta, she is a battle ax. Her silvering hair was done up in a neat but functional French twist which complemented her secretarial business suit and work pumps. The only unusual thing about her was that she was packing, meaning, she carried a firearm. I'd seen enough under arm bulges through ill-fitting suits to know. I don't know if there are ladies' dressmakers who could disguise it. Still it reassured me that no one was getting into my office if I didn't want them in.

"Thank you, Loretta." I said as I lightly shook the hand she offered to me.

She opened the office door, letting me go in alone. Alone. That was still a concept that I found hard to believe. It meant that Wilber trusted me. The office was functional with a big desk with a docking station for the laptop in my briefcase to connect to so I had access to normal keyboard and decent sized monitor. There were no pictures or anything else hanging on the walls to distract me from this business.

I took a deep breath and sat down in the black leather executive chair.

I have just this one day to prove myself. I'd had better make it a good day.

I picked up the files that had a brief review of the offers the Organization gave clients and began reading.

The soft but incessant hum of the overhead fluorescent lights filled otherwise quiet room and before long I could feel its echo in the tensing of my muscles. I rubbed my temple with my finger tips and tried to ignore it. Still, I found my attention wandering from the words on the page and when I closed my eyes the right one twitched painfully. I got up and flicked off the lights, then sat back down in the dim natural light of the row of high windows that ran along the top of the wall at my back. It was enough to work with. I plowed through the files.

I was over half-way through the stack when the door to my office opened.

Loretta informed me that it was lunch time and then looked curiously up at the ceiling. "If the lights are flickering please let me know and I'll have them replaced."

I absent-mindedly gesture to the overhead lights. "It's the hum; it gives me a headache."

She disappeared for a moment then returned carrying the brass goose-neck lamp that had been on her desk along with an office supply catalogue.

Smiling she said, "I know how you feel about those florescent lights. Infernal things. I can't stand the noise they make either. Here's the office catalogue we use. See if there's something in there that you would like. If we order before 2:00 p.m., it will be delivered tomorrow."

I glanced through the book for a desk lamp and some floor lamps to brighten the room. I didn't want to deprive her of her lamp, but when I couldn't decide quickly and she continued to stand there, I set it aside and told her I would give her my preferences later.

She gave me a motherly smile then left me to my own devices again.

I took it to mean she liked me.

My stomach began to growl. I needed a break anyway, so I put my handwritten reviews in the file drawer in my desk then went to get some lunch with Guy. There were several restaurants in the area, but I didn't feel up to sitting down somewhere. My wrist was still throbbing and my throat was slightly constricted with pain. Even walking was enough of a jarring motion to aggravate my wrist. There was no way that this was just a simple sprain. It was broken.

Guy was a little too in tune with me. He took one look at my face and ushered me into a sunglasses store. Snatching his glasses back off my face he gestured to the sunglass display. "*Bonbon*, you pick something that makes *Monsieur* Brawden go *ooh-la-la* when he sees how handsome you are."

I had to smile at that. "I don't think Wilber will ever say ooh-la-la to anything."

"Stay in this area, *Bonbon*. I will get you some soup and a sandwich. Maybe an unsweetened iced tea? That is good for the stomach, no?" Guy gestured for the hovering sales girl to come over. "You are doing good, *Bonbon*. *Madame* Levine has already ordered your business cards."

I nodded then turned my attention to the racks of sunglasses. Inside, I was stupidly happy over his praise. $400 later I had stylish 'Salavatore Ferragamo' shades which were much better suited to my face. Since Guy hadn't returned yet, I wandered around the stores nearby. It was an eclectic area with high end shops next to long established mom and pop stores. My stomach was burning slightly so I headed into one to grab antacids. Inside it was packed with knockoffs of designer names, shrimp chips from Hong Kong and all kinds of electronic paraphernalia. Further to the back of the store I discovered an unpleasant surprise, porn. Gay porn. Triple X-rated gay porn with my face on the cover hidden with a single black bar across my eyes. How did I know that it was me? I see my body in the mirror in the shower every day. This DVD was my debut into debt service.

Cinderella.

Any good feelings and self-worth that I had accumulated that day went down the drain.

I don't know how long I was in that store when Guy tracked me down but I had a black back pack full of DVD's, a knockoff portable DVD player and questionable high end headphones. I had perfected my client face so no one, not even Guy, knew how badly I was shaken. Knowing I had made videos is different from seeing them.

Did I want to see them? No. Did I have to see that first one? Did I need to revisit that incident? Only if I wanted to be stronger. Wilber needed me to be stronger.

After I returned to the office, it didn't take long to set up the player then I popped in the DVD, it started playing right away. After a few moments of my looking at the magazine and the boy catching me, that signature *boomchickawahwah* porn beat started up.

My chest tightened. It got hard to breathe. The blood pulsing in my ears grew louder and louder drowning out the music and lame dialogue. My stomach twisted and cold sweat beaded on my forehead. My hand trembled when I reached out to hit stop and powered the thing off. I didn't need to watch it. I had been there, and even if I denied it, my memory sometimes played back clearer than that little silver disk.

Lock it down. Get behind my client face. I can't break down. Not here. Wilber…Wilber wanted me in this position. I can't fail…not here.

My hand still held a tremor when I cupped my forehead.

My wrist was throbbing. I had iced it twice already and had popped some aspirins, but it only took the edge off.

I couldn't even think of eating.

I went back to work on the client files. Five of the six applications were standard boilerplate. One I could toss out. He had no collateral property-wise, and he was unmarried. His restaurant would fail. Land, warehouse, and other assets secured the other four applications. The last one, the sixth and final application, was the one that had me sitting in the dark of my office staring down at that empty DVD case still sitting on my desk. I had glanced at the file quickly this morning and the similarities were uncanny to my own. This was why I had to buy those DVDs. This was why I had to watch that damned thing even though every cry of that younger self was like a knife to my heart. This father had to know what he was getting into. He *had* to know.

I closed my eyes and leaned back in my chair staring sightlessly at the ceiling as memories washed over me of another father who didn't know better or thought he could beat the system. I remembered a night when I was lying on my stomach in Wilber's den, right beside the fire in the hearth, getting all toasty warm, as he reviewed some documents.

He gave off a big sigh and closed the folder. Taking out his red pen, he slashed the cover then tossed it to the floor. "Goth Boy?"

I turned and looked at him from the floor.

He sat in his leather wingback chair like a very old and tired king. The shadows of the gas fireplace danced on his face. "To get anywhere in this world, it's not what you know; it's who you know. I had ambition. I had skill. You've been on Collections so you know what I am capable of. I am capable of much, much worse. But all my skill and drive wouldn't have gotten me anywhere without a worthy patron. Once I got in with the right guy, I got off the enforcer track and onto the executive one. I've never looked back. Compassion is a weakness, a liability in this line of work."

"You showed me compassion," I pointed out as I turned over onto my back.

"Don't mistake ownership with compassion, Goth. You challenged me. You challenged my authority and you got my attention. Once you had my attention, I had to have you. A skinny, all arms and legs, punk ass kid with big, grey eyes had the gall to challenge me over a small debt. Don't argue with me. Compared to others, what your dad owed was chump change."

"What brought this on?"

Wilber gestured to the file on the floor. "You see that red mark. That is the end of a man's life as he knows it. I'm taking everything: his house, his car, his bank accounts, his wife, and his daughter. It would have been easier for the family if he'd just gotten a life insurance policy and got himself killed. Instead…he's killed everyone he cared for."

I pushed myself upright. "You're sending them to a brothel?"

"Don't think that your time with me is anything like what happens in a brothel, Brant. Few come out of there. Those who do are damaged beyond recovery."

I felt sick to my stomach.

"The Organization will have its money with interest, Goth. Even if I send someone to Collections, if they cannot repay, it will come back to me. It's like I have co-signed the application when I approved the loan. I get the money from them, or the Organization will take it from me. They will take my commissions, my portfolio, and my possessions. And if that is not enough, they will even take me. If you're healthy, transplants are a lucrative business." He picked up his scotch and took a long drink. "That is why I smoke and drink, Goth

Boy. One day I might fuck up. I would rather they just kill me than sell me off like a car in a chop shop."

I sat up and watched him as he stared off into the fireplace. His hands lay heavily on his knees.

"What happened to your patron?"

"He fucked up. He backed a few bad loans that all came due around the same time. If he had asked for help, I would have given him all I had. Instead, he just… disappeared." Wilber leaned forward to loom over me.

I leaned back flat on my spine. Disappearing was not a good thing.

"Brant, if I ever give you a call and tell you to run, I want you to clear out of here with just the clothes on your back. Don't look back. Don't ever return."

I was sure that Wilber was drunk. I moved from the fire and knelt in front of his chair, resting my head on his lap.

Wilber absently stroked my hair like you would a cat.

If I could have purred I would have.

"I don't want you see you cut open, Brant. I don't want you see used like that. You are too fucking innocent to be used like that."

That was probably the third time I had ever seen Wilber shitfaced. He'd leaned heavily on me when I helped him up the stairs and into bed, hanging onto me like a body pillow until sleep took him. When I shifted away and he didn't even notice, a clear sign he was in a drunken stupor. He would have woken up and dragged me back to him if he hadn't been. I went back downstairs, gathered up all his papers, and tucked them back into the briefcase. All except for the red slashed one.

He had let me read files before so I didn't hesitate to glance it over. He said wife and daughter. I knew the hell they were going into. Tears streamed down my face. Compassion was a liability in his business. Wilber still had it even if he denied it.

Why else would he have saved a skinny, black-haired brat from certain death?

Why would he get drunk tonight?

Why does he hold me so tenderly in his sleep, tucked up against him while he curls around to me as if to offer up protection?

I tucked the folder into his briefcase, turned the fireplace off, and then climbed the stairs to his room. Quietly, I slid into bed behind him until I had pressed myself up against his back. He leaned back against me in his sleep.

Wilber is an Organization man, but he's still a good man, deep inside, otherwise why would he be getting drunk over a business decision?

I reassured myself of the thought again and held him in my arms offering up my worthless comfort.

****

"Mr. Williams, Carl Dulett is here," Loretta's alto voice startled me out of my little memory replay like a gong sounding in the front of a palace. "Should I make him wait?"

How she said it told me that I wasn't as calm as I thought I was, what I hoped I was. Taking a few deep breaths, I could feel my client face settle on me like a familiar mask. I could function now.

"Sir?" Loretta's tone was one of concern.

"Not necessary. Thank you, Loretta, send him in."

"Sir, Mr. Brawden said that he will send a car for you at five o'clock."

"Thanks again, Loretta." I glanced at the clock.

Thirty more minutes to go.

Dulett was a nervous man. His skin was naturally a dark tan, but it was pale with strain and stretched thin over his skeleton. This was a carbon copy of my past life. His wife had cancer. The bills were piling up. The house was on its second mortgage. He had three children, one daughter and two sons—all nine months apart.

Mr. Dulett was a desperate man.

The Organization lived off desperation.

And for what I was about to do...so was I.

I stood up and offered my hand. He came in and smiled anxiously. "Mr. Dulett, I would like to thank you for coming down here today."

"I've been waiting for a call. You approved my loan application?" His voice was sharp as he cut right to the point.

I was going to throw up. I reached into my briefcase and pulled out the antacids I had picked up while out shopping. I popped two and chewed the chalky tablets. If Wilber gave me this job permanently, I was going to need tons of these. "Your application has been reviewed and is pending approval."

"Pending? I don't understand."

Come on Brant, don't make this personal. "The property that you offered does not cover the full loan. The interest rates alone would have to be paid weekly."

"You don't understand... Helen needs this treatment."

"I understand more than you realize, Mr. Dulett. I don't think you are seeing passed the immediate situation." I gestured for him to sit and turned the small DVD toward him. "The Organization would want security."

"Security?"

"Assurances that the loan would be paid if you defaulted on your scheduled repayments."

"What kind of security? I listed every asset I have."

"Don't look away from this, Mr. Dulett." I turned the DVD on and pulled the headphone jack out. This time when I listened to my younger self cry out in agony. Mr. Dulett had to know what he was walking into. Candy coating it wouldn't make it any easier for him but he had to know what he could be sentencing his children to.

"What are you showing me?" he whispered with his lips turning down with disgust at the images he was seeing. Then his eyes shot to me and he yelled, "What the hell are you showing me!"

The door to my office bounced open and Guy stepped in with gun drawn. Guy's eyes flicked to the screen. His face clouded and he stalked up, moving to shut it off.

I blocked Guy's hand.

He looked from me down to the image on the small screen and his eyes filled with sadness.

I composed myself and hit the pause button fortuitously halting on a close up of my pain filled face. "I'm still working with the client, Guy. Please close the door."

Dulett jumped to his feet, his face a mix of horror and anger. His hands clenched tight and halfway raised as if to punch me. "Why did you show me that... that filth?"

I turned toward him my features schooled to calmness. Deep inside, I felt something. Even if I wanted to hide in a corner and rock back and forth with my mouth on my kneecaps but I couldn't do that anymore.

"My Mom had cancer and her treatments drained our finances until we were about to be thrown out of our house; so, my Dad came here, just like you. Everything was fine for about six months then he fell behind on the payments. They were coming for my sisters."

Dulett stared at the frozen face on the screen. I could see the realization sink in. Color faded from his features as his eyes slipped from the screen up to me. "They did that to you? You were just a baby!"

"I offered myself as security for the loan. I wasn't going to let my sisters be taken like that," I said in a hard voice, gesturing at the DVD player. "I'm showing you this because I know you can't make the payments. Once you fall behind, the Organization will take your house, your business, and, when they realize that those will not cover the full loan, they will come for your wife, your daughter, and even your sons. They will be the real collateral. They will use them..." I paused a bit before adding empathically, "just like that."

"She's only twelve."

"I was fourteen and the sister they were going to take was ten at the time," I retorted, keeping my voice flat and unemotional. I had to kill any idea that the Organization would give mercy because of the age of the collateral. I wanted, maybe even needed him to understand the risks involved.

"Bastards…" Dulett dropped the player back on my desk.

I pulled it toward me then powered it off. I closed the screen my hand shook with agitation. Even though I dropped my hand back below my desk, I was certain Dulett saw. "Nevertheless, once someone does that to you, you are changed. The child you were is dead. There is no coming back from something like that. You have to become someone new to survive."

"If I don't get money, they will stop Helen's treatment." He lifted his hands and grabbed at the sides of his head. "What am I going to do?'

Now it was my time to become the devil's advocate. "Would you give up your future for the sake of your family?"

He turned and looked at me.

"As security, the Organization can take out a life insurance policy to cover the full loan. When you default, you would be killed and the policy would be cashed in leaving your family free and clear of the loan. The alternative is your sons and daughter wishing to be dead rather than enduring what they'll have to go through."

Dulett turned to me with his expression haunted. "That would leave my family with nothing."

"There is nothing to stop you from taking out your own policy."

Anger began to tint his tone. "You're making a big assumption that I couldn't repay the loan."

"You would not be here if there were other options still open to you." I gestured to the portable DVD player, "I've had the optimist fucked out of me."

Dulett returned to the chair setting down heavily on it. He ran his hand through his hair as he stared up at the small narrow windows at the top of my office wall. I couldn't even imagine what thoughts swirled through his mind.

"I can't let her die. The kids need her more than me." He sat there staring at the player for a moment and then nodded. "Take out the policy."

I handed him the pen and pointed to the line to sign. I was the Devil to his Daniel Webster.

"The money will be transferred to your account tomorrow. Mr. Dulett… please, don't make me cash that policy."

He signed the paper without hesitation then put down the pen. "Why? Why did you do that? Knowing what they were going to do to you."

My hand still trembled and the wrist of my other hand was sending stabbing pain up my arm so I kept them under the desk. "I love my little sisters and seeing how they have grown without that touch of darkness tells me that I did the right thing."

"You're still paying back the loan even having to do this?" I thought I heard pity in Dulett's voice but he was staring down at his fingertips. "Can't you go home? Does your family know what you did for them?"

No, it wasn't pity. He was trying to understand.

I shook my head. "As I said, you're changed when you get worked over like that. I contact my family but I don't belong to that world anymore."

"And this one suits you better?" There was censure in his voice as he rose to his feet. Anger was there but it wasn't directed at me. He probably felt like he failed as a father.

Wilber had said that they searched us out. They searched us out and placed themselves in harm's way. It was too much to expect gratitude. Besides, I had to make him aware that the Organization didn't show mercy and now, for the rest of the day, I was the face of the Organization.

"I just saved your children from the life I had to live when my Dad couldn't make the loan payments."

Whatever else he was going to say he swallowed back down. "Yes, you did. Thank you, Mr. Williams." Dulett extended his hand to me. He refrained from saying anything as I reached across with my good hand to shake his.

"Don't take this the wrong way, Mr. Dulett. But I don't want to ever see you again."

Dulett's expression was subdued, as he looked me in the eyes. There was still hope there that this influx of cash would save his wife.

"The same here, Mr. Williams." He turned and headed for the door. Just as he got to the frame, he paused and turned back towards me. "You are a good brother. Few would do that for their sisters in this day. Those men might have taken other things from you, but your heart is still intact."

As he passed through the door, I fumbled for my new shades. Guy came in, popped the DVD out and snapped it in half before stuffing it into the inner pocket of his suit coat. I started gathering up my papers.

Guy's gaze watched me straighten the desk's top before his accented voice questioned me. "*Bonbon?*"

I sniffed and rubbed at the corner of my eye behind the sunglasses. "Who would think that dust bunnies would be in here, too?"

"*Monsieur* Brawden is waiting outside."

I nodded, closed everything in my briefcase. Guy took the case out of my hand when I stepped out of my office door.

Loretta was shutting down her computer system and straightened quickly when she saw me. There was that iron lady mannerism as her eyes watched Mr. Dulett leave the building. Suddenly, she turned grandmotherly. "I will see you tomorrow Mr. Williams. Please get that wrist of yours looked after. Coffee preference? Donuts?"

My eyes were stinging behind my expensive glasses. At least my nose wasn't running unchecked. "What makes you think I'm coming back tomorrow?"

Loretta let out a lady like snort but it still held a lot of meaning. "You're better than that useless piece of work who was here before. Guy, don't forget that black backpack. That type of material does not need to be found here."

Guy slipped back into the office and I winced as a stream of French profanity wafted out. He had looked into the bag.

I continued as if nothing was happening. "No coffee. Diet cola and those little mini white powder donuts."

Loretta raised an eyebrow as she glanced over at my office. I would take a guess that she knew French and could tell exactly what Guy was cursing about.

"I will have them ready. Did you pick out some lamps?"

"No." My voice sounded curt. I could feel the heaviness of having the client face on far longer than I expected and the weariness of the constant pain in my wrist.

"We'll do it tomorrow. I'll have your business cards ready as well."

I nodded. Guy stormed passed by with my briefcase and backpack in one hand then held the outer door open for me. He didn't say anything but the set of his jaw was rigid with anger. He trotted forward and opened the limo door for me. When I climbed in the darkness of the interior swallowed me whole. I sniffed back a few tears. I was emotionally bruised and physically shattered and I had put in an eight-hour day. Wilber sat as still as a stoic statue.

"Are we still working?" I asked in a strained voice.

"No." Wilber replied softly.

I turned and climbed on Wilber's lap setting my knees on other side of his hips and plastered myself against his chest. He brought his arms up and under my suit jacket and pulled me closer to him.

"Loretta has given you her seal of approval. If I had listened to her from the beginning, we wouldn't have had that previous problem at the office. Are you all right, Goth?"

I rested the side of my head against his shoulder. "I can do this."

"I know you can. I wouldn't have suggested it if I had a doubt. I have always admired your strength of will. Did you have any problems?"

"No. I turned down the restaurant. Everyone else is a go."

"Even Dulett?"

"I got security." I took in a big breath. "I showed him my first DVD."

I felt Wilber's body stiffen with anger.

"I showed him the consequences of non-payment. He signed a waiver to get a life insurance policy for the loan plus interest." I wanted to drop my client face and crumbled in the seat beside Wilber.

"Where did you get a copy of that movie?" There was tightness in his voice but it wasn't directed at me because his fingers tangled my hair gently.

My wrist began pulsing heat even more. "Back of a shop on 54th. There were lots of copies but I bought them all. Guy has them in a backpack. The clerk said it's a best seller." I slipped off his thighs settling wearily back onto the seat.

My voice sounded exhausted even to my own ears. "I thought trying to get Mr. Dulett to agree to a life insurance policy would be hell because hearing that his kids would be sent to a brothel might have been a farfetched threat; but, seeing the consequences of failure was something else. It was almost like talking to my Dad, only I was the devil's advocate giving him the options and consequences. Having my DVD available was a very useful tool."

"Where is it?"

"Guy snapped it half."

I nestled into Wilber's side carefully holding my aching arm up across my body. His spicy male scent filled my nostrils. "You know, considering there was only a black bar across my eyes, I was surprised that the cashier didn't recognized me when I bought the entire lot."

Wilber's tone was filled with annoyance as his arm came up and over, wrapping me close. "Those DVDs were supposed to be pulled.

I'll look into it. Anything sold after your end of service date is yours 100%. You earned it. Money makes the world go round, and I want you to have your own so you will never be in anyone's debt again."

I closed my eyes. I'm tired. "Are you proud of me?"

Wilber kissed the back of my head. "Yes, Brant. I'm proud of you. You did me very proud today."

I closed my eyes and clung to the warmth beside me. A fist of ice gathered my intestines into a ball as I thought of what I truly wanted from him. It wasn't fair to Wilber if he couldn't give me what I wanted because I didn't tell him what it was I wanted. Why I wanted it. After two tries to get my throat swallowing correctly I could stammer.

"When I was working, when it was a really good take, you were happy with me, you'd tie me up and fuck me until I couldn't handle the pleasure anymore and pass out. I miss that. I want that. I would like you to do that to me again. That's what I wanted last night but…"

Wilber stilled. "Oh, Goth, that wasn't pride. I was reclaiming you as mine. I wanted to impress my touch on your body and soul after all those others took you. It was little more than an animal claiming territory."

I turned my head toward his face. "Then claim me, Wilber. I want you to. I miss it."

His hand came up and pressed the hair clip open. He pulled my long hair around and draped it over my shoulder. "So, this is what you were asking for before, when you asked me to tie you up. You wanted to belong to me."

"I belong with you. You just need to realize it." I tried to keep my tone light.

He laughed and cradled me close. "There are days you make me feel so old, Goth Boy. Then there are days, everything is new. I understand you now. If you need me to restrain you, I'll know what you're asking for."

I tilted my head up as he leaned down pressing a warm kiss to my lips. I invited him inside. Our tongues dueled, and I could feel him groan into my mouth. I brought my hand up to stroke his hair and accidentally hit it against the back of the seat. I hissed and pulled back.

"Brant?"

"We need to go see Doc. I think my wrist is broken."

"Why didn't you say something earlier?"

"I wanted to prove that you choose wisely."

"You never have to prove anything to me, Brant. Mikey, hospital. While Doc is okay for things that don't need police attention, you need x-rays."

I lay on his chest, my wrist cradled across my middle. He stroked my hair and allowed me to snuggle into his warmth. Compassion might not be good for business, but I needed it. I pressed my forehead up against his throat. I think Wilber wouldn't mind a big dose of compassion either. It would do us both a whole lot of good.

Chapter Five: The Enemy

While I wasn't the popular choice as point man, my quarterly earnings stood on their own merit and silenced the naysayers.

I knew that non-performance wasn't tolerated. You didn't get a black mark added to your file. You disappeared. Disappearances weren't an everyday occurrence, but they were still regular enough to ensure that all employees never forgot that big brother was watching – and keeping score. So, I worked hard.

Wilber had made a lot of enemies by my excelling in this position. Enemies weren't avoidable in the Organization, but this situation was worse because they knew what I had been. They remembered the pretty, boy toy standing behind Wilber at District meetings. I had heard things that only the upper echelon was supposed to know. As far as they had known I was there because I was just a disposable bauble. Once the bauble outlived their usefulness, their pretty corpse was found in a ditch. I had been rubbed in their faces by attaining a position of some respect and authority. I may have been Wilber's eye candy but I hadn't, evidently, been vapid eye candy. These people were my enemies too.

Ten months flew by in the blink of an eye. The lingering fingers of winter were fading with each day and the buds were beginning to come out on the trees. My wrist had been spiral-fractured. It was healed, but it ached terribly some nights that I resorted to taking aspirins to function.

I kept my Wednesday afternoon appointments with Dr. Kirkpatrick because Wilber insisted it was for my own good. More often than naught, I left the doctor's office with a headache needing extra aspirin. Wilber had questions in his eyes but I wasn't up to sharing what Kirkpatrick and I discussed each week. I had to work it through for myself.

My days had taken on the mantle of ordinary and I appreciated the monotony that normal offered. Over diet cola and powdered donuts, Loretta regaled me with the goings on within the Organization. Guy would listen to us gossiping like hens and shake his head. I noticed that my tailored pants were getting a little tight around the waist so my Shadow turned into the donut police. I was restricted to two a day. My love affair with those little white artery cloggers was curtailed.

While I was staring at the computer monitor, Guy opened the door and carried in the latest batch of applications. He brushed at his upper lip then gestured with his chin. "You look like you've been snorting the other white powder, *Petite Bonbon*."

I slapped at my upper lip and nose. He shook his head, pulled a handkerchief out of his breast pocket, and gestured for me to stand. I found it amusing that he called me petite. He had to reach up to clean my face. Then again, he had come to Wilber's house when I was a scrawny sixteen-year-old and I still hadn't finished sprouting.

"There. All handsome again. Have you planned what you are going to do tonight?"

It was Wilber's birthday and I had decided to bake him a cake. Wilber had a competent chef, but I returned to experimenting with baking like I had before… before everything went to hell back home. I had fleeting thoughts of becoming a pastry chef, once upon a time. I wanted to make Wilber's cake from scratch as part of my present. He had few hobbies other than me. I hated the opera and the theatre, which were his other part time passions. And if I got him tickets, I'd have to go with him. One Madam Butterfly performance was enough. I had found him a nice, patterned silk tie and matching handkerchief – monogrammed, of course. I knew he'd use it. But I knew that he would appreciate something handmade so baking him a cake was something I knew I could do. Now I only had to get all the necessary paperwork done so I could get out of here early and get started.

Loretta burst into my office.

Both of us stared at her because she was normally a stickler for manners and propriety. Her eyes were wide and her face was pale. "Mr. Williams, Mr. Constantine is on line one for you."

Guy blanched. I knew the name. He was Wilber's Boss. Technically, he was mine as well.

"Why would he be calling me?" The expression on both of their faces set my inner alarm off.

"I don't know. Don't keep him waiting." Loretta voice wasn't exactly shrill but it was way above her normal register.

My voice was surprisingly calm when I answered. Client face equated to client voice as well it seemed. "Williams."

"I am sending a car for you. It should be there shortly. We are going to dine at the Golden Leaf. I understand you have been fully trained." The voice was smooth, masculine, and very silky yet it froze my blood.

Fully trained? What? What did he mean by that? I was shocked speechless. *Did Wilber pass me off to Mr. Constantine? He said I was private stock. What's going on?*

"Are you still there?" The tone was now amused.

"Yes, sir."

Constantine continued as if he were ordering fine wine. "You will not need your bodyguard. You will not need to be armed. You will not call Brawden."

"Mr. Williams, a limo is outside." Loretta whispered.

"Come outside now, Mr. Williams." The receiver went dead.

Does that mean he's in the limo outside? What the hell is going on? Was there something wrong with the reports?

I stared at Loretta.

The color rushed back into her face and she turned into the battle axe who guarded the inner sanctum. "I don't know what is going on, but you don't make that man wait. Get up. Guy, get his jacket."

Loretta fussed over me, straightening my tie; brushing my bangs back from my eyes, shoving a snub nose .38 in my waistband.

Wilber insisted on my learning to shoot. Once a week, we went to the shooting range. I didn't like it, but I learned. I hit the target every time. That was good enough for me. Shooting paper. I wasn't doing anything else. I couldn't do anything else or maybe I should say I wouldn't do anything else but shoot paper. I may have fallen a distance from the light but I wasn't in complete darkness, at least not yet.

I pulled the gun out of my belt and handed it back to my secretary. "I won't use it."

"Don't be stupid, Brant." She shoved my hand back.

"He said no weapons." Reluctantly Loretta accepted the gun back.

Guy helped me on with my suit jacket and handed me my sunglasses. "Be careful, *Bonbon*. Where you going?"

I shook my head. If Guy called Wilber, and he would, Wilber would storm the Golden Leaf and that didn't seem like a good idea. I slipped my shades on just as Constantine's bodyguard opened the outer door. Apparently, I was being a little too slow. Both Guy and Loretta stared after me as if it were the last time I would be seen. Fear clutched at my stomach.

Maybe it was. Maybe I did something wrong.

"Mr. Williams." The bodyguard led me toward the passenger side of the long, stretch limousine. I glanced back into the store front and saw Guy frantically dialing his cell phone. I slammed my client face down and locked it in place as I adjusted my sunglasses before stepping into the back of the car.

Augustus Constantine II was the man in charge of the Organization. He took over after his Father's assassination when he was merely twenty-six. He was more vicious than the competition and had total control in less than three weeks and has kept it for these past twelve years. Those that had opposed him disappeared, along with their family, servants, and pets.

Now at thirty-eight, he was in the prime of his life, at the pinnacle of his game, and he knew it. A private meeting with Mr. Constantine was a terror and a privilege. A private meal was unheard of.

"Prompt, obedient, intelligent with a sense of discretion and stunningly handsome. Those are attributes, I admire, Mr. Williams.

James, go ahead." That telephone voice was more devastating in person. My insides quivered as he spoke. It was more an act of self-preservation that I laid my hands on my thighs and kept my gaze forward.

"Beauty and grace, something else I appreciate in a dinner companion."

I felt a butterfly's brush against my cheek as my cell went off in my jacket. Constantine lifted my shades from my face. Falling back deeper into the opposite seat I automatically reached for my phone. I knew who it was. Only Wilber called me. Guy had gotten a hold of him.

Constantine's voice shifted from compliments to one of iron command and expected obedience. "You will not answer that Brant Williams. If I had wanted Mr. Brawden in on this conversation, I would have invited him."

It was physically harder to sit there and let the cell phone ring eight times. It stopped. I bit my lower lip. Since Wilber first let me out of his sight, the rule was the same. If his call was left unanswered, I ended up with another bodyguard travelling with me. I had worked hard for the freedom of just one Shadow so it was excruciating not to answer and listen as the call transferred to leave a message mode. I felt sick to my stomach. It started to ring again.

Constantine held out his hand. I handed my phone over.

"Mr. Brawden, this is Augustus Constantine. You will refrain from calling Mr. Williams. We are going to have lunch, then a lengthy conversation. Your constant interrupting is a distraction that I will not tolerate." The tone was deceptively calm. There was a stillness in the man's form that radiated harnessed danger.

My stomach clenched hard.

I was so dead.

"As I informed Mr. Williams, if I had wanted you to be privy to our conversation, you would be here. I am now turning off Mr. Williams's cell phone. It will remain off until our meeting is adjourned. Good afternoon, Mr. Brawden." Constantine snapped the phone shut, powered it off then tucked it inside his own suit coat along with my sunglasses.

I spoke to break the unbearable silence, "Sir, is there a problem?"

"Yes, Mr. Williams, may I call you Brant? You may call me Gus."

"That is inappropriate, sir."

"Well-mannered as befitting a gentleman." Constantine leaned back on the leather seat and crossed his leg so his ankle was resting on his knee. His shoes were custom. His suit was tailored. Everything about the man across from me screamed wealth and power.

"As I was saying, we have a problem, Brant. Mr. Brawden forced you into a position that was ear marked for another Organization member. I have reviewed your performance records, and I find you very well suited to the job. Everybody likes you. The clients trust you. You've brought that location up to the potential it originally was supposed to be. However, the fact of the matter is that you are not Family. That member who was supposed to be instated there has bitched about Brawden's whore for the past ten months and has finally gotten backing from his father and a few other board members."

"If you were useless, it would be easy to remove you and place that individual into that office." Constantine suddenly moved and caught my chin in a strong grip. "However, removing such beauty from the world would be a slap in the face to God himself."

What the hell is going on here?

I moved to break his hold but he tightened his fingers so they dug up under my jaw painfully.

"Appease me, Brant."

Confusion must have flashed across my face.

"After all you have endured, you should have broken into a thousand pieces; yet, you are still an innocent. That is simply amazing. Brawden missed his calling as a trainer. Now, give me a kiss, Brant."

"That contract has been fulfilled. I don't do that anymore." My voice came out calm and rather hard, which surprised me because I felt neither.

"Remember who I am, Brant." Constantine shoved my chin up but released me.

"I am just an employee. This could be considered sexual harassment." My fingers curled into the leather to keep from feeling my jaw. His finger strength was surprising.

He slowly reclined back into his seat. The hard stare of his green eyes pinned me in my seat. "I hold your fate in my hand, Brant and you're getting lippy with me? No doubt you have heard how brutal I can be. You should know by now that there are those who follow the rules and those who make the rules. I know where I fit. Which category do you fall into, Brant?"

Constantine's shoe pressed up against my calf. There wasn't going to be any believable show of nonchalance on my behalf so I shifted my body away.

"What do you want from me?"

Constantine was striking, it was undeniable, and it was more than just physical. His sharp features went with his cutting tone of voice but the aura of danger seeped off him. I was terrified. My insides clenched tight. We might have some similarity in body type and size but that was about it. His hair was coal black and cut into a businessman style, but his eyes were green like a cat that looked right through me, classically handsome; feral and deadly.

His eyes glittered with intent. "I already made my request. A kiss. Make it passionate."

I was as far from safe as I could get.

Laughter filled the small dark cabin as the car came to a halt in front of our destination. "I will get one from you later, Brant. Right now, we will go into the restaurant and speak of mundane things. After desert and coffee, we will get down to the core of the meeting."

I couldn't even attempt to pretend to be pleasant company. When I was working, it was cum and go. I didn't have to interact with the

Clients beyond the physical. By the time the applicants got past Loretta it was more along the line of "please sign here" and they were off with their loan. Constantine didn't even bother to ask what I wanted but went ahead and ordered for the both of us. In the next half hour of Constantine's constant dialogue, I pushed my food around the plate and drank a lot of lemon ice water. I wasn't even going to try to eat because I would end up tossing my cookies on the crisp red linen of the table. I knew I amused him. He watched me struggle to maintain composure, but I couldn't keep my client face on. He unnerved me so completely.

Dessert was a mango mousse with fresh fruit. I excused myself to go to the bathroom. I think I had drunk about fourteen glasses of water in the span of an hour. When I got back, my dessert was still sitting there with another full glass of water.

Constantine had moved on to coffee.

Wasn't this ever going to end?

I grabbed my water and drained it.

"Eat."

"I'm not hungry." My stomach growled.

"Lying to me, Brant?" There was an arched eyebrow accompanying that question that was supposed to indicate humor.

My stomach twisted into a tight knot. "I'd be sick if I try to eat anything."

"Honesty. That is refreshing." Constantine tapped an envelope on the table.

"This is about the matter that Mr. Brawden brought to my attention which in turn brought you to my attention. Your series of videos have been a highly lucrative venture. I would say the sales alone cut your debt in half. The rest you worked off in a ten-year period, which was extended far beyond what is normally expected for debt repayment. Mr. Brawden made sure that you were not too overworked."

He paused.

What was I supposed to say? He was right. You can't argue facts.

117

"Those DVDs you found were pirated copies. They were stealing from the Organization; no, they were stealing from me. No one steals from me. It took us some time to track down the distributors but in the end, we shut them down. The paper trail was a train wreck and it took more time deciphering it than burning all those disks." He pushed the envelope across the table.

I took it and carefully opened it. There was a check inside. I had to blink twice to make sure that I was reading it right.

"My forensic accountants have estimated that, at a minimum, this is your cut."

There were five zeros following a five. Five hundred grand? Made out to me. My hand shook. "What is this? What does this mean?"

Constantine took a lingering drink of his coffee. "It means that you are free from whatever hold Mr. Brawden has over you. As I stated, this is the minimum of your royalties. My accountants have said that this group were either the worst or were genius at hiding cash flow. On my way over to your office, they called to tell me that they had found another two leads and once again your Cinderella flick was the leader of the pack. They are running over everything with a fine-tooth comb. The final tally might be double that."

I think I was in a state of shock. I just sat there and stared down at the check. *What did this mean?*

"Which brings me to the meat of the issue. You are a good loans officer, Brant. Better than expected. Since you were being so truthful before, I will be truthful now. I fully expected you to fail the first day. Everyone has known that Brawden kept you on a short leash, even when you were whoring yourself for money."

The waiter came up and pretended not to hear that last statement by turning on his heel and walking back the way he came.

"I actually began to question Brawden's faculties when he put your name forward, until I checked into your background. He educated you. He trained you. He turned you into this desirable creature that you are today. It's because you turned out to be more than just competent that all those rumors of Brawden reaching above his station started up."

I blinked. I think the tension was finally getting to me. I was getting tired.

"…so it comes down to merit versus Family, and unfortunately, Family always wins."

What was that I missed?

"I have to fire you, Brant."

"Fire… me?" *Why were my words slurring?*

"But, I have a new job lined up for you. You start today."

"Job?" I shook my head. "Job?"

What was the matter with me? I was so tired. I could barely keep my eyes open.

"This is a good thing for you, Brant. I normally would order a disappearance but that would be a waste of all the work Brawden did on you…"

My head nodded forward with so much weight I had to steady myself with a hand on the table.

Constantine continued but now his voice sounded so far away. "I am married, Brant. I have a lovely wife and two children who are the light of my life. My wife comes from a well-established Family and knows the pressures this type of life inflicts on men such as myself. She prefers that I don't bring my business life home. In the past, I have had mistresses who have understood the score and accommodated my less than familial desires. Unfortunately, this last mistress thought she could blackmail me with a bastard child that wasn't even mine. She upset my wife. I love my wife and I don't like to see her upset so we agreed, Carmilla and I, that my next mistress would be male. No chance of a child popping up here."

My thinking was sluggish. *Wait.*

"You drugged me."

"Yes, Brant. In your water."

I lurched to my feet swaying like I'd had a liquid lunch of the alcoholic variety.

"Wilber..."

"I get what I want, Brant. I even have my wife's blessing. She has impeccable taste as always. Carmilla saw your picture and thought you were a beautiful boy. Meeting you in the flesh, I can't do anything but applaud her choice. This is solving two problems with one solution. The whiny bastard gets to be point man and I get a professional who knows the score."

Wilber. I needed to get to Wilber.

I lurched away from the table. I knew I was staggering and wobbling, as I was trying my damnedest to walk in a straight line. I had to find Wilber.

Wilber...

Constantine caught me. "Don't forget your check. You earned this money." He leaned forward and whispered into my ear, "I cannot wait to try out all the skill and technique you performed before the camera. I'm sure you can teach me a few things."

I took one step, then another before darkness overwhelmed me. Constantine and his drug had won.

****

There was a loud moaning echoing though my head. It rang like church bell inside my skull.

Wait. That was my throat.

I tensed and fought against the lingering hold of whatever drug Constantine had slipped me. I was being molested. A hot body was pressed against my back and inner thighs. Fingers rubbed at my nipples that lit an unwanted fire in my groin.

I cried out as a hard cock was forced into my body. I tried to grit my teeth as the pain hit. I had a rubber gag in my mouth. My left nipple was rolled and pinched between two fingers. I tried to pull back from that spike of pain and ended up impaling that cock deeper in my ass.

"God, you are so tight." The rapist bucked his hips forward, grinding deep into my ass.

I groaned around the gag.

"From the number of cocks up your ass every night, I thought you would be all stretched out. But you're so... tight... and hot... and gripping... me... so...beautifully."

Every pause was a hard thrust, until he was buried completely.

Leather cuffs held my wrists chained to the headboard. My ankles were spread wide, locked to the bedposts.

Helpless.

Constantine was raping me.

He jerked my cock, forcing my hips up and back against him. Tears streamed out of my eyes.

I've survived this before. I could do it again. I would do it again.

Constantine knew his way around a man's body. I wasn't his first conquest. He alternated his nipple pinching with his hip pumps and cock strokes. I tried to resist but the lingering effects of whatever he gave me just left me in a whirl of sensations and pleasure. He made me cum. While my body shook with orgasm, he took a rough hold of my hips and began to jackhammer into me. I landed face-forward on the pillow, and the force of his fucking drove my peaked nipples against the bedding, rubbing me into another level of wanted bliss.

Finally, he just collapsed on me, pressing me down into the pillows and mattress. My own cum was wet and sticky beneath me. I shivered as he stroked my hair and exposed my neck. He suck-kissed my shoulders and licked the sweat from my flesh. When the rubber bar-bit was loosened, and I spit it out. My jaw hurt. The nasty taste of the rubber was clinging to my lips.

"You are everything I hoped you would be and more." Warm lips pressed against the nape of my neck. I shivered with disgust.

"Are we done here?" My voice was low and filled with more than a touch of self-loathing. My body twitched with post orgasmic sensation. I only wanted to respond like this with Wilber. I closed my eyes.

"Can I go home now?"

"You are home." A hot tongue swept up the sweat of my shoulder.

I twisted my head to look back as best I could. "What?"

"I don't share my mistress. This is your penthouse while you are with me. Unfortunately, I have a feeling that you will run from me if I let you loose, so these…" Constantine lifted my wrists. He pressed his lips to the leather cuffs. "…are going to stay on for a while. Bondage does suit you. I can see why your DVDs are in such high demand."

I closed my eyes as his hands trailed over my nakedness.

"Beautiful." He leaned over and kissed the swell of my ass then stood up. The bed rocked.

"What do you want from me?" My voice was low from the effort to keep groans of pain in check. I'd been raped but I've also suffered worse than this.

The sound of a cap popping and the effervescent bubbles sounded unbearably loud.

What the hell did he drug me with?

Gulp, gulp.

"I told you I have a new job for you. You are now my Executive Personal Assistant. I have healthy appetites, and I like to indulge them when they arise and I'll be using that business degree you have. Think of this as a step up, Brant. Wilber Brawden is a thug who has a mind for business, but he has risen as far as he is going to go. His associations in the past were with the wrong people and the Board of Directors has a very long corporate memory."

I heard the bottle tap on the top of a glass table as Constantine moved around the bedroom.

"I'll send my tailor to you and dress you to fit your new station. You will be coming with me to important negotiations and you will be more than just eye candy. I'll get someone else in to dress you more appropriately for afterhours endeavors. I do like you in black leather especially with your pale skin. Make sure to dress to please me when I call on you."

I felt my chest tighten. I didn't want to hear this. "I never said I was going to take your job offer."

A hand tangled in my hair and wrenched me upright, as far as my chained wrists would allow. "From the moment, you caught my attention, your father, and sisters as well as Brawden and his men's fates have been in your hands. The Board was in a deadlock over swatting Brawden into the ground over this little power play of his. If I hadn't stepped in with the offer to mediate the situation, his whole crew, you included, would have been taken care of by now." Constantine let my head drop and the crick in my neck sounded unreasonably loud to my ears.

"It is not wise to make an enemy of me. You will go farther if you appease me." He trailed his fingertips along the side of my face, lightly brushing my skin.

"You don't need Brawden. He has kept you bound to him through illusion. He can only hold you back now."

Constantine dropped his weight back on the bed stretching his limber body out beside mine. "You have a great prospect before you, Brant. Even you recognize that your many talents were being wasted in that little front office. I will take you to places Brawden has no hope to even darken. You are intelligent and diligent. You're easy on the eye, and you're great in bed."

I wanted to throw up.

Constantine stood up and disappeared. The sound of the shower began clearing as the drug burnt its way out of my system. Along with the return of my hearing, the full amount of pain crept in, intensifying with each passing breath. The feel of his assault was still in and on my body. I jerked on my bonds once and it started the phantom agony in my wrist and forearm. My fracture was long healed but I could still feel the pain, I let myself drift into it.

At least I had something of Wilber's that couldn't be taken away.

123

I must have drifted off with the lingering drugs after affects because Constantine startled me as his hands released my ankles.

"I get what I want, Brant. I get it because I will do what I need to ensure I get it. If getting your cooperation means threatening your sisters, even that little cutie, Erris, I will; but I know you've figured out that Brawden's life in your hands. I want peace in my House. You must be removed from that office and all association must be broken with Brawden. Coming to me and my bed, is my offer. Do I need to state the consequences if those conditions aren't met? You have until tomorrow to give me your answer."

"I can give you my conditions now." Tears that had been threatening to fall retreated behind an icy ball of anger that formed in my gut. My hips creaked as I pulled myself upright and closed my legs. The feel of cum seeping out of my ass made me nauseous. I felt bruised on the inside.

"Conditions…I didn't give you any options."

I jerked on the cuffs. "We are in the negotiation stage. Walk away from the table now and you will never be able to take these off because I will head out at every opportunity."

"Enlighten me, Mr. Williams." I expected anger from Constantine but this undisguised amusement set me on edge.

"First and foremost, all the monies coming from those DVD sales are going to be put into a scholarship fund for my sisters. They are going to be untouchable by the Organization."

"There should be enough for your sister's granddaughter's granddaughters. Agreed, it is your money after all."

"Next, you will personally oversee the protection of the staff at that office. My replacement's reputation less than stellar; there is no reason good people need to be run out of there."

Constantine surprised me. "I'm not expecting him to last long. Your performance records are a hard bar to match. Is that all, Brant?"

"You never come near me again without a condom." The anger and loathing that I felt was absent from my voice. For the moment I was grateful for the client face's protection.

That demand was met with a scowl. "There are limits to my generosity, Brant."

"For my safety as well as yours." *I don't know where you've been.*

There was a moment of silence then Constantine gave a slight nod. "There is to be no contact with Brawden."

"That is a given." Constantine would be nothing more than a client. I could handle a client. Give in gracefully and the ordeal ended faster.

"Sass…not what I expected from you, Mr. Williams. Agreed, safety first and foremost." Constantine dressed with a satisfied air, the manner of a victor of a hotly contested struggle.

Those green feral eyes caught my gaze in the mirror as he adjusted his tie. "I'm not expecting you to fawn all over me…and I won't stand to be treated as a client. I'll win your affections. Don't pretend to like me when you don't but I won't stand for you undermining me. Never forget that I saved your Mr. Brawden from an early grave today. Anything else you want to include in this negotiation?"

"You've met my conditions." I don't know how confident I looked laying there debauched and bound but Constantine looked at me satisfied.

"I thought for sure you would have set a time limit on our arrangement." He soothed his tie and vest over his trim waist then picked up his suit jacket.

"No need, you'll toss me aside when you lose interest."

"What makes you think my passion will wane?" His only physical response to my deliberate taunt was a raised eyebrow.

"You said you've had mistresses…I expect to be one of many."

"While you might not think it, I value loyalty. If my dear wife did not give her approval, I would have to have a very good argument to make my case. A smoking hot bod on long lovely legs…" Constantine cupped his hand and stroked the inside of my thigh down to my knee, "is not enough to compromise my marriage."

I kept my thoughts on loyalty and marriage hidden behind my client face. "I'm satisfied with the negotiations. I belong to you."

Constantine undid my wrists. A wince of pain broke my mask as I rolled to my side. Constantine's fingers stroked my cheek then swept my hair over my ear. "I asked you for one thing today. Give that to me we will stop for the day."

I sat on the edge of the bed aware that a mix of Constantine's cum and my blood oozed out of my abused ass. I met lips then teased his lips open, allowing my tongue sweep into his mouth and intertwine with his. I held my body away from him. I didn't want him near me any longer than necessary. If I touched him, I would ruin his suit and he would have to get naked and change…and he would probably fuck me raw again.

"That's it. That's the greeting I want from you, Brant."

My client face was firmly in place as he ran his thumb over my bottom lip.

"Randal and Michael are your bodyguards. You go nowhere without them. For this week, you do not leave this penthouse. Everything you need will be brought from Mr. Brawden's estate."

"Understood, Mr. Constantine. I assume you have the gold locket that was in my vest pocket?"

Constantine pulled his jacket on smoothly then reached into the inner breast pocket. There was a simple glint from the electroplated gold as it swung in the light of the, no, of my, penthouse.

"Then there is nothing else that I need from Wilber's estate."

He coiled the heart and delicate chain into the palm of up upturned hand. My fingers closed over it.

Constantine kissed me again. "Don't defy me and I won't drug you again. Get cleaned up. The tailor will be here in the morning."

Constantine lightly tapped my cheek. "Your sisters are very lucky."

He blew me a kiss as he left the bedroom. I could hear the door open to the penthouse and close behind him. My client face faded as I wiped my mouth clean of his kiss. I knew I was a damned good brother. I'd proven that time, and time again. I knew I was a damned good loans officer. I got more loans covered with insurance policies than anyone else and I didn't have to resort to showing that DVD after that first time.

Low voices filtered from the other room which told me that Constantine was going to make sure that I didn't return home.

It hurt to walk but I had suffered through worse. Constantine's mark of ownership was still deep within me. I wanted to scrub myself raw to free me from his grip. Water rained over my head and shoulders as I stood in the large walk-in shower, wrapping myself in the memories that would have to sustain me. Wilber was gentle in the rough way that I liked. He whispered through my hair that I was damned good lover and that he was lucky I chose him. My hand would be dwarfed in that big-scarred mitt of his. Warmth burned deep in my chest for him because of what he showed me I knew the definition of cherished now.

I'd heard stories and rumors about Mr. Augustus Constantine II when I just eye-candy and a low-level executive. The bottom line was no one touched what was his.

Was I his?

Physically; but, not in the way that truly matters.

Oh, hell no.

Only his enemies and fools dared to cross this ruthless man of the underworld and I was no fool.

Another trickle of cum slipped down my inner thigh. That phrase *'keep your friends close but your enemies closer'* clicked with me. For a few fleeting moments, I had everything I ever could have wanted and now it was all swept away by this man's whim. Constantine chose this route so I was going oblige him and make sure I was a damned good enemy. How was I going to prove that?

I shivered as I switched the shower to cold.

I was going to fucking kill Gus Constantine.

Chapter Six: Shade

There are those who can say that time flies by - one blink and a year passes. Not so with me. I felt every one of these last one thousand and ninety-five days.

I've been the EPA of the Head of the Organization from 8:30 am to 5:00 pm, sometimes as late as 11:00 pm, almost 24/7. Legitimate business crosses time zones and illegitimate business never sleeps. The successful don't beg for leniency.

Constantine's behavior towards me had changed over these years. I was more than just a convenient fuck toy: more of a 70/30 split of my time toward business. When he turned his attention to me, it was as if I was back in the studio filming a porno. I was trussed up like in a bondage film – wrist cuffs, neck brace and blindfold. Even if every other toy was discarded, the blindfold remained. I guess he didn't like to see the results of his handiwork. He was stupid if he thought he could keep that innocence I had even after Wilber had me for ten years.

God, it feels like centuries ago.

Constantine got this body. He even used my mind but if he wanted my heart…it was gone, long ago. I don't even know where it was anymore. Probably dragging after Wilber somewhere. My thoughts wandered further down this unforgiving path.

Did he even think of my anymore? Maybe the questions should be, did I even want him thinking of me? I sure as hell wasn't proud of what I'd become. I was now called Ice.

When Constantine's name was mentioned his Ice associate was always linked to it. Wilber and my family were still a chain used to keep me in line yet I now had a staff of ten beneath me for work that lined the coffers. The staff only saw what was accomplished in business and they aspired to be my *Icemen*. We basked together in the glory of being efficient but if there was a mistake…I alone faced Constantine's disappointment.

Business is business whether it is above board or beneath it. Constantine worked very hard so that meant those under him worked even harder. My reward system was based on merit. If a job is well done and a bonus is warranted, I personally cut my staff a check. I wasn't buying their loyalty, I was showing my appreciation for the fact they gave it willingly. If they fucked up or someone wasn't pulling their weight for whatever reason, I ripped a strip off in front of everyone. So, mistakes weren't often but when they did…well that was the first and only time that Constantine had taken matters into his hands and he made sure that I learned the consequences of an underling's failure.

Mr. Sterling was a potential shining star that I called up from the pool of outstanding talent from the lower floors. He had high honors in school and had previously supported a couple of lucrative projects so I had no problems promoting him. Only problem was that books smarts and cunning didn't get far within the Organization when laziness and an air of entitlement came with it.

Constantine was dealing with an Italian company for exclusive rights to a fashion house when the shit hit the fan. The sales figures were six weeks out of date and projections were just a slight re-working of the previous year. The current intel was that the House's matriarch had a debilitating stroke that she was not expected to return from and the heir apparent had been burning through the resources, aka models and designers like there was no tomorrow. Luckily the deal fell through. Constantine was royally pissed, rightfully so, and since it was my job to provide him information, it was our fault; which was my responsibility.

I apologized for Mr. Sterling's mistake but Constantine stopped my words with a vicious slap to the face that split my lip open. Blood flew everywhere. His curt command of "get out" made me turn on my heel with the bad data under my arm. The silence that met me when I came back to the office was something that didn't need to be discussed. Everyone jumped when I threw the file across the room and it hit the wall with a loud thump.

"Mr. Sterling, I believe it was your duty to provide this company with the most up to date sales and projections. Would you care to well what the hell you were doing with the time that you have been paid for because it clearly wasn't analyzing sales and projections?" Aside from the initial throwing of the file, my body was still and my voice even. This is where the Ice moniker came from, a full form of the client face. I found it to be more effective to be calm and collected than ranting like a madman.

"I...did. You must have picked up the wrong research..." The bastard dared to try and blame this snafu on me. The rest of the team backed from him.

"Don't compound your incompetence with more lies." I turned my attention fully on him. "I know for a fact that your workstation has been used for social media and it exceeds 60% of your weekly work hours. Your social commentary that you leave lacks the sophistication of a high school student. The only reason you have remained here was that when you work you are efficient and accurate."

The door to the office opened behind me. Mr. Glass, Constantine's personal security, aka thug, stepped forward. There was a sharp stab of tension in my stomach as the man entered. Mr. Glass made problems disappear...permanently.

Only now, was I considered part of the problem?

My attention, all of my attention, was brought back on the younger man paling before me.

"I...I...have the data...I did it...I mean, I thought I sent it...Mr. Williams!"

The squeaking soles of Mr. Glass's approach echoed around the small room. It felt as if the walls were closing in on us. Sweat beaded on Mr. Sterling's face. Forcing my shoulders to relax was a herculean task when a strong hand clamped down on me but I was given a quick squeeze and released.

I wasn't the problem today.

"Boss shouldn't hit your face. You're already starting to bruise…" Mr. Glass continued passed me.

He halted in front of the young executive. Glass wasn't a physical monster like Wilber but what he lacked in girth he made up for through intensity. Sterling backed up into the boardroom table until there was nowhere else to go. "You get on the fast track and end up disappointing Mr. Williams and the Boss. You might have thought you were hot shit up here in the rarified air but you are about to find out how far you have to fall. Now, Mr. Sterling I am going to escort you from the building."

"What…what about my things?"

"You came into this building with nothing, you leave the same way."

The young man opened his mouth to say something but I cut him off. He had a death wish. My tone was cool and biting. "Right now, at this moment, you are little more than chum in the waters and you should realize that. It would be in your best interest not to be heard of again."

I wasn't going to ask just how bad this was going to be. I truly didn't want to know. Mr. Sterling walked out under his own steam to whatever awaited him.

"You're bleeding, Mr. Williams." Mr. Glass gestured to his lower lip.

I wiped seeping blood from my lip with a linen handkerchief as the door closed with a quiet click. That had to be the most ominous sound in the world. There was complete silence remaining in the room. I regarded the remaining team with my client face firmly in place. "We fucked up. Don't disappoint me again."

And we didn't. Constantine shouldn't have any complaints about my department. I earned their trust and respect by working alongside them and even later into the night. That was something Wilber had taught me right from the beginning. "You get what you give." I might be Ice but if I said we had to work through the weekend my staff would do it without complaint.

****

"Williams." Randal's voice called to me from the main room, "Boss is entering the building."

What the hell? He never said anything about dropping by tonight. I wiped my face dry.

Time to start job number two. There was a breakfast meeting early in the morning so at least this wouldn't be a whole night stay.

The image that stared back at me in the mirror was a portrait of an aging cover model. I could see the lines and tiredness around my face but the reaction I got from Constantine's clients was still one of lustful appreciation. I had made it clear that I wasn't entertaining but if a smile and leer sealed a lucrative deal, I wasn't above offering it. Rubbing my towel through my hair a final time, I caught movement in the bedroom as Randal got the custom bondage gear prepared on the bed.

I was tired of this shit.

Constantine had gotten pissed when I chopped my hair off at the end of the first day of work. Since there were expectations of accomplishing work I was determined that I wasn't going to be dragged around by long hair in a business setting. I've never denied him anything else, so since then, his personal barber has been keeping my grooming routine up to corporate standards.

"Brant." Randal called from the bedroom again.

Constantine, the lazy bastard, didn't even have the courtesy to tie me up himself anymore.

Well, this just ensured that face time with him outside of work was shorter.

That last business trip combined with a vacation with the wife and kiddies to Singapore was a godsend to me when I got left behind in favor of a translator. Really, you don't take your fuck toy with you

132

on a family vacation. Not even Constantine has those big balls. I took
my vacation time and went home to visit Dad and my sisters for a bit,
yet I was always under the watchful eye of my handlers. Little
Madison was growing like a weed and running everywhere with
grabby. Erris was going to be the taller than her oldest sister and she
wasn't done growing yet. Dad, looked old but the contentment that
radiated from him when we were all the dinner table was real so all
this was worth it.

Remember why you're doing this.

The sound of a clearing throat brought me back to the present.

I stood still as Randal buckled a black leather collar around my
neck. He didn't say anything. I didn't need to either. Randal finished
buckling everything up, but didn't lock my hands behind me. "Mr.
Constantine didn't leave instructions."

Well thank God for small mercies.

I didn't have to be locked into stressful positions for minutes on
end. Randal gave me a half-hearted smile. This meant he didn't have
to watch me suffer while we waited for the Head of the Organization
to arrive.

"There's some left over 'Death by Chocolate" cake on the
counter."

Randal shook his head, "You should open up a bakery, Brant."

My response was more bitter than I intended. "And when would I
have the time to do that? The boardroom and the bedroom kind of
take up most of my day."

"Maybe it's something you should think about in the future."
Randal called out as he left the bedroom.

I frowned. What did he mean by that? I went and stood by the
window looking out, past my reflection to the lights of the city below.
Constantine liked me in black. My naturally pale skin made me look
ethereal. My neck was now covered with a high collar forcing my
chin up and my head back. If I tried to look down, the edge dug hard
into my shoulders and jaw. The air conditioning vent hit me and my
exposed nipples tightened to hard pulsing nubs accentuated by the

tight PVC tank wrapped around my torso. Constantine would like that. The rest of my outfit was, for the lack of a better word, specially made, easy access leather breeches. I was a beautiful fetish doll ready to be played with again. I leaned forward and rested my forehead against the window.

I was 30 years old today. I've been a whore for more than half my life.

"Wilber…" I dared to whisper his name. That was the extent of my rebellion against Constantine now. A whisper in an empty room to a lover, no, to a man who I wanted to be my lover. We didn't even have the time to truly explore what we could have been. I felt my core turn cold.

Business was business and what was going to happen in a few minutes was going to be that.

Constantine had taught me well.

"Brant, front and center. Now!" The bellow from the other room set my stomach in a clench because this wasn't the norm when he came calling.

Moving as fast as I could without making the collar dig in any further than necessary, I stumbled to a stop at the bedroom door when I saw more men that the Boss crowded into my living room.

My voice was calm even though my stomach muscles were clenched tight. "Our agreement was exclusivity."

Constantine turned around with a full glass of scotch in his hand and computer tablet in the other. He glanced up from the tablet then did a double take. "Why are you dressed like that?"

"What are you usually here for?"

"Well, not today."

I could feel the eyes of the five other men who had come into my penthouse ogling me. The one with the razor stubble for hair tried to hide his mouth with his hand as he licked his lips. My guts clenched again. "Then I can take this off."

"Not yet." Constantine shook his head then tapped the screen once more. I could see the glare of his gaze at the screen from across the room. Someone had his attention, and it wasn't going to be good.

"What's going on?"

"They are here as backup to you as you are taking care of this…" Constantine tossed the tablet my way but the bondage paraphernalia restricted movement and it hit the floor, hard. I couldn't look down at it.

"Randal, get that off him."

My breathing became easier when that damned high collar fell away. Constantine took a deep drink then grimaced. Picking up the tablet, I caught Constantine downing the rest of the glass in one vigorous head toss. His abuse of alcohol was not a common occurrence. Not good.

"The Board has decided to reward you, Brant. You discovered that discrepancy in the reports in Zone C and upon investigation, the whole barrel is tainted."

"The Board wouldn't reward me."

Because they know who Cinderella was and the nickname of Ice still didn't make up for the fact that I was bedded goods.

Constantine met my gaze. "It is standard practice when corruption is this wide spread the entire Zone is cleansed."

My heart skipped a beat. Cleansed. That meant everyone disappears. "What about the girls? They're just paying back family loans. They have nothing to do with the corruption."

"Nobody else has your prospective, Brant. They are regarded as acceptable damages and loss."

My anger skipped my cautionary button. "Bullshit."

There was an undisguised snort from the huddled crew. I ignored them as Constantine continued explaining why he was here on my usual entertainment free day.

"Which is why you have a three-hour window, now an hour and a half." Constantine shook his empty glass in the air and razor stubble head moved to the opened decanter on the coffee table and filled it back to the rim. "Think of this as another test of your character. Cleanse the problem as you see fit. Get going."

****

Whoring is whoring, so say those who haven't had to do it.

I was fortunate enough to get the status of escort back in the day.

A brothel was a step below streetwalker in the Organization. These young women and men would have been listed as a troublemaker, such as a runaway, to get sent there. Physical unattractiveness would not be a drawback if there was a hole to be filled. Nightly quotas would be set and clients would arrive at their door where the possibility of refusal was nil. To have the pimp skim from the brothel affected the overall payments these workers were making; the compiling interest would be driving the possibility of debt closure from their grasp. When it was shown that the outstanding debt couldn't be recovered…well, that worker was transferred to medical where they disappeared through organ donation.

A hot shot of agony ripped through my stomach. These crooked bastards were killing these women and men without a thought to the hell they had already gone through.

I thought I had known about the Organization from Wilber's dealings but he was of a far higher caliber that these lowlifes we were coming to.

"Mr. Williams?" Razor Stubble glanced up into the mirror with that same unnerving look of lust in his eyes. He probably had worn out of the Cinderella DVD from the vibe he was giving off.

"We are here to secure the Organization's assets. There will be no further damage to the goods. Is that understood?" I had pulled on the Ice cloak along with one of the expensive tailored suit Constantine's stylist had filled my closets with. The way Razor

136

Stubble looked at me I might has well have been back in the PVC tank and leather pants.

"I'm here under Mr. Constantine's orders." He returned gruffly which told me nothing.

Randal turned the car into the dilapidated six-story hotel. "Mr. Williams, the limousines will be here in ten minutes. Should we wait for them?"

So much horrible could happen in ten minutes.

"Mr. Williams?" Randal called to me again.

"No one gets outside the building." I directed my order to Razor Stubble.

I pushed the door open and stood in the night, the air was heavy with the stench of decay and human waste. If there had been a heyday for this hotel it was well and surely gone. Even the neon proclaiming the name of the hotel was flickering and humming inconsistently. From the amount of monies that should be coming in from the number of girls registered under Gordon Kelley there could have been improvements to the establishment.

Randal moved up to my side. "Brant?"

"Get the girls into the lobby. Kick the johns out." I glanced past Randal to Razor Stubble and his five other associates. "You know these men?"

"Heavy hitters, every single one of them from the Board itself." Randal's voice was low and wary.

"Meaning?" My stomach clenched with dread.

"It's not good."

"My priority is the girls. As soon as the limos get here, usher them out. Every single one of them. If they need medical attention get them to the Doc as quickly as possible."

"I'm not leaving you here by yourself."

"I've got his back, little man." Razor Stubble stepped close then nodded. "Men are in position, Mr. Williams."

Cockiness and over indulgence in drugs and alcohol made this test of character simpler than it could have been. A few of the pimp's henchmen men ended up with knife wounds but there was no gunfire to bring the authorities down on us. Harsh words and bruised egos were the worst of the injuries until Gordon Kelley was dragged out of a room in little more than a silk shirt and saggy underwear. His partner, an underage crying teenager, was wrapped in a sheet and ushered into the arms of her fellow girls. It was easy to see that all sixteen of them were various degrees of healing. One blonde haired girl wore an eye-patch.

"Is this everyone?"

"Sammie's down in the dungeon." The eye-patched girl called out. "I haven't heard anything from her, she might not even be alive."

Randal pointed at another of Constantine's men. "Show him down to the dungeon. Everyone else, line up. We are headed out to the limos. Those needing medical attention in the second car."

This is when Gordon Kelley decided he had enough.

"What the fuck do you think you are doing? Do you have any idea who the hell you are fucking with?"

One couldn't miss the way all the assembled girls cringed at the abruptness of that bellow. I re-acted. The heel of my foot caught him full on in the face and the room echoed with the crack as his jaw dislocated. Those men who had been holding him, let him fly to the wall. The ice in my veins cooled my anger and my thoughts as I tore into him. The gargled scream didn't touch my core as my fists pounded into that face or my leather shoes broke bones.

A hand caught my forearm and jerked me back as I reared back to send another punch. Razor Stubble tightened his grip even more to get my enraged attention. "Now is not the time to bloody your hands."

I glanced down at my fist and finally realized that it was red with blood. I don't think that his remark meant anything about my beating that scum into the filthy carpet.

Razor Stubble whispered into my ear. "Cleansing is my specialty, Cinderella. Salvage is yours."

"What?" Whimpers from huddles of girls brought my attention back to the moment. There was a wheeze from the pulp of a man on the floor.

"Let go."

Razor Stubble took his own sweet time releasing his hold. His thumb trailed over my bloody skin then he sucked it into his mouth. There was another face I wanted to punch in.

Randal came up and wrapped my knuckles with his handkerchief. "Sammie didn't make it."

A lump formed at the base of my throat. "Bring another car for her. She doesn't stay here."

"Understood." Randal glanced down at the floor. "You might want to say something to the girls."

Terrified eyes stared at me. I must have looked a sight, so different from the corporate executive that had walked into this hellish brothel. The throbbing in my hands was starting to get passed by the fading adrenaline rush. I'd never beaten anyone before. I'd defended myself when I had to but to out and out punish someone was a new low for me.

"I am a representative of the Organization. We were unaware that this place was being operated under these conditions. This type of repayment service was not the intention. This place is now closed. You will be taken for medical attention if required. After that, you will be settled in better establishments."

"You mean we're still nothing more than whores?" Eye Patch cried out.

My voice continued calm and composed. "Your families signed a contract and then were unable to fulfill the terms…"

"Answer me…"

"Until the full…"

Eye Patch forced her way to the front of the crowd. "Bullshit…what the fuck do you know about the hell we've been through. They killed Sammie and all she did was bag that fat greasy fuck who wanted to cut her…"

"Shut up!" Randal jumped in front of me.

"Lisa disappeared and Miki! That fucker probably killed them too!"

There was the sound of a watch alarm beeping in the sudden silence after the girl's outburst. Razor Stubble raised his wrist then pushed the button to make it stop. "Your window is officially closed, Cinderella. You need to be concerned about the living and not the dead. By the grace of the second hand, I'll give you one minute to clear out with the assets before a full cleansing begins."

He stared me right in the eyes and I knew that this was not an empty threat. Razor Stubble was not part of Constantine's sphere of influence and that beep was the sign that his leash had been released.

"Go."

Randal protested. "But…"

"Move it out!" I barked out.

Constantine moved in the higher echelon, the rarified atmosphere of the board of directors who would never get their hands dirtied, or bloodied by something so trivial as debt collection, aka prostitution. I'd never kid myself that I knew what the girls or boys forced into the brothel system endured. I just knew that I had been damned fortunate when I walked into Wilber's district. Medical attention was little to nil and from our brief encounter I would estimate that most of these women were in need.

This was still an underworld show so it needed a under the radar doctor, and the only one I trusted was Doc back in Wilber's domain.

"Brant, your hand?" Randal's voice broke through my thoughts.

"What?"

"I asked if you broke your hand?"

Flexing my fingers, I knew if they were broken but they were simply cuts from Gordon Kelley's teeth. "I just bruised them."

"We'll get the Doc to look at them" Randal wrapped a clean handkerchief over my knuckles.

"The girls will need him more."

"I am under strict instructions by Mr. Constantine that you are not to be injured."

"Don't worry. He can still fuck me." My guard was down so my dark thoughts came to the surface.

"Mr. Williams..."

The undisguised shock in his voice told me that I had gone too far. "Ignore me, Randal. I'm in a pensive mood."

The ride continued in silence until Randal broke it again. "Mr. Williams, don't let the Angel of Death into your condo."

"Angel of Death. Who is that?"

"Nico Cavello." Randal glanced up into the rear view mirror.

"I have never met a Cavello."

"The bald guy who licked your hand. He and his crew work exclusively for the Board of Directors."

"You mean for Constantine."

Randal shook his head. "No...Mr. Constantine is the Chairmen of the Board of the Organization but the Board runs on its own sometimes. People disappear when the Board has Cavello bring his attention on you."

What the hell is going on now? I've done everything I was capable of at headquarters legal or otherwise. This 'test of character' was nothing more than a hope that I would fail from those men from the shadows. I've tried to stay in the background...

"Mr. Williams, we're here. The Doc will see you first."

"Me?"

"Your hands..."

It was on the tip of my tongue to argue but then I could see the girls being lined up the stairs. They needed medical attention more than me but if Constantine's favorite toy was broken, it was deemed easier to be moved to the head of the line. My fists were aching but I had lived through worse pain.

The chatter dropped down to silence as I headed up the stairs. One of Constantine's men opened the door for me then closed it

behind me. The entry way to the Doctor's office was still in a slow
rate of decay and his call from the examination room was just as gruff.

"Take your clothes off and get up on the table..."

"It's just my hands." I replied holding them up for him to see.

He turned on his heel and his bloodshot eyes widened. "Holy
shit."

I laughed. "I've been called worse."

"Brant...you got a haircut." His hand reached up for a moment
but he never touched me. His eyes took in the rest of my appearance.
I was an executive after all.

"Among other things."

"I get a call saying District 1 is sending girls for attention but I
never expected...I mean...why the hell would District 1 be calling me?
I guess now I know. Take off your pants and we'll see what damage
was done."

I shook my head. "It's just my hands."

"You get in a fight?"

"More like handing out retribution."

Doc looked at my hands. "We going to need x-rays?"

I flexed my fingers. "Nothing's broken just a little chewed up."

"Knuckles on teeth can do that. When's your last tetanus shot?
If you can't remember it's better to be safe than sorry." Doc worked
quickly and efficiently and soon my hands were wrapped in sterile
white bandages and my butt cheek stung from the injection.

Doc slipped off the vinyl gloves and tossed them in the trash.
"District 1 girls on my stoop and you looking all fine and dandy
means it ain't just rumor that you're up at Headquarters. Mr.
Brawden wasn't looking so hot for a long time after you stepped up.
I've heard he's been looking for your replacement."

I didn't need to hear this. It was that little wanting spark in my
iced heart that begged Wilber to wait for me. After all this darkness
of humanity, I was still a romantic.

"He's like that prince going around trying that glass slipper on
every hopeful..."

I cut him off. "Charge the maximum on every girl you see. Send the bill to me. I'll take care of it."

"Why me? District 1 has its own hospital staffed with underworld doctors."

I flexed my hands ignoring the pain. It was more than likely going to hurt work in the morning. Straightening I met Doc's eyes evenly. "Because even though I was a whore, you never treated me like one. These girls are just repaying family debt and they've been run through hell. They need to be treated like they matter, because they do. Just because someplace else has the latest equipment doesn't mean it offers the best care."

Doc nodded then turned back to his office. "Send in the worst first. Not going to promise miracles but I'll do the best I can."

"That's all I ask."

The new few minutes were spent getting Constantine's men organized. Constantine prided himself on the loyalty of his employees so these guys I could trust not to make the situation worse. The cell phone buzzed in my breast pocket. The number was unknown and with that knowledge my stomach sent a sharp spasm through me.

"Williams."

"My beautiful Cinderella…" The voice was the Angel of Death.

Hanging up was not an option. "Report."

"It is complete."

Silence. What could I say to that?

"Your broken dolls have been identified."

A stab of agony in my stomach almost bent me over. "Understood."

Deep breathing filled my ear. "I know you cut your hair, but you looked much better when it was long."

I didn't want to the deal with this. "If there is nothing else left to report…."

"Now, now. Don't be like that, Princess. I would like to take you out for drinks."

143

The icy tone froze my voice. "I seriously doubt you have drinks on your mind."

"You're right. I want Cinderella flat on his back, moaning as I ram my cock deep into your ass. I watch your video every night and want to bring tears down your face as I fuck you."

A shiver of apprehension ran down my spine.

"Silence is agreement, Cinderella."

This verified that Cavello wasn't Constantine's man. None of them would have even dared to speak to me this way. "Debt repayment services are now null and void."

"You're still under contract."

"It is a private agreement."

"Mr. Constantine might have some say in the matter for the moment but the wind is saying that change is coming."

"Don't beat around the bush, Mr. Cavello."

"I want you. When your patron tosses you to the wolves, I'll be there…"

I hung up. *God, what else is going on?* I noticed I was doing my Napoleon gesture, hand to stomach, and forced myself to stop. Image was everything. This was not the first time that a business associate that come on to me but to become the target of the Angel was Death, a loose cannon only commanded by the whole of the Board of Directors, was a concrete threat.

"Randal, let's go."

The girls were milling as I headed down the stairs.

"Hey, Cinderella! What happens to us now?" One of them called out.

"You will call him Mr. Williams." Randal took a step towards the dark-haired woman. Bruises were still very colorful on her face and body. A younger thug grabbed her by the back of her head and shook her until she screamed in pain.

"Enough!" The thug shoved her back in line at the sound of my voice.

"After you see Doc, you will be divided up to different brothels to finish out your contracts. Your contracts will be altered accordingly once the final tally is discovered."

"So, what do I have to do to become the new Cinderella?" The dark-haired girl grimaced as she cradled the back of her head.

Randal yelled back at her. "I said, you call him, Mr. Williams."

I walked forward then carefully extended my bandaged hand forward to tilt her face to the streetlight. Bruises upon bruises and I was about to add more. "You don't. You ran away from your first posting and because of that you ended up in that brothel. Once you're in a brothel, that's where you stay until you either finish off the loan that was borrowed or you cause too much trouble and disappear. One way or another, the Organization will get its money back; and right now, it's entirely your choice how that gets done."

There was nothing but silence behind me now as I headed back to the limo. My stomach pain flared up as I sunk down into the seat. My hands were throbbing. I felt like hell.

"Brant?"

"Home."

The dividing panel rose between the cabin effectively cutting me off leaving me in solitude. Those girls didn't see this as a rescue. This was just another way to screw them over. I'd have to look deeper into the files and see how much monies were embezzled and apply it accordingly toward each outstanding debt.

This was a hell of a day.

****

I heard murmurs of different voices, but I didn't try to make out the conversation as I walked back into my condo. I mentally sighed. It would have been too much to hope that Constantine had gone home. My day has been long enough and I just want sleep. When I woke up next morning, I could get started on the first day of my new decade. I could only pray it was better than the last one.

Constantine sat in a dark brown leather club chair holding his usual drink, scotch on the rocks.

"What the hell was the reason..."

I caught Constantine's hand motion. I was a valued assistant in public, but he treated me like a dog in private. This place might be listed as my penthouse, but we both knew who ruled the roost. I dropped down in a submissive position. My knees spread to about shoulder width, shoulders were pulled even to balance a pole across if necessary and my back was rigid. My head was arched up almost as if a steel cable were attached to the top of my skull straight down through to my pelvis.

I was rewarded with a chink of ice against the side of Constantine's glass. If I needed correction, he gave it quickly.

Glancing over to the side of the chair was I was surprised to see a young man on his knees. He had shoulder-length brown hair that hung forward over his face as he huddled in a piss poor attempt of submission. There was another man in the room hidden by the wide back of the other leather chair.

There was a strained silence in the room. The only sound was the boy's ragged breathing, and Constantine's scotch glass.

Constantine took another drink before addressing the unknown man. "While, I find your offer tempting, Brant is more than just a sex partner. He is heavily involved with the business side of things. Your boy is beautiful and seems to be on his way to be a well-trained submissive, but I really can't see him filling Brant's shoes."

"He's not here to fill Brant's shoes, just your bed."

Wilber!

I don't know how I kept my head from popping up. I could feel Constantine's eyes on me as I stared down at the marbleized lines of the slab floor tiles.

Wilber is here!

I closed my eyes forcing down the hope that attempted to flow up from my wounded soul. It was easier for me to accept disappointment by denying it first, than to have Constantine rip it away.

Wilber's tone was even as if he were talking about an inanimate object. "Besides, Brant is looking ragged."

"I have noticed that, Brawden." I heard the ice in his glass chink together, as Constantine took another drink. "If only he'd been Family. I appreciate talent, no matter from which arena that person first came."

God, they were discussing me like I wasn't here. I glanced sideways at the boy who was meant to replace me. The boy was shivering. *Enough.* I got up off my knees and walked toward the poor kid. It was shades of me sixteen years ago, when I walked into the dragon's den.

Wilber, what the hell have you done?

"Brant?" There was amusement in Constantine's voice until he saw my bandaged hands.

I met his gaze evenly, "Have some compassion."

Grabbing the kid's upper arm, I pulled him to his feet. His flesh was ice cold. All he had on was a pair of pants that were so thin he might as well have been naked. The boy flinched in my grip. Bruises were fading from his body, but I could tell that he had more bruises than Wilber had ever left on me at one time. A hand closed around my heart. This kid had come from the brothels.

Constantine shifted his position and lifted his leg so his ankle was resting on his opposite knee. His green eyes took on the glow of a predator. "I don't need compassion: I need stimulation. Kiss him."

What? I couldn't have heard right but the boy stiffening next to me proved that I must have.

"You know what happens if I have to repeat myself." The amusement was gone from his voice. I still hesitated. There was a tone of warning in his voice, "Brant."

The boy lifted his head up. He couldn't be more than seventeen. He was pretty in a street punk kind of way. He looked like he could

147

be smiling at you, while sticking a knife in your ribs and stealing your wallet. The brothel had kicked that out of him only a bit; the fear in his eyes was still fleeting. He may be bruised, but he was far from being broken.

"It's okay." He reached up for my face with his free hand, catching me around the neck and urging me forward. He only came up to my nose. I caught his hand, pulled him off and pushed him away.

I might have to lie down and take it, but I wasn't going to hand it out. I wasn't built that way.

"Brant." Wilber's voice sent a shiver down my spine.

I didn't dare turn towards his voice, even though I wanted nothing more than turn around and allow my parched eyes to drink in his face. If I ran to him like I wanted to, Constantine would make someone pay. Right now, I had a feeling it would be this kid.

Wilber continued to speak. "You know that we don't force them into these deals. The family walks in of their own free will. It's only when they fall behind something like this happens. Have you forgotten?"

Constantine was still sitting there in deceptive ease. "Mr. Brawden wants an exchange. This boy for you."

Wilber added lowly, "Nicky would rather stay here in this penthouse than a brothel."

My chest clenched tight. I finally turned and met Wilber's gaze. His face was unreadable. Nicky jumped back up on me wrapping his arms around my shoulders. I wasn't prepared for it. I staggered backwards then tripped, landing hard on my ass. Nicky took advantage squirming up on me. His warm lips slipped against mine then he dropped his head down to whisper into my ear.

"Please." His impassioned whisper stilled me. "Don't send me back to that place."

I worked an arm between us and pushed him up and off me. Considering his face his eyes were a warm sepia tone, but they were turning dull. Just like mine. Old beyond his years… on their way to dying. It took me sixteen years to hit the lowest of the low. He wasn't going to last long working in the lower ranks of the brothel.

Could I help him? Was I so broken now, that I couldn't even do that?

"Please, Brant." He begged me with a choked voice.

I raised my hand and caught him by the back of the neck. I pulled him down on me and began to kiss him, tenderly, teasingly, mercifully. I doubted Nicky had seen much of any of this. I licked at his lips until he opened his mouth to me. I let my tongue dart inside his mouth. He tasted of strong mint. Nicky squirmed on my body, pressing his hardening groin down into my stomach. He was shorter than me and far too thin for his height. I guess they don't feed their whores down in the brothel. He was such a small thing.

I flicked an eye over and saw Constantine watching the floorshow with interest. He nodded once.

Damn it. I'm not that much of a pervert. No matter what the hell I had become, I was not taking a child.

I closed my eyes. "He wants a show."

Nicky stilled. I could feel his stomach contract with fear.

"Do what you want. I won't resist you." My voice was an even unfazed tone even if my own stomach tightened in disgust.

"You... you don't want to fuck me?" The kid was honestly puzzled that I wasn't all over him.

What kind of hell had he been through?

"No, I don't do children. Make it interesting, and you just might end up here in the sky."

His eyes were truly puzzled. "You want me to fuck you?"

No, I didn't want him to fuck me, but the alternative was worse than what I could live with if I did nothing. If the price of keeping this child out of the brothels was me rolling over, then I'd do it.

I closed my eyes. "Do whatever you want, Nicky."

"Brant." Someone whispered. I was fanciful enough to think it was Wilber.

I made sure I reacted enough for our audience to appreciate it. I had been a porn star after all. I shrugged off my jacket and vest. Nicky had no such qualms getting down to business. I could take small comfort in knowing that Wilber had found the boy… not trained him. I allowed myself to be turned over onto my hands and knees. Nicky swept his hands up under my shirt and pinched at my nipples roughly. I grimaced with pain. He was rough. This was probably all he knew. He took my hips and ground his hard cock up against my ass. I just hung my head and let him push me into any position he wanted. He was desperate. Not for sex but to get away from the brothel environment. His nails raked down the sensitive skin of my lower groin as he shoved his hand down the front of my suit pants. A hiss escaped my throat.

"Enough." Constantine set his drink aside and stood up.

Nicky stilled but he had his hand wrapped around the warmth of my cock. "I can see that I've been missing something for quite a while. Nicky, come and kneel by my chair. Brant, stand up."

It took a moment to untangle, then I climbed to my feet. My groin was pulsing. The kid had scratched me.

"Mr. Williams, you've been perfect these last three years. You've been obedient. You have done everything I have ever requested without protest. You don't like me though."

"Was I supposed to? That was never part of the deal…" My head whipped as Constantine's hand cracked across my right cheek but I stood my ground. I was pissed that someone so young was lost down the same road I had taken.

So young and already unable to turn off it.

The iron tang of my blood from my cut inner cheek tainted my mouth. My fingertips tested my lip but there wasn't a trace of red on them. "With respect, Mr. Constantine, I gave you exactly what you told me you wanted when we first met. You said you wanted a trained companion who wasn't in competition with your wife for your affections and I gave you that."

A dark eyebrow arched. "And you think you're competition?"

I stood before him, disheveled in a undone shirt and unzipped pants. "I'm a business whore. I'm not even in the same league."

There was silence only broken by the chink of ice and the hum of the heater kicking in. I could feel his predatory eyes on me but I had the art of aversion down pat.

"I can see now that I've been bedding a shade... a beautiful pale ghost. I've broken him, Mr. Brawden. I gave him every physical convenience, but I didn't see that I wounded his spirit so badly. Do you still want our Brant, even like this?"

"Yes." Wilber's simple word just... just... I couldn't even articulate what it meant to me.

Constantine reached up. I flinched. His green eyes flicked up to me. Even at his worse, I had never flinched from him. Slowly he reached out and touched the red mark he left on my face. "You can't be freed now, Brant. You understand, right?"

His hand tightened around my jaw and pulled me close to whisper in my left ear. "You know too much about me and the Organization. The safest thing to do would be to put a bullet between your big, grey eyes... but I think I have taken enough from you. It's time I gave something you want."

He straightened then turned and regarded his new acquisition. "Nicholas...whatever am I going to do with you tonight? This penthouse belongs to Brant."

"I don't want it." I pulled my executive personal assistant "Iceman" persona around me. My voice was calm even though I was shaking internally.

Constantine reached down and ran his fingers through the boy's brown hair. "Then sell it."

"Give it to Nicky."

Constantine turned back towards me his eyes narrowing a bit to let me know that he was beginning to get irked at my obstinacy.

"Generous gesture, Brant, but you earned this little perk. My Nicholas will earn his own rewards. Mr. Brawden, you might want to set our little ghost here up in a kitchen. I've had him cook for me a few times while we were travelling for business. Excellent selections and perfect presentations. He has hidden talents."

Constantine caught me unawares. His palm cupped the back of my neck and urged me forward toward him even as I tried to back up. "I will have one last kiss from you, Brant. You have been taught how I want it. Show Nicholas what he is supposed to do."

I felt my face flush with embarrassment. I didn't want to do this in front of Wilber.

"Now… Brant."

I forced myself to lean into his body. Constantine kept in shape. I knew this because he set my workout schedule to coincide. He was ripped. I've seen him lifting free weights that I couldn't handle. He was stronger than me, but he only used enough strength to keep me in line. As I said, he didn't need to; I wasn't stupid but I was cautious around Constantine.

Kindness belonged to his family. As I've been reminded countless times, I was not family by blood or by bond.

Constantine wrapped his fingers into the back of my short hair and yanked down hard. My mouth opened in a gasp and he stuck his tongue deep inside. I closed my eyes. I still didn't want to have to look at him. I began to French him the way he liked it. He pulled back dragging his teeth over my bottom lip. "You fuck like a professional, Brant."

That was supposed to be flattery? I wanted to vomit. The burning agony in my stomach stepped up a notch.

Constantine let me go. "Are you taking him with you, Mr. Brawden?'

"That was the plan, sir."

"Then with your permission, Brant, I would like to use your penthouse tonight. I will get Nicholas his own quarters tomorrow."

I nodded. I didn't trust myself to open my mouth. I just might start screaming.

Wilber's voice was gruff as he spoke to me. "Get what you need."

Constantine started getting his groove on before Wilber and I left the main room. I darted into my bedroom and grabbed from the closet a pair of shoes and an old, old brown sweater from way before the start of these hellish three years. I met Wilber at the front hall. "That's it?"

"I don't need anything else from this place."

Wilber turned and headed toward the door.

Randal pulled it open and held it for us. "Good dinner, Brant. Call me if you open that restaurant. Me and the boys would be regulars."

I hop-jerked my shoes on as I followed Wilber out the door and down the hall toward the elevators. I caught up to him just as the doors began to open. I struggled into the sweater. It was over my head when Wilber caught me by my arm and dragged me blindly into the elevator. I hit the far wall. He jerked the sweater down and twisted me around, so I was back first against the paneling. His huge hand came up and pinned me there by my throat, then it slid down and rested on my chest.

"You cut your hair." His eyes ran over my face. His other hand came up and stroked the back of his fingers along my temple before catching up a jet-black strand. When I hacked it off with a sharp knife, there had to have been at least an arm's length lying on the kitchen floor. Constantine had not been impressed. The hairstylist wasn't that impressed either while trying to fix my whack job.

"I didn't want him touching it."

"Why didn't you come back?" His voice was tight and angry.

I looked down at his hands. They were all there... his fingers were all there. I knew that but relief ripped over me like a tsunami. A sob escaped my lips then I began crying in earnest with tears, stuffed up nose, and the works.

I startled him with my breakdown. He let go, and I slid to the floor as my knees just gave out. "Brant..."

Tears burned at the corners of my eyes, and my throat tightened up, "I tried... he sent me a finger. I thought it was yours."

"Goth Boy…"

"I thought it was yours," I brushed the side of my hand across my eyes to clear them. "Constantine had told me to be good and… and…"

Wilber knelt and pressed a hand to my reddened cheek where Constantine had slapped me. "Guy went missing not long after you disappeared. We never found a trace of him. Some said he ran but I knew he wouldn't have. It was probably him. You're coming home with me, my Goth Boy. You're safe now."

"I thought it was yours. I thought it was yours." It was like a mantra I kept repeating.

He held up his hands and flashed all his fingers at me.

"You are too much the martyr, Brant. I'm not your sisters. I don't need your protection." Wilber gathered me to him like I was a fragile piece of spun glass and I wrapped my arms around his shoulders burying my face against his shoulder.

"I knew Constantine took you, but I couldn't do a damned thing about it. I couldn't get any information. Then suddenly there you were in designer suits and short, short hair. I would see photos of you with him, and I knew you weren't happy. I could tell. Your eyes were different. They've seen too much. They've seen things you shouldn't have had to. Things I'd protected you from."

"I thought it was yours," I repeated, unable to form a better response. The simple old spicy scent that I associated with Wilber filled my nostrils as I turned my face toward his head and hair. Reflexively, my hands tightened, trying to meld his body into mine so we'd never be separated again. The white of the bandages stood out so stark against his black jacket.

Wilber gathered me up against his chest. His hand came around and cupped the back of my neck to him.

"I thought it was yours," I whispered into his shoulder. I dug my hands onto his back, clutching at him to make sure that this was real. That he was here with me now. That he was here in my arms.

The elevator came to a halt, and Wilber pulled me to my feet but I couldn't get my hands to let go. The doors began to close as he snaked an arm out to get the sensors to open again, then basically pulled-carried me out into the lobby. I wasn't letting go for fear of waking up and finding this all a dream.

For being late May, it was chilly. The wind swept up my back under my gaping shirt and baggy sweater. The door to the limo was opened and waiting. Wilber peeled me off his body with the same ease as always and set me on my feet.

"Get in, Goth Boy. We're going home."

"This is happening, right?" I plead, "It's real. I'm not dreaming?" I needed it to be real.

Wilber leaned forward and pressed his lips against mine. His thumb stroked my cheek that was still pulsing hot from Constantine's slap. "Does that feel real?"

"Wilber..."

"I'm here, Brant."

"I love you." I shook my head as he opened his mouth, emphatically cutting what I knew he was going to say off, "Don't tell me I don't know my feelings. I fell asleep with you in my thoughts every night. I woke up every day and sent prayers for your safety. I did what I had to these years. I love you."

Wilber ducked into the back of the car and pulled me in after him by my wrist.

"Please tell me you believe me, Wilber."

"I believe you, Brant." He pulled me onto him. I willingly climbed on his lap, spreading my thighs, and pressing my weight into the leather seat. I buried my head against his shoulder. His hand came up and settled across my lower back, easily slipping under my sweater.

"A lesser man would have faded to nothing in Constantine's care. I will take you as a pale shade of what you once where. Patience and care will see you bloom again."

155

I secretly inhaled his spicy scent that I missed so much. "You make it sound like I'm a flower."

"You're a delicate blossom that has been obscured from everything that gives life. You've gone dormant while you've been in the shadows, but what makes you special is still alive. I will return you to the sun, Brant."

I was beginning to think I heard more of what I wanted to hear rather than what Wilber was really saying. He couldn't be this forgiving; this understanding. Not after everything that I'd had to do for Constantine these past few years.

I tried to slide off Wilber's warmth back onto the seat, but he locked his hands around my waist. I turned my face away staring out into the darkness of side window. My words were whispered but Wilber heard them. "How can you even stand to touch me? I've... the things I've done..."

His ten fingers framed my face and turned me back to his gaze. "I am honored, Brant. I am honored to know that you consider me part of your family. You did what you have always done. You protected me like an older brother should but, Goth, I'm not your brother. It is my job to take care of you. I came to Constantine every month with offers for your release. He turned me away without even listening."

"So why did he let me go this time?" I asked with my eyebrows drawing together as my lips turned down a bit.

Wilber shifted me off him then picked up a weekly magazine lying on the seat and opened it to a high-gloss photo. It was shot of Constantine and me walking through some art gallery during its grand opening. I was staring at a painting with such unguarded sadness in my expression about three feet behind him that it surprised me. My client face had cracked. I didn't even know a photo had been taken. I remember that painting. It was just blocks of color, but for some reason, it reminded me of home. Wilber's home. My home.

"After this picture came out, Constantine called me. He told me to find a replacement if I wanted you back."

"He let me go?" My voice was a little incredulous.

"I think his wife asked him to. You cannot ignore this photo, Goth. Heartbreak has never been caught so poignantly."

"I want to go home." I laid my body heavily across the seat and rested my head on Wilber's lap. Just the sound of his voice gave me a sense of security that 2.6 or even 3.1 million just didn't give.

"Brant." A hand touched my bare neck.

"I'll grow it back."

"Only if it's what you want. You are not a slave. You are not a toy."

"May I be your lover?"

"Yes, Goth." Wilber urged me back up until I was enfolded in his arms. He opened his legs so my ass was sitting on the seat but my knees were hiked up over his thigh. I'd gotten too heavy to really sit on his lap by the time I'd hit seventeen. I had reached my current height of six-foot-two but was still a little underweight at one hundred and thirty pounds but every inch of that was lean muscle. Wilber kissed my temple.

"Happy Birthday, Brant. I lit your candle on your birthday cake and made a wish before I came here today."

"You made a birthday wish for me?" I'd never heard of that before.

"I'll do it every year from now on."

"Why?"

"Because my wish came true. Welcome back, Brant. Welcome home."

I tilted my head back and angled my head to receive his kiss. I kept my eyes open to know that it really was Wilber I was kissing. That it was him I was touching and being touched by.

What did he say? He lit a candle for me? He wants to lift me to the light? He wants to set me in the sun. Just looking up into his strong distinctive face was enough to light up my world. I felt like the moon emerging from behind the earth back into the warmth and radiance of the sun. The shade I had been for three years burned away in direct light. It just couldn't survive in the face of brilliance.

I knew I was too old to be clingy but I never wanted to let him go. The fear lingered in my mind that this was just a hallucination or a dream seemed all too real. The limo began to slow then turned into the gateway. Home. Looking at the Wilber's house was now a sight for sore eyes.

We untangled ourselves as Mikey came back and opened the door.

"Take off." Wilber ordered and Mikey flashed me a wide smile then closed the door behind us. The car pulled out before we even got into the front door. As we walked toward the house, every window was dark.

Where is everyone? I frowned and Wilber saw it as he unlocked the front door.

"I told everyone to clear out for the night. If I succeeded in bringing you home, I didn't want any interruptions. If I failed... well, you know I drink alone."

I felt shy. I was startled when I felt Wilber's fingers brush at the tear tracks that still stained my cheeks. "The time for tears is over. You are home."

"I'm 30 years old today. I'm not a boy."

"No, you're not. You've turned into a hell of a fine executive for the Organization." Pride beamed in his face and he kissed a tear stained cheek.

Wilber walked into the dark house flipping on a light as he reached the kitchen. I followed him like a grateful kitten plucked from the curb. I had wanted to try this so many times in the past but was afraid of being rejected. After three years with Constantine, I wouldn't let any opportunities pass me by again.

I leaned my body onto his back and wrapped my arms around his chest. I breathed in his scent and felt the warmth of him through his jacket. In my folly, I swear I could feel his heart beating against my cheek. He stilled.

I tensed for a moment and almost stepped away, but then… I brushed my face back and forth across his back and tightened my grip.

Being faint of heart won't get me what I need, and I needed Wilber. His strength. His kindness. Maybe he just wanted my body, but that was enough. I could love enough for the both of us.

His hands came over mine, and I expected him to peel me away. But instead his hands clasped mine and held them tighter to his chest.

"Thank you," I whispered into the material of his jacket.

"For what, Brant?"

"For not pushing me away."

"I will never push you away. You've been away too long. Come here."

While I claimed to be thirty years old, but right now I had the emotional control of a hormonal teenager. He turned in my arms and pressed my head against the side of his. I clung to him and cried with relief. All my wishing and hoping and waiting and wanting had finally come true.

"You're home. You *are* home."

His hand come up and rested on my bare neck.

"I'll grow it out again." I could feel the warmth of his hand beginning to melt the ice my soul was encased in.

His thumb stroked up and down my nape. I shuddered – but not in a good way and he stopped. "I can't imagine what you have gone through, Brant, that a simple touch makes you stiffen. I will not ask. If you want to tell me, I'll listen."

"I don't want to talk about Constantine."

"When we won't." Wilber gathered me in his arms, and I felt something I haven't felt in years. Something I had taken for granted until it was wrenched away from me. I felt safe. In Wilber's arms, I felt safe.

"I want you to do something for me, Brant."

"Anything, Wilber."

He shifted his torso and reached into his suit pocket. He rummaged for a moment then pulled out a lighter. "Even though it's your birthday, grant me this wish." He relit the single candle that sat on a sea of white frothy frosting. I been crying in varying degrees since the elevator ride from the penthouse and now I was down to sniveling. I had to wipe my runny nose on the sleeve of my sweater.

"What do you wish for?"

Wilber pulled me in front of him and wrapped his arms around my chest. He gave me a hug with just enough pressure to make my ribs feel like cracking. "You. A wish for a wish."

The flame flickered and danced. I pressed back against Wilber then closed my eyes.

Thank you for caring about me enough to come and get me. Thank you for not cringing away from my touch, the touch of a whore. Thank you, Wilber. Thank you for not forgetting about me.

I let out a puff of air, and the candle winked out, leaving a dancing trail of smoke.

"You want some?"

"Sure."

Wilber reached forward and ran his thick finger through the icing then brought it up to my lips. He painted my mouth as if it were a picture from a child's coloring book. Then I watched absolutely fascinated as he sucked that finger into his mouth.

Wilber's lips quirked slightly then he moved forward, slowly. His tongue flicked out and lapped the icing off the corner of my mouth. "Wilber..."

"Have you had tenderness from that man?"

I closed my eyes.

"Have you been treated with the care that you deserve? I'll remedy that. I'll give you everything you deserve and more."

Lick... lap... Ummmm.

"Wilber..." My tongue came out and licked some of the frosting into my mouth.

His hand came up between us as he pulled back his fist full of cake. A broken laugh escaped my throat. Wilber wasn't a sweets kind of guy. He took a bite from the cake in his hand then pressed it towards my mouth. His eyes were bright; his gaze, intense. A shiver ripped through me. I remembered that look; Wilber wanted me. I matched his gaze and leaned forward taking a mouthful of cake from his hand. Vanilla and cream cheese icing. I loved this taste. So many found it bland, but I liked it.

I ran my tongue around my lips to gather every bit of that sweetness and smiled, whispering. "You remembered."

"I remember everything, Brant. Just because I don't spout poetry at every opportune moment doesn't mean that I am a callous bastard. I know what brings you joy."

I flinched again as his knuckles ran up the back of my neck. His jaw firmed.

"You've been through an ordeal. It's time for you to get some rest. Your room is just were it has always been."

What? I don't want to spend my first night back under Wilber's roof in my small, lonely bed!

Wilber wiped his hand clean on a tea towel. I stood behind him, scared that he was going to leave me alone and scared of being scared.

"Brant?"

I pulled myself to my full height. "I want to sleep in your bed, in your arms."

Taking a deep breath, I added, "I missed being with you, Wilber."

"Are you sure?"

"With all my heart."

Carefully, he took the tea towel and wiped my face clean. How many times had he done this as I grew up? He might have procured my clients, but that was to service the debt. This was for us. He took my hand and led me through the kitchen down the hall and up the stairs. Three years had passed and nothing had changed in the house. It was as if time had stood still. If only that were true.

Wilber guided me into the bedroom, and there he paused, looking me over as if he was unsure how to proceed but I could see desire in his eyes. I was too well-trained as any man's whore not to notice that he'd been hard as a rock ever since I sat on his thighs in the limo ride over here. But this was Wilber… my Wilber, the holder of my heart and the key of my existence. I knew I was alive when I was with him. Why? He made me feel it. He called me his flower, how true. I blossomed under his care. I thought I had wilted under Constantine's thumb but it seemed as if I had simply gone into hibernation. He had gotten everything he wanted from me, as a subordinate and as a mistress. If it wasn't so sad I would have laughed at him. When he got what he wanted he didn't want it anymore. I traded my bed with that brothel escapee and he was grateful for it. That was a testament that my core wasn't as pure and untouched as I thought it was. Would Wilber want this thing that I've become? I hope so.

I leaned forward and pressed my lips to Wilber's. Rarely had I taken the initiative. I may have wanted Wilber's attention, but I used to wait for him to give it. I brought my hands up and held his head, angling mine to mash our tender flesh together. It was a kiss of need and wanting but it was also, truthfully, a kiss filled with desperation.

All the while we were Frenching, his breathing had gotten deeper and his eyes darkened. His hands slid up my arms to my shoulders, gently pushing me back and breaking the kiss I honestly didn't want to end.

"I wanted to give you a night of peace after the hell you've been through," he admitted.

"Welcome me home, Wilber." I lay back on the mattress and held a hand up for him to join me.

In the pale light of the moon, I saw his hulking shadow pause. "Only if you truly want to be with me." His voice was gruff.

Before, I would have pulled my hand back when he didn't reach for it right away but this time I lifted it higher, opening my palm.

"Welcome me home, you will give me peace," I told him with the kind of honesty that burned into someone's soul.

My throat tightened. "There is cold and then there's COLD. I've been so COLD for so long. I want to be warm and you are the only one I will allow to do that for me."

Constantine had taught me how to be bad... well, his kind of bad. I gripped the hem of my sweater and jerked it off over my head. My body had become more defined over those past one thousand and ninety-five days. I'd filled out more and bulked up. My body had matured to match my height now.

I met Wilber's eye and ran my hand down my throat to my bare chest, over a pebbled nipple and down my muscled stomach, slowly lingering over zones that got my body hot.

The faint lingering scent of Old Spice filled my nostrils, and I inhaled gratefully. The tailored suit pants showcased my hardening erection. I let my fingers slip into the low waistband, the tips just brushed at the base of...

My seductive show halted abruptly when Wilber caught my wrist and yanked away from my body.

Unable to help it, my eyes contacted his just long enough to hear him say, "This is *not* you, Brant."

He jerked me off the bed a whole lot easier than I expected then, without warning, I found myself wrapped in his arms as we stood in the middle of the room. "This is not you... this is *him*... this is Constantine," he whispered softly in my ear.

I looked away confused and more than a little ashamed that even though I was in his arms I was still writhing to Constantine's tune. My throat tightened as I admitted the truth, "I can't remember the me I used to be. The client face became my daily one; by day and by night. I had to use it or he would have won."

Wilber's arms tightened around me, offering comfort. "I remember you, Goth Boy."

"Then show me, Wilber," I whispered, "and rekindle the fire inside me so that I'm not cold anymore."

He pulled away just enough to look at my face, "I don't want to hurt you."

The only way you can hurt me is by not touching me or leaving me alone.

Turning my gaze back to his face I drank in his features, pulling those special feelings close to me like a warm blanket. Aloud I said, "I love you, Wilber. You can't hurt me."

My flesh was shivering as his hard-meaty hand swept slowly down my spine, from my nape, past my shoulders, down my back, slowly dipping into the crevasse of my buttocks. One finger slid under the waistband caressing the skin gently.

I stared into his eyes and thought it strange in my memories and fantasies, that he's so much taller than I was; but then again, most of my memories are from the time when he was a giant and I was just a kid. His eyes searched my face for any signs of discomfort or fear. I pressed my upper body closer to him as I angled my head so I could kiss him the way I wanted to. No, the way I needed to.

Wilber pressed his mouth up against mine and gently prodded my lips open with his tongue. I submitted but kept my eyes open. I wanted to see, no, I had to know who I was kissing. Wilber pressed me down hard into the mattress. I brought my arms under his as my hands clutched at his back as he continued to coax me into sweet juicy kissing.

His palm rubbed against my erection, and I moaned low. With the button undone and the zipper down, he peeled the pants off my butt and down to my thighs. His hand closed around my cock with gentle, easy strokes. His touch was so warm and so welcomed after Nicholas's frantic clawing and Constantine's cool ownership. I arched my body up to his, offering up my groin to his touch. Slowly, he began to move his head down my body. His lips and tongue wet the skin of my neck down to my collar bone. My breathing deepened as he sucked at the shallow hollow of my throat. I speared my hands in his hair. He paused, shaking his head free. In the light of the bedside lamps, it seemed like his eyes were glowing.

"Let me. Just feel, Goth."

"Wilber..."

I buried my hands into the sheets as he suckled my nipple into his mouth. His teeth gently grazed the taut flesh then laved it with his tongue. One hand flicked his thumb back and forth over the other. Each sensation ripped through me, cracking open places that I'd had to board up. Tender places I'd had to seal just to survive. I moaned but kept my eyes open.

This has to be real. It had to be, or this would be just too horrid to bear.

What?

I sat up startled as Wilber's mouth took me deep. I could count on one hand how many times Wilber had gone down on me. It wasn't something he liked doing. His shoulders pushed my thighs wide to give him access. I'd thought I wasn't capable of true pleasure any more, not having received any in so long. My cries were just for Wilber. They've only ever been for Wilber.

This was a treat. A special gift just for me. Too intense. Too much pleasure. I... I... too much. Too sensitive.

"Wilber! Stop... going to ..." Hands cupped my buttocks and pulled me deeper into his mouth. I tried to forestall it but Wilber swallowed me. He'd never done that before. Before he'd pulled off toward the end to watch me spurt. I sat there, dazed in the afterglow of orgasm. I was more than a little dazed now that he had done this. For me.

"I will never take anything that you do not offer, Brant; but, I want to be in you." I watched, still out of it, as Wilber wiped at this mouth with his thumb. I frowned. I was naked, and Wilber was still fully dressed. "Brant?"

"I want to feel you in me." I spread my thighs and pulled my knees back towards my chest.

I watched, splayed lewdly before him on his massive bed, as he pulled off his jacket and tie. I appreciated the fact that he threw his clothes to the floor with disregard. His attention was on me. I should have been embarrassed to be holding myself in this position, especially with Wilber's spittle drying on my reawakening cock; but,

I wasn't. I sucked on my fingers then prodded my ass opening myself to receive him. My love shucked his pants.

"Tell me if I hurt you, Goth Boy. That is the last thing I want to do to you."

For a big man with a gruff appearance, one wouldn't think that he could touch with such tenderness, such gentleness. I never compared him to the clients I serviced. There was no comparison, but I endured that *bastard*, I knew. Wilber was my ideal not because his penis was larger and thicker, it was because he had never truly used it as a weapon. If I earned punishment from him, it was usually sharp slaps across the tender flesh of my ass. A spanking doesn't sound as horrendous as it can truly be. The pain was fleeting but the memory of sprawling across his knee and frustration that lingered because I failed to meet established standards coupled with the disappointment on his face was far more devastating. He pulled my fingers free and substituted his own, working my body gently but with urgency until I was shuddering and gasping, lost in a world of our own making. Wilber pulled me up to my knees and turned me so I straddled his thighs, leaning my back against his chest.

"Tell me what you're feeling, Brant."

I gasped as he breeched me. Oh, so slowly, Wilber began to push up into me and his hand came around to stroke my stirring cock. My body was flush. My hands grabbed at the sheets as Wilber rocked into me. He searched for that special spot. When he hit it, I twitched as I cried out loud. He continued to stimulate my prostate with each stroke.

"I want to get deeper into you." Wilber's words whispered along my sweaty skin.

I shivered as he pulled himself free. Carefully he helped me ease forward to my hands and knees then pressed his warm huge body at my thighs and then one hand bracing his weight as he laid his torso across my back. Wilber's body hair was wiry and brushed against my skin in little tickles. He placed his hand over mine then laced our fingers together.

"Here I come."

I shivered with anticipation as he pressed the head of his cock back up against me. "Brant."

His fingers tightened around my own as he breeched me once more.

I felt love and tenderness for the first time in one thousand and ninety-five days, and I reveled in it. Wilber brought his arm around my waist to hold me steady as he began to speed up. His pressed a kiss to my exposed nape as he jutted hard into me one last time. His release into me fractured the ice I had encased around my heart. He jacked me until I came a second time collapsing forward, tears streaming down my face. I began to cry. These weren't simple tears of distress like I had in the limo ride home, but tears from years of repression and grief and triumph.

I was home.

Wilber said nothing as he gathered me to him, pressing my body gently against his sweaty flesh. He never said anything, but he was there. He had always been there. He cuddled me to him like I was still the skinny growing boy who had first come to him.

When the sobs finally stopped shaking my frame, he laid us back on the bed and tucked me close to him, curling around me like he used to. Cocooned in his arms, I was protected by his body.

I used to think that this was a sign that I was simply his possession. I knew better now. He would never say it. Actions speak louder than words, and he had been telling me for years in his own quiet way only I just wasn't able, or willing to listen.

I pulled a pillow to my chest and rested my tear streaked cheek on it. His aftershave filled my senses. He kissed the exposed nape of my neck and then an arm came over my waist and splayed across my stomach. Wilber loved me. My heart had returned to me. I felt my stomach settle down from its usual rolling agony. A deep warmth feeling I'd half-forgotten started to beat in my chest. If I stood in his glow long enough, maybe life would return to my eyes.

Chapter Seven: The Illusion of Freedom

Freedom is a rare and fleeting thing.

For one romantic and glorious night, I was thought I was free with Wilber. My Wilber was everything I had ever wished for deep in my heart. He was kind and attentive. He seemed in tune with me. He even had a birthday cake just for me. Lying awake in his bed in the light of morning, I let my thoughts drift back and couldn't remember ever having a real birthday cake.

Sure, I'd had misshapen cupcakes that Emily had made in her light bulb oven, but I'd never had a cake made just for me with my name written on it real, thick icing and pretty two tone icing flowers. I thought I had secretly cried over the fact that every one of my sisters had gotten a birthday cake and party when their special day rolled around. My birthday came with a trip to the ice cream parlor with Dad. Mom always had something else to do. Dentist appointment. Doctor's visit. Just too damned busy to show up.

I guess I finally had the reason I never had my birthday officially celebrated: I'd ruined Mom's life. But if I hadn't been born, who would have been there to save the rest of the family? That had to even things out, right? A couple of ruined lives for some happy ones, an eye for an eye... but I'm done now. Right?

I turned to my side and hugged Wilber's pillow to me. His scent was on it. I inhaled deeply. It smelt like home. I was finally home. I could live for me now. I had money to rely on. I let a small smile crack my lips. I had Wilber.

Last night, he'd planned to leave me alone. My tears always did distress him. But somehow, he'd known that I'd needed him, and not in our old rough and tumble way. Constantine may have treated his female mistresses with respect, but not me. I was a possession. He'd use me roughly, then, set me back on the shelf. He respected me in the work place, but he didn't respect a toy after hours. It didn't matter if I was feeling ill when Constantine wanted his rocks off, he got his rocks off. I think he even fucked me when I had a high fever from the flu. I can't be sure it even happened.

Every bit of me was aching anyway, so really, what was the difference?

I was free now.

The phone extension rang beside the bed.

Wilber had given me a sweet kiss on my shoulder and played with the back of my short hair before he left for work this morning. He'd left the curtains open, so I was lying in a shaft of warm, morning sun. With Constantine, I had been starting to forget how to feel. I turned my face toward the light and just basked. Sloth was a luxury I just never appreciated before. I could do sloth for a while. I closed my eyes and snuggled back into the sheets.

There was a knock at the door. Huh? The door opened. "Brant, telephone."

I used my fingers and wiped at my eyes. I didn't know how wound up I had been until I relaxed. I felt boneless right now.

"Good morning, Rick. Is it Wilber?" I pushed myself up letting the sheet puddle around my waist.

"Constantine, Line One."

What? Every good feeling, I had been enjoying just burnt off like flash paper. *What did he want? Nicky couldn't have worked out? In one night?*

"Brant?" Rick gestured to the phone on the night table.

"I…" I panicked.

"He knows you are here, and he seems annoyed."

My hand literally shook as I reached for the phone. Damn it. At least my voice sounded normal. "Williams."

Constantine started in with his clipped words, "Work started half an hour ago, Brant."

Yes, he was annoyed. Crap.

"But…"

"You were replaced as my mistress, not at my PA. Where is that Cicero file? The damned temp can't find a damned thing. Better yet, my car will pick you up in half an hour."

"I… I…" It usually took me a while to get my brain up to speed to have to deal with Constantine's demands, business or personal and right now I knew I wasn't firing on all cylinders. Wilber and I had reacquainted ourselves almost until dawn.

"I told you last night, Brant. You can't be freed. You are now a part of my Organization. Not 'the' Organization, MY Organization. You are still at Brawden's? Do you have any suits there?"

My mind was catching up with the situation, "I'm not sure."

"I'll have the chauffeur stop at the penthouse and pick out something suitable. You can change in the car. We still have the meeting with Universal Conglomerate at noon. I'll forgive you this lapse today, but you will be docked pay. You will be at your desk tomorrow morning on time."

My stomach had started burning as soon as Constantine had started talking. I was going to be sick. "Yes, Sir."

I couldn't get my head around this. I thought… wait. I sat on the edge of the bed and rested on head on my hand. What had they said last night? "He's not here to fill Brant's shoes, just your bed." Damn it. Damn it. I scrambled out of bed. Carmine, Constantine's chauffeur, was punctual and he didn't like me. Carmine would be early.

I felt like I'd just taken a kick from a mule to the chest. The illusion of freedom was worse than getting trussed up in a stress position and left waiting for minutes on end. At least, if the stress was too much, eventually my heart would give out and I would die. It would be kinder to cut my heart out and let me watch it stop beating. I stumbled out of bed into the shower. I was done in ten minutes.

Amazing how short hair cuts down on preparation.

My old room was still here, kept as if I had just stepped out for the day, instead of three years.

Oh, Wilber…

Apparently, I had put on some muscle. I snapped a t-shirt over my head but had to go back into last night's pants. I never noticed by my thighs were wider than before. I slipped on socks and a pair of runners then grabbed a baggy, black hoodie from the back of the closet.

Rick and Mikey were in the kitchen when I came thundering down the stairs. I needed a shot of caffeine. Guy's absence was a heaviness on my chest. Guy had disappeared. Not long after I'd gotten a finger on my breakfast tray. It didn't take much for me to connect the dots.

Rick pushed a cup of coffee towards me. "Mr. Brawden said that you are to have a good breakfast."

"I'm late for work."

"So I gathered." Rick returned lowly. "I thought you were retired."

That was a polite way of saying I had hung up the bed and walked away from the life as a whore. I took too big a gulp and scalded my tongue. "As Mr. Constantine pointed out, I am still his Executive PA."

A bowl of oatmeal was set in front of me. I stilled. Guy would take away my powdered donuts and shove an oatmeal bar at me.

"Was he killed?"

They didn't bother pretending. They knew who I was talking about. "Probably."

"Was it my fault?" I slid into the chair and looked down at the gloppy mess.

Mikey slid some toast on a plate towards me. "I don't think so, Brant. Guy disappeared while he was out on collections. We found his car. It looks like he got taken out by just a street gang." They shared a look across the table but said nothing else.

"That is a risk that we all take." Rick hit Mikey on the shoulder and gave him a glare. A small glass of grapefruit juice was set down next to the stack of toast.

My stomach was burning again, and I really didn't want to eat. But the guys had done so much work, and Wilber had asked them to take care of me. Then again, I'd thought Wilber had made me his lover, yet he was still treating me like his charge. I nibbled at everything. I couldn't eat too much with the way I was feeling, or it would end up on the floor.

A new guy walked into the kitchen. Mikey made the introductions. "This is Terry. He came onboard when …uh, Guy disappeared."

"Limo out in the driveway." The man's appearance was like one of the federal agents that surround VIPs motorcade, black suit, white shirt, black tie, and black sunglasses, but his voice was pure gravel.

I glanced up at the clock. Twenty minutes. I knew Carmine would do this. I couldn't recall Constantine's schedule of today off the top of my head. I didn't know when I'd be back home, but I would be back. I'd find a way.

"Terry's your Shadow." Rick added.

"Are you ready to go, Mr. Williams?"

Shadow? Constantine didn't give me a Shadow. I'd had the guards at the penthouse, but that was to make sure I didn't run more than for my protection. Then again, Constantine was constantly surrounded, so I didn't need my own bodyguard when I was plastered to his side most of the time. I guess it made sense for Wilber to want me to have someone of his own watching my back. I really didn't rate the kind of protection a mistress had, and now that I wasn't even in that category any more, I might be a target because it looked like I was in Constantine's inner circle.

I grabbed my coffee cup. It had cooled enough, so I drained it. I had gone the work day on nothing but coffee before. It wouldn't help my stomach any, but it could be done. I had left the penthouse so fast the night before, I didn't have any ID. My cell was there, which was why Constantine had to call the house. I didn't even have a watch.

"Let's do this." I was dressed like an oversized teenager heading out to cause some havoc at the skate park or someplace else he shouldn't be. I don't remember ever being young. That was just kind of sad.

I stood up. Rick dropped a hand on my shoulder. I looked over at him. "It's good to have you back, Brant. Mr. Brawden has not been the same without you. Maybe he can relax again. He was on a fast track to a heart attack."

I kept my alarm to myself. My client face had become my everyday face. No one could tell what I was thinking, what I was feeling. The scary part was that I could feel myself flicking switches into the off mode as I headed to the door.

Happiness, off.

Tenderness, off.

Compassion, off.

I think the hardest part was going to be turning them back on again when I got home. But I was coming home.

My Shadow got the kitchen door for me. "Nice to meet you, Terry. I'll tell you right now, the chauffeur is a dink of the worst order, but Carmine is Mr. Constantine's dink, so we have to play nice."

"Mr. Williams." Terry gave me a slight smile as I prepared myself for the fireworks.

Carmine was standing at the car and pointedly looked down at his watch. I was early, but it didn't matter to him. He would now take the slow boat to China to get me back to the office. The wily bastard knew his boundaries. When it was just me and him, he pushed them as far as he could without being called on it. Carmine got me where I needed to be, but he was never pleasant about it.

Terry walked out ahead of me. He looked the person who should be climbing into the back of the limo.

Carmine ignored the muscle and just stood there with that grating, little smirk of his. Terry made a point of getting up into the chauffeur's face then turned his shoulder so he was blocking him and opened the backdoor for me, "Sir."

I never got a sir from Carmine. Half the time I didn't even get an acknowledgement of my existence.

"Thank you, Terry."

I slipped into the back and found everything I needed to transform into the highly efficient Executive Personal Assistant to Mr. Augustus Constantine, II. As I said, Carmine knew his boundaries. If I showed up looking like a bum, it would be his fault, because he had been ordered to get my clothes. Terry kept the door open as he laid out the new rules of conduct to Carmine. It felt good.

"Carmine, is it? I'll give you directions to get Mr. Williams to the office from here."

"I have the route planned out…" Carmine was a little taken a back, but recovered quickly.

"I am Mr. Anders. I oversee Mr. Williams's security, so you will be following my instructions for the day."

"Security? Mr. Constantine did not provide security for…him."

Terry caught that pause. "I'm sure that Mr. Constantine's oversight will be brought to his attention when we finally get to the office. Time is wasting, Carmine. I'm sure you would like to explain to Mr. Constantine why you can arrive at Mr. Williams's home in twenty minutes, but the return trip takes much longer."

I really liked Terry. He closed my door and waited for Carmine to start walking to the other side of the car. Then he gave me a finger waggle before climbing into the front, passenger seat.

Getting into the tailored, three-piece, charcoal grey/ black pinstripe was like donning armor. Constantine was an underworld giant, but he also played hardball in the legitimate arena. Just because we were thugs, didn't mean we had to dress down to the stereotype. Today was game day with an international monster. No wonder he was pissed that I wasn't at my desk.

We reached the office in sixteen minutes. Now I was dressed like a young executive but I wasn't mentally ready. I almost would have rather had the detoured route.

Terry scanned the area then again blocked Carmine from reaching for the backdoor, which would have been another first, and held the door open for me. I stepped out as the consummate business man. I flipped my sunglasses on as the mid-morning sun reflected brightly off the glass building of *Moda Monde Logistics* – the legitimate front of the Organization. I might have been losing who I was, but I knew what I looked like. The upper echelon of the Organization knew I was Wilber's find and Constantine's whore, but the rest of the employees of MML didn't. To the salaried workers, I was Constantine's hard-ass, right-hand man. I earned respect from them based on my work.

I passed security inspection then waited for Terry to get patted down. They took his gun. I would have to get permission from the Head of Security to allow him to carry inside the building. I could ask Constantine, but favors were cashed in quickly with him. I knew the kind of currency he would want from me, even if he did have Nicky to mess with now. I may have been too good of a mistress.

When we got to the top floor Mr. Rizzo, our usual temp from the secretarial pool, jumped out of my chair and ran up to me, quickly blurted out what Constantine wanted, and fled from the floor.

I don't know exactly when I stopped caring what might happen to me. Maybe the news that Dad had finally sold the hardware store and retired or that Emily was pregnant with child number two or that Sarah was engaged or that the rest of my baby sisters were on the right track to a life of light and happiness. They had futures. Everything single one of them.

Couldn't I have one too?

I remembered the day that Constantine discovered that he no longer instilled terror in me. He had gone off on a rant, because some ocean freighter had been hijacked in the South Seas, even though agreements had been made and money had changed hands to safeguard the cargo. He'd been venting and everyone else had scurried off or found something to occupy them.

I had just stood there and waited for the tantrum to be over. When he had seen that I wasn't cowering, Constantine had gotten up in my face. I'd had nothing to do with the deal, and I wasn't going to take responsibility for the snafu. After he'd finished spitting on me from all his shouting, I offered him a breath mint. That had stopped him cold. Everyone who still had had the nerve to stay in the office had stopped cold.

I'd paid for my '*insolence*' that night.

Constantine might have treated his former mistresses with care. That night, he'd taken me to the edge of my endurance and set hairline fractures through my body and mind. I'd defied him. Not only had I defied him, but I'd done it in front of witnesses. After the fact, way after the fact, I realized that I had challenged his authority before my staff. So, when he disciplined me, he pulled out all the stops.

Randal had been reluctant, but he had been given orders. My mouth was to set in rigor with that damned rubber bit. Pleading for mercy just pissed Constantine off, so the opportunity had been completely removed. My hands had been locked behind me in leather wrist cuffs. My ankles had a matching set of cuffs and, for the first time, that high leather collar had shown up. I'd been set on my knees with my ankles connected to my wrists by a black pole only six inches long. The strain on my lower back had been excruciating. After about ten minutes of that, Randal had come back in with another pole. This one had attached my wrists to the collar. I'd been strung tighter than a bow. My legs and back had ached, but when I didn't keep them flexed, I'd pull on the collar which would cut off my breath. I'd been barely aware that Randal had still been in the room. He hadn't wanted to be there. True sadists are very rare.

I'd been struggling to breathe. My limbs had begun to cramp. My sweat had turned cold. To make matters worse, Randal had been given more orders to follow. As he'd moved toward me, jingling more restraints, my chest had heaved with the effort not to panic. If I'd panicked, I would have been dead. I would have crushed my own throat. Randal had added thigh cuffs that locked to another pole which kept my legs spread open. To add to the final humiliation, Constantine's favorite toy had been lubed up and shoved into me. Then Randal had moved off to leave me in my increasing agony.

I'd been completely out of it by the time Constantine had finally arrived.

At that time, I had reached the point of not caring if I lived or died. All I would have had to do was let my legs relax and I'd have strangled myself. My heart rate had been elevated and it had pounded unmercifully in my ears. Death had been very inviting.

Then everything had been turned upside down. All the restraints had been removed but my muscles had cramped from the strain of the stress position. My world had been pain. I had known that HE was talking to me but I'd been too far gone to understand anything other than my ache. I'd defied my master and been shown the error of my ways.

My inner light had dimmed that day.

Constantine had always made sure to leave no scars on my body. The ones on my psyche were deep enough. Even after all of that, he had pulled out the hard rubber toy and screwed me into the mattress. I hadn't even had the resolve to weep as he did it. He could have been fucking a corpse for all he cared. It had been a lesson that had to be taught and a lesson that had to be learned. He had done it the most horrible way possible, so it never had to be repeated.

It was no wonder my eyes had faded. But that was then and once I recovered I knew how to *handle* this king of the castle. I knew that he knew what I was doing and only allowed me a certain leeway when it came to business and he let me know he allowed me to steering him in that direction. What resulted from this was we discovered our boundaries.
I never questioned him in public again.

He stopped torture fucking me.

It took me one work day and the weekend to resurrect the perfect Executive PA and pull my client face back into position. Physically, I couldn't move the next day so it was marked down as a sick day leading into the weekend. A doctor came and inspected every inch of me and declared me physically sound. When he finally left, I had gathered up enough of my moxy to ask to be left alone. My listlessness and unresponsive behavior set my bodyguards into high alert but that was more that my body screamed in agony even when I breathed. I honestly think I wasn't left alone because Constantine feared that I might do harm to myself. That was the farthest thing from my mind. I was too busy shoring up what was left of me. If I had been going to contemplate suicide, it would have been a hell of a lot sooner than this.

Come Monday morning, the corporate Iceman was back at his desk before Constantine arrived. The bruises at my wrists extended down to my hands and those at my throat were higher than my dress shirt collar and tie. It was useless trying to hide them so I ignored them and my subordinates made inquiring glances but knew enough not to comment on them at least within my hearing.

Constantine arrived right at 8:30 and paused at my desk. I could feel his gaze on me but didn't bother to look up.

A cup of green tea from the coffee shop on the ground floor was set on the corner of my desk.

"Upon reflection, I was out of line." Constantine never apologizes. He admits he's wrong and that is the end of it.

"Bring in the Odessa file and get that translator up here for the nine o'clock meeting,"

Business life continued with a hitch. Constantine's after hours attention lessened to a visit every three days. This limited service, I could handle.

I shook off my flashback. Constantine didn't belong in my private life. I was with my Wilber again. I felt a little spark of warmth in my chest. I was with Wilber. I unlocked the top drawer of my desk and pulled out the lost Cicero file, re-locked the drawer then walked into his office.

Constantine called out with a big booming voice. "Ah, there you are. You don't look that rested for coming in so late. Brawden keep you busy last night?"

He was playing the charming host today. I pasted a fake smile on my lips. "Here is the Cicero file. You must get ready to leave in half an hour for the meeting with…" I laid the file down on the desk and opened my day planner.

"I asked you a question, Brant." The jovial tone was dropped in favor of his usual curtness.

"Yes, he did, sir. Croswell Industries. The situation with…"

"Did he wear you out?" I glanced up at him. His eyes had that feral glow. Apparently, Nicky didn't wear him out.

"Yes, sir."

"Did you like it?" He kept poking at me like a scientist, or more like a kid with a stick and road kill that was dying but not quite dead yet.

"Yes, sir."

"Why so formal?" Constantine stood up. "We are beyond those constraints, you and I."

He touched me. His hand spread out on my chest as he moved around behind me. He began to rub at my right nipple through my shirt as he slipped his other hand inside my jacket and vest to move down around my waist, across to my stomach and dipped into the waistband of my trousers.

"You don't get to do this anymore." My word was tight as I was hit with a heat of anger. I shrugged my shoulder and the motion pulled his hand out of my waistband.

Constantine pressed a kiss to the nape of my neck. I twisted my head away and took a step backwards. "You have Nicky now."

Constantine cocked his head slightly as his green-eyed gaze narrowed. He was playing with me. He had no intention of pursing me but he felt he had to test the waters. What kind of man did he think I was? I indulged myself in a glare.

He straightened to his full height as a dangerous smile quirked his lips. "I have a best-in-show dog right here. He's just a pup."

Constantine made a show of allowing me space as he stepped backwards so he could lean back against the desk and crossed his ankles. "I wished it was you under me last night."

"About the meeting…" I wasn't taking the bait.

"I want you, Brant." His green eyes darkened.

"No."

"No?" His voice had a laugh in it.

I snapped my datebook closed. My words were clipped and sharp. "You accepted delivery of my replacement. I'm nobody's whore."

Constantine sat up crossing his arms across his chest. "You're Brawden's whore."

"I'm his lover."

"Are you sure? Couldn't it be just a case of nobody plays with my toys?" Constantine's voice had that dangerous quality seeping into it.

"I'm not your toy." The door was closed. My subordinates weren't anywhere near to hear this banter. Then again, I didn't have to fear him anymore. I didn't belong to him. I was home.

"You were."

"I never was your toy. I was a possession just like the exotic fish in your tank."

He moved fast and I found myself sprawled face first across his desk. I went with the roll and landed on my knees by his chair. His hand tangled at the hair at the nape of my neck as he jerked me upright until I was resting against the front of his thighs.

His voice was calm and even as he held me tight against him. "What if I told you that I still want to continue our arrangement?"

"No." I stared straight ahead. "I am done with that service."

"You are done, when I tell you you're done. Suck me off."

"No." It came out a sharp bark.

Constantine rattled my head back and forth for a moment. "That seems to be the only word you can say, Brant."

"It seems to be a word that you don't understand the meaning of."

He punched me in the back of the head but let me go. The force of his blow knocked me onto my hands.

"Sass, Brant. I can see that Wilber has a strong influence on you even after all this time. Just remember your place. I'm not above

181

teaching it to you again if you forget." He sat back in his chair, and I could hear him lighting up a smoke.

I climbed back to my feet. The back of my head was throbbing, and the heels of my palms hurt from breaking my fall. I reached down and picked my appointment book up off the floor.

"That poor excuse for a secretary was the best that they could send me. I think he got the short end of the straw. Whatever have you been telling your staff about me, Brant? Truly, I had intended for you to have at least a two-week honeymoon period, but business waits for no man." I made sure my face was blank as I regarded him. His green eyes raked over me, and I knew that he knew that I was deliberately hiding my thoughts from him. When I had been his, it hadn't been acceptable. But that was then it wasn't the case now. He blew smoke up into the air, but not at me. He didn't need to make that petty, little display of power gesture. I knew who wore the pants in this office. Besides Constantine had other ways to fuck you up all of which were worse than his just blowing smoke in your face.

"You are an asset to my Organization, Brant. If I must forgo your other talents in order to exploit that mind of yours, so be it. However, you are going to have to pass those talents on. It's going to be on-the-job training for Nicholas it seems." Constantine's whole aggressive demeanor changed which meant he had gotten the answer he was looking for.

"Your go-to-guy, its Reynolds, isn't it?"

"Yes." I straightened my shirt and vest.

"You're grooming him to take over for you?"

My tie was twisted. "More like someone who can fill in for me when I'm unavailable."

"Good, bring him in beside you starting tomorrow. When you head out to take care of Nicholas, Reynolds will step up into your position."

"Meaning what?" My tone was still clipped.

"No need to get your knickers in a twist. Reynolds has as much appeal as Brawden --competent but unexciting. Your hours are going to be shortened here. Nine until two here in the office, then from two to five you will take Nicky in hand."

"I don't understand?"

"I want my show dog to teach the pup how to perform." He said it so matter of fact. I doubt if he even realized he referred to both Nicholas and I as something less than human.

I was going to be sick. How insulting could he get? I had a feeling I was going to find out.

"If Nicholas keeps me happy, I stay off you. I've gotten used to easy access. Nickolas's a street punk. If he's going to replace you, you need to upgrade him right away. For three hours a day, you will take him under your wing and show him what I like."

I shook my head because I really couldn't believe I was hearing this. "You... you want me to train that boy. I thought you preferred to train your possessions on your own."

"He's not you, Brant. You had a base to work off. He's just desperate. Nicholas has potential to be a kept toy after I'm tired of him, but he doesn't have the brain to replace you. His debt is five years. He's already serviced three weeks. His enthusiasm last night was gratitude to get out of the brothel. You train him right, and he'll be fully repaid in less than two years. From there, he will probably be able to get himself a sugar daddy. He does have a certain physical appeal."

Asset or liability. That was Constantine's world view when it came to business and right now Nicholas was business. What was I? An asset or a liability?

"You want me to train that boy to be your whore?" I caught control of my emotions and reined everything back in, back down to that client face, Iceman cometh level.

"It is been proven that the best teachers are those who have walked the same path. You will be providing Nicholas with a future, because right now, if Brawden hadn't rescued him, he probably would have had to endure 20 clients a night, every night for five years. Boys don't last that long if they owe that kind of money." Constantine's lips curved as his eyes snaked up my body to halt their climb at my mouth, "Think of Nicholas as… your little brother."

I didn't care if I got knocked around for it. I couldn't keep the distaste out of my voice. "You are one sick fucker."

He stood up and grabbed my face. "I have never claimed to be anything that I'm not, Brant. Train Nicholas to my specs and I'll keep my hands to myself. I would like him here eventually as your assistant, or a gopher if he can't do anything else. I did like the afternoon delight we shared. I would rather continue the tradition, be it with Nicholas or with you but one way or the other, I will have one of you keeping the tradition alive. You choose who will do it."

He pressed a kiss to my forehead and let me go. "I'll need the latest stock quotes on UC before we head out for our meeting."

Just like that. Constantine laid out the plan, and that was it. I headed back to my office.

"Oh, and Brant? Your man can be armed, but I find it offensive that Brawden sent him without my approval."

I straightened my backbone. "Wilber was concerned for my safety."

Constantine frowned. "He doesn't think I can protect my assets?"

"I'm not your asset anymore."

Constantine broke out into a laugh. "Touché."

His tone dropped back to a serious bent. "I was going to suggest it anyways. There are several agency dogs sniffing around my business lately. It looks like we have a disgruntled associate within our ranks and they have been selling my goodwill like dime store candy. I've got people tracking that hole down but I'm asking the key people to keep an eye out and keep their heads down."

"I'll pass that on to Wilber."

"Call for the car. We leave in five minutes."

I left his office. Terry was standing outside the door to my office. I let security know that Terry had clearance for weapons then I sat heavily in my chair. I had thought I was free of him. For twelve glorious hours, I'd basked in what freedom could be. I'd been outside of Constantine's sphere of influence. I'd been a fool and the ache in the back of my head reminded me of how much of a fool I'd been.

My cell phone went off, and I pulled it out. It was a text message… from Wilber. I didn't know he was such a technophile.

Are you okay? There were no short forms or misspellings that weren't standard English.

My fingers tapped out my reply. *I am good. I will be home by 6. I love you, W.*

I love you too, GB.

A sob escaped my mouth. Electronic declarations of love. I felt myself break. My inner core just shattered. I sat at my desk as tears ran down my face. The freedom I thought I had proved to be just an illusion but I still had love that was real.

Wilber's first declaration of love.

I took a deep, cleansing breath and wiped at my eyes and cheeks. After all I had done, he was there for me. He had been there for me all along, even when I thought I was all alone. I wasn't withered emotionally. The warmth burning through me right now told me so.

Wilber didn't want my protection. He didn't need my protection, but there was someone who did. Nicky. Nicholas. Constantine was a bastard, but he was the lesser of two evils. I remembered the desperation in Nicholas's eyes as he wriggled on me. No, I'd never been to a brothel, but if I could keep this kid out, so be it.

I pulled out the card for Constantine's tailor. *Treat him like a little brother, eh?*

Constantine wanted to play on my Dr. Kirkpatrick's identified martyr complex. Something identified, catalogued, and compartmentalized really doesn't rule the world anymore. Yes, I'm a dammed good brother but that is to my family. Calling Nicky my little brother doesn't make him part of it. That punk might be scared now but once he finds his footing, he'll come out swinging and Constantine put me right in harm's way. Unless little Nicky opens his eyes and realizes it – there was a chance I wasn't out of that penthouse. I've felt Wilber's warmth after so many seasons of perpetual winter. What would I do to stay in the warmth? I was going to find out.

I arranged for a little army to descend on Nicky at three. This would come out of Constantine's personal discretionary fund and it should because training mistresses really wasn't a business expense. Step one: Change what you look like in the mirror. You can pretend it's not happening to you if you don't recognize who is staring back at you. I shut everything down and was gathering up my laptop when the door to Constantine's office opened. If I had to show Nicholas how to be a rich man's mistress, so be it. If it would give him a better shot at a different life, I would do it.

I followed Constantine out of the office as he prepared to wreak a little havoc in the world of high finance. Terry, a sign of Wilber's love and protection, trailed after me. I clutched my cell phone tightly in my hand.

I had his heart's declaration so I had freedom after all.

Chapter Eight: Master

The crowd that gathered within the confines of the penthouse main room went silent as the body hit the floor. Now the only sound I could hear was the pulse of blood pounding in my head and the unceasing whirr of the air conditioning. This was one of the few times in my life that I'd hit someone with the intent of hurting them. I'd used my size, strength, and training to intentionally punch someone. Nicky crumbled like a rag doll to lay still and silent for a few seconds.

His bratty attitude which had just pushed and pushed me to the edge was gone now. Fear looked back at me. Pain was pulsing through my fist. My stomach was burning a hole through me again. The situation had gotten this bad because I'd allowed it to. I tried to be his good-natured mentor. He threw that back in my face reminding me that I had rolled over for him to be fucked like a bitch the night before. Nicky was just a little tiny fish in this great big pond. He was trying to undermine my credibility with the makeover team.

Leave it to Wilber to find someone with a quick brain. Take advantage and twist the knife deep. His vocabulary was going to have to be upgraded as well.

Constantine would be coming soon and this lack of progress was unacceptable. I channeled the inner agony into something I could use.

"Out!" My voice was harsh and tinged with my lingering anger.

The stylists, tailors and even Nicky's private guard, courtesy of Constantine, skittered out of the room. Nicky made to move off his back. I took one step toward him, and he turtled in on himself, his arms cradling his head instinctively.

Good, at least he had some sense of self awareness.

"Position." Nicky stayed huddled on the floor. "POSITION!"

I took a stomp towards him and he suddenly scrambled to his knees, hunching into the standard pose Constantine liked. Not good enough. It wouldn't do.

"Straighten your spine. You're not a dog. Head up. Chin down, more. There. Hands on your thighs. Spread your knees. Wider. Now stay there."

I stood looking down at the trembling youth. Nicky knew he had hit the jackpot you only had to look around this place. A luxury apartment for an entry level underworld mistress. Nothing like the penthouse I had been given but then it seemed to be awarded based on merit. I stared down at the top of his brown curls. You could see the wheels turning in his head. He had street smarts. Street smarts let him survive in the brothel. Streets smarts kept him alive in that cut-throat place. However, street smarts didn't cut it in Constantine's world.

Constantine didn't have the patience or inclination to train his new mistress. If Nicky couldn't provide the entertainment and sexual release in the ways Constantine wanted, he would be damned lucky to go back to the brothel. If not, he would just disappear just like Guy and I would resume my old duties on my back.

That wasn't going to happen. It wasn't.

I watched the boy struggle with the stress of the position I set him into. I knew what I was doing. I was saving my own neck at the expense of another. Wilber was someone I thought I had lost. A dream I didn't dare reach out for. I didn't reach for because I deliberately sabotaged myself. Most of what Dr. Kirkpatrick told me over our hours together I thought was bullshit claptrap designed to keep me coming back week after week but once I sat down and honestly took a look at things I could admit that the Doctor was right. Identify the behavior and you can correct the problem. If I was going to throw myself on another cross it was going to be for my benefit this time.

In all my years with the Organization I understood my sacrifice was the exception, not the norm. Husbands threw their wives to the wolves for a reprieve. Mothers willfully abandoned their daughters to a hell no one should endure. In my short time in Collections a mother and father had left their three daughters behind to face their debt. I moved heaven and the underworld to find them. I left the little girls in the custody of their grandparents and authorized organ extraction on their parents. It paid back the original loan and the interest. There was even enough commission due me to set up a trust fund for the girls who were better off orphans.

Maybe that martyr condition was not as obliterated as I would like it to be but it wasn't ruling my actions.

I had Wilber, and I was discovering I had something inside me that was willing to do what I had to, to keep him. I discovered that I have a vicious hidden bastard within me.

So far, the compassion I showed Nicky was treated with contempt and disregard. Two hours were wasted. All we'd accomplished was a more appropriate haircut for his mop and measurements for some new tailoring. That was it. I had one hour left to get some manners into this little punk ass before Constantine came for inspection.

Nothing was not an acceptable concept to Constantine.

"I'm…" Nicky's voice was full of uncertainty and had dropped down to a younger raange that he would deny to his grave.

Brutality seemed to work with him and if that was how he wanted to continue from this point forward, so be it. Deliberately I made my tone cold and harsh. "Don't speak until you are asked a question."

"But…"

I slapped him on side of the head knocking him off his knees and breaking his pathetic attempt at first position. I was annoyed with both of us. "Position. What part of 'don't speak' don't you understand?"

"I got to pee," his voice wheedled.

That was going to annoy Constantine real quick.

"Position. Hold it." I stepped up behind the boy and forced my foot between his crossed ankles and butt. I stepped into him. He tensed.

"Your perfect position is contact from my shin to my waist." I took him by the shoulders and pulled them back so they were straight. I reached around and took a hold of his chin and pushed his head back

189

until it rested on my vest. I tugged his chin forward and down. I knew what muscles screamed in agony after a few minutes of this pose. I had hated it, so I knew Nicky would too.

"Hold this position. This is how you greet Mr. Constantine when he comes for a visit. You stay in this position until he releases you."

"Please Mr. Williams, I have to pee.". He had spat on my efforts to be a mentor so now I was going to be his master. Coolly, I gave him an education in Constantine-like discipline.

"Every break in position will result in an additional thirty seconds. Every break in silence another thirty seconds. You are up to four minutes, Nicholas. Four minutes from being allowed to rest and to go to the bathroom. You have anything else to add?"

I was answered with labored breathing. This position always hurt my neck. I would stink of liniment right after Constantine left. He came back once for his briefcase and possibly a little more but I'd reeked of muscle cream. After that smelly incident, I got that damned, high leather collar. It was more like a neck brace than anything else. I checked my watch. Three minutes down. I could feel the muscles in Nicky's back begin to quiver.

"Tighten your stomach muscles. Don't let your back do all the work. You're going to have start working on your abs or you are going to be in a whole world of pain. Shoulders…keep the contact."

Nicky was just a punk ass who didn't know how fleeting kindness was if he didn't jump a few levels of sophistication. Today was a waste. I glanced around the apartment Constantine had given him. It wasn't a penthouse, but it wasn't a slum either. Far better than a cot in a brothel.

"Good, boy. Break position. Go to the bathroom. Come back here right away. Make sure to wash your hands."

He groaned and leaned forward resting on his hands. Slowly he climbed to his feet. I closed my eyes. If I was doing this… it would have to be done right. "Acknowledge me, Nicholas, before you make another move."

"Uh?"

"Position."

His voice was hurried and he couldn't look at me. "I don't know what you mean?"

"Every time a command is repeated…" Nicholas got down on the floor but seemed confused on which way to face. His attempt was still far from perfect but it was better than a hunched back and droopy shoulders.

"I am your Master. I have given you permission to do something you want. You thank me for my kindness."

"Thank you…" His voice trailed off.

"Mr. Williams."

"Thank you, Mr. Williams."

"Go to the bathroom."

Nicky bolted away from me. I waited until the bathroom door closed and collapsed into a club chair. I still felt like I was going to throw up. My head tilted forward.

Concentrate on breathing.

Nicky could probably handle another half an hour of training, but I was toast. The burning agony that was my stomach was not being calmed with the antacids I'd been chewing. It felt as if my esophagus was on fire. I expected smoke curls to come out of my mouth.

This was too much.

My hands had a tremor. Damn it. This burning my stomach seemed to come on when I was under pressure and yes, training Nicky was definitely stressful.

I heard him come out, but there was no way I could pull myself together before he could see me. I was a wreck. I'd already exceeded the maximum dosage of antacid tablets for the day. Maybe there was something else wrong if this pain came on like this. My smile came out like a grimace as I thought of Wilber's expression if he saw me like this. He would have me flat on my back on the way to a legitimate hospital in two shakes.

I could feel eyes on me, but I couldn't lock down my emotions. I pressed my hand to my stomach and just rested my head heavily off my shoulders.

The trembling tone that had crept into Nicky's voice was gone now. That streetwise smart mouth was back. He had recovered a hell of a lot quicker than I thought he would. "I know you. Even without that long black hair of yours, everybody has heard of Cinderella. Even in the lowest of the brothels, we know you -- Top Bitch."

As Constantine said, Nicholas was a street punk and if given the opportunity, he would try everything to screw me over. Any ground I had gained with punching him, I'd just lost.

Damn it. Lock it down. Lock it down now.

I pulled myself together and hid the stabbing pain behind my client face. I blinked the sting of unshed tears away and sat up staring at him. I had my face schooled to neutral externally; but, I horrified internally. I thought being sold internationally was bad enough but to have punks like this see it meant that there was still sales underground.

Slowly I murmured, "Cinderella?"

"You bypassed the collectors and went right to the Big Guy. You must have had some skills to get him to take you right away. You've never stepped one foot inside the brothel. You don't know what it's like. I've seen your place. You're high in the clouds, Mr. Williams. You don't know the hell it is down in the dirt. You don't know what it's like to be raped."

"I know rape, Nicholas."

Nicky snarled back at me. "Don't call me that. They called me that just before they shoved some drug up my ass that turned me into nothing but a whore hole. I don't remember half of the stuff they did to me, but I remember the pain and humiliation that came back when I was lying in my own blood and pools of cum. Don't you dare look down on me! You just got lucky cause you're a pretty face." By the time, he got to the end of his breath he was practically screaming at me.

"Really?" The next voice that spoke was calm but froze both of us as Constantine stepped into the room. "Really Brant, I can hear you two doors down the hall."

"Position," I hissed at Nicky. Instead of obeying, he just looked over at Constantine with terror in his eyes.

"Position!" I hissed at him again, giving him a hard shove to snap him out of it. He dropped down to his knees. It was a poor attempt. His whole body was shaking. I could only assume that Constantine had been his usual less than charming self the night before.

"Brant, I'd expected some progress." There was a tint of censure in Constantine's voice.

"We got the hair and manscaping done. Mani and pedi were a nightmare because he chews his nails."

"Toenails too?" Constantine's voice was a little lyrical which meant he was pissed off royally.

"I'll leave that up to you to discover that talent. We also got the measurements to get started on an acceptable wardrobe."

Constantine gestured off handedly at our tableaux. "And this?"

"We've just started on manners."

I stepped up behind Nicky and corrected his posture, holding him tight against me. He shivered.

Constantine looked over at us and shook his head. "Unacceptable. Brant, would you please show our little Nicholas what elegance looks like."

My stomach muscles clenched. Damn it. While it sounded like a request, I knew what he really meant. Defiance was not an option. I moved in front of Nicky until I was facing him and lowered myself with a whole lot of refinement into the same pose. I'd done it often enough these past few years.

I heard Constantine move forward until he was behind me. He stepped close and checked my position. I touched him from shin to waist, buttocks to the nape of my neck. Constantine brought his hand down the side of my face to my cup my chin.

"Look over here Nicholas." Constantine's voice was soft, and that was terrifying. "Nicholas, is a lovely name. Get used to it."

Tear-filled brown eyes looked up as he physically shivered in fear.

"Cinderella? Truly? Beauty is fleeting, little Nicholas. Brant worked very hard to get where he is." His index finger stroked the side of my cheek while he talked in that deceptive tone.

Sure, enough he was pissed. I tried to pull back as his fingers tightened around my jaw like a vise. My hands few up to push his arm away but he dug his little finger up pressing hard into the soft underside of my jaw.

"That is not where your hands should be Brant."

Arching my head back into his stomach and forcing my hands down at my side rewarded me with lessening pressure.

"Yes Nicholas, Brant here had a touch of luck and got himself a patron who put him through school. His Mr. Brawden recognized that Brant was more than a prostitute. But, Brant built on his beauty and his education transforming what he had into something so rare that it's valued and I nurture it. He is more than just a toy to play with. He is what you should strive for. He is the ideal. He is the pinnacle. You've already spent three weeks as a brothel whore. Do you think you can last five years?"

"No, Master." Nicky blanched and the remnants of defiance in his gaze faded as he turned his eyes to the carpet.

I got a light slap to the face. "Good, at least you got some progress. Get up, Brant." Constantine backed off me and came around behind Nicky. "You need to work on position, Nicholas."

I watched as Nicky swallowed down his fear. He pushed himself up and squared his shoulders. "Better. Not elegant but a good first attempt."

"Progress report, Brant."

Nicky's eyes flicked over to me with a pleading expression floating in his eyes.

Mentally, I snorted. *Lying just makes it worse for everyone.* I shook my head. "Little to none. We only accomplished a quarter of what I had on my agenda because of his…well, let's say an attitude adjustment was required."

"Stay." Constantine sat down in the club chair and held up his hand and, automatically, I went and poured him a whiskey tonic. When I handed it back to him, he gestured for me to stay where I was. He kept his eye on Nicky as the boy tried to keep the position. "Do I need to hire a professional?"

A professional. A shaft of fear struck through me as a flashback to a brightly lit grey room, a single metal chair and where a heavy-set woman with large hands and thick strong fingers waited. That one session with a professional was more than ten years ago, and it still resonated with me. My rebellious phase with Wilber ended that day. Once with a professional was all I needed. "I think we have come to an understanding."

"Meaning?"

"As you said, Sir, Nicholas needs to work on his position. I will make him understand that just because he is here, doesn't mean he stays here. Unless he vastly improves."

"Can he take over for you?" This innocent question was accompanied with the clink of ice against cut crystal glass.

I frowned. "I don't think he's got his grade 12."

"Not what I meant, Brant. Your cultivated, brilliant mind is very rare in regular folk and I doubt I'd ever find something like it in the gutter by chance. Brawden was lucky enough to find you and smart enough to develop you. I sincerely doubt that I will be so lucky."

"Nicholas seems…"

"I'm not interested in his intellect right now, Brant. Can he be my mistress?"

I watched the boy shiver. Twenty customers a night or one sadistic fucker for a couple of hours? Was there a better alternative? "I think you should ask Nicholas."

"I've asked you."

"You will twist him. You will break him. I don't think he's strong enough to survive your sexual depravities." I voiced my honest opinion.

"I can." Both of us turned to Nicky. There was a mix of pleading desperateness and a quip of defiance in his tone. "I won't go back to that brothel. I can be your mistress. I won't mess with Mr. Williams anymore."

Constantine took a drink. The ice clinked in the glass. That green cat-like eyes glanced over my way and then he drowned that slight smile in the whiskey glass. I knew right then that he didn't give a flying fig if I had gotten Nicky prepared today. Constantine wanted that simple very devastating admission from the boy.

"Are you willing to train him, Brant? The better he's trained, the more opportunity he has to survive."

He was going to walk all over Nicky and the kid didn't have a clue. "You're giving me an option?"

"Nicholas's fate is in your hands."

I clenched my fists tightly. Casually I sighed, "Did I ever tell you you're a stone cold bastard?"

"Yes, you have. Countless times but only in the appropriate setting. I have learned to appreciate your honesty and candor, Brant."

He broke eye contact with me and glanced down at the kneeling boy. "Brant has earned the right to say that to me and any problem he has with me he brings up with me directly. I don't tolerate rumors and innuendos from those I allow close to me. You realize you have a hell of an opportunity before you, Nicholas. If you hate the brothels so much there are other ways of making payments on the money that's been defaulted on. Providing organ transplants has proven to be a lucrative business."

Nicholas blanched. I just stood there with my jaw line aching and watched the realization of his situation sink in. Constantine and his sadistic style of debauchery was the lesser of the aforementioned evils.

"I *can* be your mistress."

"Of course, you *can*. The question is *will* you? Brant is the ideal you should strive for. Nothing was given to him. Everything he has, he had *earned*. You've got miles to travel before you are granted the same privileges, Nicholas. Understood?"

"Yes, Mr. Constantine."

"Another thing, you will never speak to Brant with such disrespect in your tone ever again. Beauty is a dime a dozen. If I just wanted a whore to pound into, I could pick anyone one. Brant's patron, Mr. Brawden, handpicked you out of all the brothels in the city. He saw something of Brant in you. So, you have potential. I expect progress." Constantine set his glass down and tented his fingers together. He peered over them at with what dangerous feral gleam in his eye.

"You have three months, Brant. You have three months to get him ready to be seen with me. If you fail, you automatically come back to me. You are free from my bed only because Nicholas is supposed to be your replacement. Discipline him as you see fit, only not the face. It's his only redeeming feature."

Both of his toys stared at him. This was his trademark 'carrot and stick' motivational tool. Nicky got the reward of a luxury apartment and a single client. I got the threat of discipline if Nicky didn't succeed. Surprisingly, it didn't bother me.

Constantine caught me in his gaze. "So, I ask you this question again. Do I hire a professional?"

"Mr. Williams, I can do this." Nicky pleaded.

"I can see your handiwork." There was a bruise turning yellowish blue on Nicholas's jaw.

I offered up a wry smile. Nicky had goaded me hard enough to shake the Iceman business persona. That was a talent unto himself.

"You pulled your punch. Nicholas, Brant is a double black belt in karate. He is also a certified master instructor in firearms and I mean he can pick you off as a sniper. I know that he also knows how to knife fight. If any injury happens to him it's because he allowed it, not because he couldn't stop it."

Nicky's head turned slightly. I could see the wheels turning his head as he re-evaluated the infamous *Cinderella*.

"If Brant takes something on, he does it to the best of his abilities. He masters it. He owns it. That is his strongest asset. That is his core. Brant sees a problem and tackles it head on if possible but he gets the job done." Constantine brought his gaze up.

"Nicholas, go take a shower and wait for me in the bed room."

I watched as Nicky quivered unsure if he could get up or not. His eyes flashed over to me.

"What do you say?"

"Thank you, Mr. Constantine." Nicky stumbled a bit as he climbed to his feet. The burning muscle in the upper thighs would cause that. He staggered off towards the bedroom.

"Well some progress was made today." Constantine took a drink of his whiskey. "By the way, what's today?"

"The twelfth."

"The day."

"Wednesday."

"Yes, so why are you here?

I frowned. I couldn't follow where Constantine was going with this. "You asked me to see to Nicholas."

"Dr. Kirkpatrick's office called looking for you since you missed your appointment. I spoke with him and he was rather concerned. He never went into specifics but he seemed to make it a point that he asked you to do something and you haven't. He said you didn't offer any excuses, you just didn't do it. This does not seem like your usual tackle the problem head on attitude. You need to take care of whatever *it* is, Brant. You've done enough with Nicholas today."

"I'm heading home."

"No, you are either doing what your Doctor asked you to or you are going to the rescheduled appointment."

"Rescheduled?"

"You have the last appointment of the day. Do what you've been putting off or go to the doctor. My wife and kids… and you, are the only ones who say no to me and live undamaged, Brant. Well others do also, but you usually take care of those scenarios for me quite effectively."

"Sir…" I protested. My stomach tied itself into knots and pushed the flame of agony higher.

"The longer you put it off the later you are going to be getting back to Mr. Brawden." Constantine reached over and picked up his drink.

Flicking my eyes back to Constantine told me that he knew. Of course, he would. Nothing got passed that feral gaze.

"Treat it like work, Brant. No matter how unsavory things get, you always bring it back to even keel. Get it done today and get on with the rest of your life."

As if that were that easy. I didn't go to Mom's funeral. How the hell can I just casually walk up to her final resting place fifteen years later?

Chapter Nine: Mom

It felt like everything was slipping out of my grasp as I stumbled out of the high rise toward the sedan where Terry was waiting. He leapt out of the car as soon as he caught sight of me and made a motion as if he was going to come and get me at the entrance then diverted his path to the back door of the car to hold it open. I must have looked like hell to have Terry do a double take and question his actions. He was so damn cool with Carmine. Leave it to Constantine to fuck up my equilibrium. That talent is part of what makes him a formidable opponent in business.

I slipped into the back of the sedan and leaned heavily against the door. Dr. Kirkpartrick is a professional. There was no way in hell he would tell Constantine anything about what happens in our sessions but he also was no match for the head of our Organization. The man was like Achilles dipped into the river Styx except instead of invincibility he had charm. Kissing the proverbial blarney stone couldn't have matched Constantine's ability. If he didn't get anything out of Kirkpatrick, his receptionist would have been the lamb lead to slaughter bleating confidential secrets all the way to the killing floor. I'd seen it happen too often not to believe that this was the scenario. And she would never be the wiser that she did something she shouldn't have.

"Mr. Williams?" I could see Terry's eyes trace over the bruises formed on my jaw line. He looked really upset.

What the hell had the guys back at the mansion told him about me? I'd known him less than a day and he looked like he was ready to rip someone a new one on my behalf.

"Sir? Shall we go home?"

A wry smile crossed my face as I settled back into the seat. I've been given my assignment. Knowing him, Constantine would have someone waiting there at the cemetery to report that I actually went.

"Mr. Williams?"

"1400 Riverview Street."

"I'm not familiar with that area, Sir. I'll take me a moment to get the coordinates into the GPS."

"Take your time."

Riverview Cemetery. I'd never set foot inside of it but I knew exactly where it was. If I wanted to I could have directed Terry to it but, I wasn't in that big of a hurry. I'd been seeing the psychiatrist for almost four years now. Every Wednesday at 3 o'clock for 192 days I went to his office in that brownstone building and probably three quarters of the time I told myself that he was spouting bull crap at me. I told myself that it was Wilber and Constantine's money that made him so desperate to keep chipping away at my client face.

The car pulled away from curb. My stomach roiled again. Pulling out my ever-present package of over-the-counter antacids, I ignored the recommended dosage and chewed a couple more ignoring the chalky taste as the scenery passed unseen by my eyes.

There were many terms that the Doctor had come up with, but the ones that struck too close for comfort were male sexual abuse survivor and martyr complex. The emotional waters were muddied for both of those. Technically, Wilber was my abuser even if he never touched me until I came of age but he was my lover as well. He was more than a mere lover, he was my touchstone, that little light of mine who shone for me in the darkest of hours. Thinking of him meant that I could reach down inside me and find enough strength to make it to the next day.

Kirkpatrick spent a lot of years convincing me that I was too young to have known what the hell I was doing. I was grasping for anything to make my life make sense. My mother had just died. I was just a child and the responsibility of keeping the family together and functioning had fallen to my shoulders. I was entitled to my anger and resentment.

Anger.

I didn't think I had any anger until a blank sheet of art paper and a box of crayons were set before me. That turned out to be an eye-opening session. It felt like my anger was a bottomless pit, a volcano just beginning, no, that had been rumbling for years waiting to erupt. The Doctor thought it was centered about my abuser and my parents who had failed to keep me safe. Kirkpatrick was partially right.

I wasn't angry at Dad. He made Mom smile. He knew how to make my sisters squeal in laughter. What could he have done with a black-haired boy who just stared at him? Mom never smiled when it was just me and her. Even a kid knew what happiness should look like and Dad gave it to her. I resented him for crumbling when the rest of us needed him but I didn't hate him and I wasn't angry at him. It was like Wilber had said so long ago. Dad was doing the best he could only it wasn't good enough.

I wasn't angry or resentful with Wilber. Even at the beginning it was just business. No, it was more than that even at the start. If I was simply business, he could have had me work off the debt in less than five years but…there wouldn't have been anything left of me. I would have been one of those unfortunates lost in drugs, alcohol and dangerous sexual situations best left un-thought of. He protected me. He might have called me a business asset but I was cared for and nurtured.

The next possible target was the other male in my life who had supposedly abandoned me. Without me naming names, Kirkpatrick got the story of how I got to be who I was, what I was and then he told me who I could be. If I wanted it. When I stalled on his suggestions, that's when Kirkpatrick started to throw around the term martyr. I wasn't a victim, I was a martyr and that was worse because I chose to be in situations that left me bruised, battered and emotionally frozen. That opened up a big case of denial over those remarks…but they rang true.

I walked into this life.

I stayed in this life when I had the opportunity to leave it.

Kirkpatrick said my question that I had to figure out for myself was "Why?"

Why was my martyrdom a need for penance?

Why did I feel the need to show sorrow when I had done no wrong?

This is the big why we were on the way to visit Mom a decade and a half after she was buried.

Terry's voice called back to me from the front seat. "Mr. Williams…"

"Hmmm?"

"Sir, we are at a cemetery."

"That we are."

It was a rather beautiful site overlooking the river that lazily flowed past. The old growth trees were in still in full leaf. The place was well tended and looked like it cost a fortune. I closed my eyes. Dad had wasted money to get Mom a plot in this place.

"Mr. Williams?"

"Drive up to the thirty-fifth row and park it, Terry."

Kirkpatrick had expected me to vilify Dad. He thought that all my anger was directed at my male support figure who failed me in a spectacular way. Only Dad didn't. He couldn't. How can you hate someone who wasn't even capable of being what was necessary in the first place? Dad… had led with his heart. He always led with his heart and by doing so he tried to make things better only to make them worse.

A sad smile reflected at me in the partition window. In my time as loans officer, someone like Dad was tagged "*easy pickin's*". He had the house. He had the hardware store and he had children. The smile faded.

"Sir?" The car stopped.

"I'm getting out here."

"Sir, Mr. Brawden distinctly said that I was not to leave your side."

The smile returned to my face. My Wilber worked so hard to shield me from life. "I'm going to talk to my mother, Terry, and that is a private conversation."

"That still means…"

"Stay in the car and wait for me." I pushed the car door open and climbed out.

"Sir!"

"Don't make it harder than it already is. I need to get this done so I can go home." My tone was clipped and short.

How hard was it to walk in a cemetery? This place had winding paths through beautifully maintained grounds and stone benches dedicated in the memory of loved ones. There were some stone monuments that stood out of place with the natural surroundings but those where up closer to the entrance. Prominent names of important families with more wealth that most people would ever see. The further I walked away from the gates a serenity descended to wrap its arms around you in comfort. Still, my legs felt weighed down as if I had shackles on my ankles and ten pound balls of iron dragging behind me. I'd survived Constantine when he was being his insensitive self so why the hell couldn't I walk faster than a snail? I knew where her stone was. Sarah had made drawings of the view that Mom had from her resting place when I found excuse after excuse not to accompany the family here after I was done with the repayment.

Finally, reaching the small stone marker was rather anti-climactic – outwardly anyways. Dad had wasted money on this upscale cemetery but her marker was low to the ground with a laser etched lily of the valley flower as a background for her name. It took me fifteen years to get here.

What was I supposed to feel now? Angry? Hollow? Did I hate her?

Staring out across the manicured grass down to the gently flowing river, I struggled. What was I supposed to say? Kirkpatrick had stressed that I had to do this to move on. He had called me a survivor of child abuse and survivor of sexual assault which had led to my current psychological trauma. I denied it at first. Mom had never hit me, never locked in a room, never withheld meals or anything of that nature. Wilber had not assaulted me. I was punished but I knew why it was going to happen. He didn't lash out for any rhyme or reason. I had walked into debt payment willingly. Yet, yes, I was numb. Yes, I was disassociated from society except when I was with Wilber. Yes, I was living in fear. That was Constantine but I had learned to play him with the minor influence I had when I needed to and he allowed it.

Kirkpatrick pissed me off when he brought these up in session but in the privacy of my room and an DSL Internet connection, I found out I was a textbook definition.

My stomach was roiling in agony as I stood there before my mother's grave stone saying nothing so the silence weighed heavy on my heart.

As far back as I can recall we had never been the hallmark family. It had been Mom, me and Poppy, my grandfather. My strongest impression was that I was happy because I spent all my time with Poppy when mom went to school or to work. I pressed a hand against my stomach. I'd forgotten about my grandfather. I had loved Poppy. He always had a pack of gum in his pocket for me but I only got it when I asked for it like a proper gentleman. Please and thank you was important. I can't believe I forgot him. He smelled of bitter cigarillos that he smoked out on the porch of our little house.

"Long time no see." My voice was tight and low. "…Mom."

I just got the answer to my big one asked question. I didn't hate her but I was angry. Kirkpatrick validated that I had the right to be angry. Mom was so young when she got pregnant. She would have been fifteen when she had intercourse but she was sixteen when I was born. She didn't know what to do with a child and she really didn't want me. Why didn't she get an abortion? Why didn't she give me up for adoption? Poppy only had Mom. His wife had died giving birth. He had made it clear that if he could raise a child on his own, she could. He worked residential construction in the summer and I remember chasing those tall legs around in the winter as if I were a little pull toy. I was four when he disappeared from my life in a car accident.

Mom was twenty.

Twenty. Babies having babies. Mom was a single mother and now she was left alone with debts, a mortgage and a high school education. She could have dumped everything and walked away. At the very least, she could have abandoned me into the depths of social services.

"You got yourself a nice view." I closed my eyes and let out a deep sigh. It took me fifteen years to get here and I was making small talk with a chunk of stone.

"I didn't even know I was doing it but I've blamed you for everything that has gone wrong in my life for so long. If you didn't get sick. If you didn't die. If...if...if. If only you loved me." I put my hands back in my pockets. "...but you did try to love me, didn't you? Only I had his face."

After finding out that Dad wasn't my biological father, I had done a search on my birth father -- Brandon Rodriguez. I was the spitting image of him. I had even found a photo in the high school year book where he posed in his basketball uniform with his main squeeze, cheerleader Mom. He was seventeen and had been considered a rising star, a shoe in, to university on a basketball scholarship and an NBA career. What would a little white trash girl with a mixed blood baby have to offer him when greatness waited?

He was an asshole and Mom loved him so much.

"Looking at me killed you didn't it. As I grew, I looked more and more like him. By the time I was fourteen you couldn't bear to be in the same room as me anymore. I didn't understand. I couldn't see your pain because I was lost in my own." I shrugged my shoulders and let out another big sigh. "You probably didn't know it but one day Poppy got me all dressed up in my Sunday school clothes and took me over there to that great big house while you were at work. The woman took me to a bedroom that had all the toys I could ever want and said I could play with them when I lived there. Then I heard Poppy and that man yelling. Poppy was pissed. I was scared because I had never seen him so mad. He came and got me and carried me out while the woman was crying and that man was still screaming at us. Even though Poppy was mad he put me carefully in the truck in my booster seat. I remember his big hands and how rough they were but he was so gentle with me, like I was made out of bone china."

I remembered being confused and scared as his nimble fingers buckled me into my seat.

"You're not a puppy to be bought now the best in show is sterile. They wanted nothing to do with you when you were born but they want you now. You're my boy, Brant. We might not have the biggest house. We might not have the newest car but we are still richer than people like that. Family comes first. Remember that. Blood is thicker than money."

My words dried up. Poppy had been an important part of my childhood. When he died everything just went haywire. Mom married Dad in a rush. We moved out of the only house I had ever known to the one I was finally able to give to my sisters. Before Christmas that year, Emily was born. It was the best Christmas present I ever had, well, until Sarah and Tanya and Erris came home.

"Maybe I did hate you. Nothing I did was ever acknowledged. I tried hard to get good grades in school. You didn't care. You never came to any of my school events even if I was the star in the play. You never came with Dad to any of my basketball games. What was the point? So, I quit trying. You didn't care one way or the other. But then I noticed Emily copying my bad behavior and Sarah started copying her and I knew I had to smarten up. I couldn't make you love me but my baby sisters did so I had to be a role model for them."

Tears sprang to my eyes as my throat tightened unbearably. "I'm angry. I hate but I love you too. Dad loved you but I don't think you loved him the same way. Maybe what we wanted from you was something that you were incapable of providing. Maybe that Brandon

208

boy broke your trust and faith in others so much that you couldn't see that we loved you and needed you."

I let the tears stream down my face. "You failed me. These feelings I have, I'm entitled to them. But it doesn't mean I'm a horrible son. Do you understand the depths to which I've crawled to keep your daughters safe? My precious little sisters. I've walked into the den of inequity of my own free will. I've survived it because I had an underworld angel watching over me. I now kill international companies with the stroke of a keyboard. I put thousands out of work with my pinkie on the enter key."

Far off to my left a bird began squawking out a territorial warning to another winged interloper. The wind picked up and I could feel it play with my hair. Nature was alive all around me as I stood before a small rectangle of stone.

"I've been called a lot of things, Mom. The one that fits me best is monster. I might have started this path for Poppy's "blood is thicker than money" credo but what I do now is for myself, me and my new family. I live in the dark, Mom. I belong there and I have discovered that I can make people do what I want when I try."

Dr. Kirkpatrick has been pointing out my behaviors and explaining my unconscious motivations to me for years. I just shut him out or ignored him because I didn't want to deal with it. I was stuck in a playback loop of my own devising. I was comfortable in it so I didn't see any reason to change. Wilber had my back. I could rely on him to give me comfort and support. I used him. In my heart of hearts, I did love him and I worried about him, but I used his honest emotional offering to my advantage – he let me. Constantine was another kettle of fish. Denial was not in his makeup. If there was a problem, solve it by any means necessary. I had a business degree and I was presented with the opportunity to use it. Cinderella wasn't going to cut it in the head office. The Iceman was born and I took tottering steps down the road to recovery that now lead me here.

"Mom…" The heaviness in my heart lifted as if a burden had been taken away. "Unfortunate things have happened to me but I didn't court them and I've survived. I'm NOT a victim."

That classic disco song "I will survive" started playing in my head. My laughter dried my tears but it didn't do my stomach any good. I reached into my pocket to grab my ever-present antacids when I felt a sharp burning sensation hit me in the back of the neck. It was like a bee sting. I slapped it and drove whatever the hell it was deeper into my neck. Yanking it out was as if I suddenly disconnected my knees from the rest of my body. I dropped on my ass.

A dart…what was with…what?

It was getting hard to think. My fingers went numb and the piece of feather and metal tumbled to the ground beside me.

I heard quick footsteps come up the grass to stand beside me. "You seem to be in trouble. Do you need help?"

I fell over onto my side.

"Looks like you do."

Another voice spoke hard clipped words. "Target is acquired. Move in for pickup."

This voice crackled over a mike. "We've been spotted. His man is on the move."

Vision shifted between focused and unfocused as I lay on the grass. I could see Mom's stone nestled on the ground less than three feet from me but I couldn't get my body to function. Hands closed around my upper arms pulling me towards the sound of squealing tires. My feet dragged behind me as two men carried me between them. I was dumped face first to the hard floor of a dark van then it rocked as others climbed in. The door slammed shut and the van accelerated forward.

"We got him?"

"It's Constantine's right hand man." A hand yanked on the back of my head forcing my face up. "Brant 'The Iceman' Williams."

"Bag'em and tag'em." The cold bite of handcuffs snapped around my wrist then my world when dark as a black bag was forced over my

210

head and the drug from the dart dragged me into complete and utter blackness.

Chapter Ten: The Path Less Taken

Awareness swam lazily around me, brushing against me lightly enough to rock me with ethereal touches. Car movement. Hushed voices. Sharp bright light stabbing into my eyelids.

By the time, I'd truly surfaced, I was sure I was in a hell of a lot of trouble. I was confined, strapped down like a mental patient to a hospital gurney and I keenly felt the IV butterfly needle taped to the back of my hand.

What happened? My stomach had been killing me... the cemetery. Something stung me...no someone shot me full of something in my neck and now I'm here. A hospital? No. I've been kidnapped!

I was too damn weak to even pull against the cuffs or the belt across my chest and hips. My thinking was fuzzy. My mouth felt like it was stuffed full with cotton. I groaned as I tried to blink things into focus.

"Sleeping Beauty is awake." The voice was accompanied with a metallic click. Two-way radio?

I stared up at the ceiling. No, not a ceiling. There were exposed girders above me. So, I'm not in a hospital. Those men who attacked me, who were they? A rival organization? Who was stupid enough to challenge Constantine while he was at the height of his power? Better yet, why would they target me? Maybe they didn't know I've been kicked to the curb. My Wilber was a District Director in the scheme of the Organization but his territory was small compared to most. I am Constantine's executive assistant without the bedroom duties now.

My head felt like my brains were swimming and sloshing with each movement; I wanted to be sick.

Wilber... he'll be searching for me.

The pale blue curtain surrounding the bed was pulled back, and three suits walked in. Off-the-rack suits. The lead man wore a brush cut from the 50's. The one on the left was trying to imitate Crocket from Miami Vice and the one of the right looked like an accountant.

God, they were cops. Then I noticed that all three of them had spiral wires hanging from their ears. Wrong, these were the Feds that Constantine had warned me about.

"Greetings… Tell us your name." Brush Cut sat down beside the bed.

I steeled myself to resist. I wasn't going to say anything, but I heard myself answer, "Brant Ellis Williams."

"Any aliases?"

"Cinderella. Goth Boy. Ice." I could hear scratching of a pen on a note pad. I paused for a moment frowning as the accountant continued setting ink to the page.

Why am I talking to them? I know far too many dark secrets of the Organization which is why Constantine said that he wasn't ever going to let me go.

I tried to lift my hand to shade my eyes but was pulled up short by the handcuff around my wrist. The other end was snapped around the metal guardrail. Both my hands were trussed like this. There was a stabbing pain in my brain and closing my eyes didn't help. The lights were too bright.

"You drugged me." My words were slurred slightly.

"We saved your life, Mr. Williams. Bleeding ulcers, four of them. Left untreated, you would be in very serious trouble. Whatever you're involved in is not sitting well with your moral code."

I have to get out of here! If Constantine finds out the Feds have me…

I jerked weakly on the cuffs at my wrists. "I want to go home."

"Where is home, Mr. Williams?"

"Wilber."

There was a flipping of paper and the Accountant spoke clinically, "Wilber Cassius Brawden. A District head but only a minor player. He's the one who recruited Williams when he was twenty-five. Record for assault almost thirty years ago, but nothing current."

"No…"

Stop talking.

"No? Brawden isn't a minor player?" Brush cut brought my wandering attention back to him.

"Wilber didn't recruit me. I offered myself to him to save my sisters."

Shut up. Shut up! Shut up! Why can't I shut up?

I began tossing my head back and forth. I wanted to sit up. I needed to get up and go home. Wilber. Wilber was my home. I always felt safe and warm in his arms.

A sly voice sounded close to my ear. "You used to make videos for Wilber, didn't you?"

I opened my eyes and found the Don Johnson wannabe leaning on the mattress. "Yes."

"How old were you in the first one, Cinderella?" He reached out and touched my hair.

"Sixteen." I pulled my head back and turned my face away from him. Brush Cut swore and sat up straight. The look of disgust on all their faces was enough to make me try and harden my resolve not to cooperate. They'd kidnapped me from a cemetery of all places and drugged me with truth serum. I was so tired and thirsty. The bed shifted slightly as the "throwback to the eighties", who had been leaning against it, stood up. I heard the curtain being pulled back around the bed and I was left alone for a moment.

I closed my eyes. I had no sense of time. How long ago did they pull me from the cemetery? Minutes? Hours? My stomach ached but it wasn't anything like the agony from before and the back of my hand was bruised from the IV insertion that was still taped into my hand. I bruised so easily that I couldn't count on that as a marker of time. As I laid here in silence, I was aware that my stomach was rather calm. Right then I knew that I should have gone to a doctor sooner, but I was so scared of finding out I had Mom's cancer. I was going to do it tomorrow. I had to have a tomorrow to make sure that I woke up the next morning.

How sad was that? Who knew that sodium pentothal made lying to myself impossible as well?

214

The curtain rattled and the questioning began in earnest.

Good cop. Bad cop. Poor little sexually abused Brant who should cling to anyone who offered a kind word. Wisely, I kept my smirk to myself.

Wilber had faith in me and Constantine didn't suffer fools within his inner sanctum. Even though I hadn't wanted to be there, that is where I'd ended up. If I couldn't do the job, there was no doubt in my mind that I would have just disappeared. I got dragged into the lion's den but I was still standing three years later. I might have four holes from surgery in my gut but I was still standing. Constantine didn't give anyone quarter, so this meant that I had to get out of this on my own. I told Mom out there in the cemetery that I wasn't a victim. I might not be as cunning as Constantine and I wasn't as brutal as Wilber could be but when push came to shove…I was the one doing the shoving.

The Feds were trying to play me for a victim.

Brush Cut leaned in over me showing me a very concerned face. "Brawden is small potatoes. We don't need him. Our target is Augustus Constantine, II. Now, Mr. Williams, did Constantine make any videos using you?"

"No."

"How long have you been with Augustus Constantine?"

"Three years."

"We didn't know Constantine was bi-sexual until he made a rather extravagant real estate purchase for you. Do you enjoy being his lover? You do know he has a wife and children. You can never be anything more to him than a dirty little secret. You know you can never claim him as your own." Buzz Cut was trying for the sympathetic listener approach.

How stupid did they think I was?

"I'm not his lover."

"What are you then?"

"I'm just his Executive Personal Assistant."

"He bought you a penthouse condo worth 1.6 million dollars and you're just his PA? I find that hard to believe."

"That was for his convenience."

"It's your name that is listed as the owner."

"He had to have easy access."

"To you. His lover."

I was laughing. Somewhere along the line, I started laughing and I just couldn't stop. "What's so funny, Williams."

"You think I'm his lover."

"What do you think you are to him?"

"Just something to hurt. I don't want to talk to you anymore. Go away."

"Mr. Williams…Brant, you can help us get to Constantine."

"I don't want to talk to you. Go Away!" I shook my head.

"You can get even with him for what he did to you."

I looked at Buzz Cut dead in the eye, "You don't get even with Constantine."

"Now that's where you are wrong. Constantine is just a man. He's not a god. He uses fear to control everyone around him. It only takes one to stand up against a man like that, and everyone falls into line behind you. You help us. We help you. We get Constantine, we put you into witness protection. No more whoring. No more hurting. You get a brand new life."

My eyes narrowed briefly, "Liar."

"Why do you think that, Williams?"

I said nothing…which was a surprise.

How long does truth serum last?

I didn't feel compelled to keep nattering with these men.

"Gay shit. That is just fucked up." A voice sounded off to my left and 80's man raked a hand over his hair. Closing my eyes, I turned my head away from Brush Cut.

"Shut it, Conner."

Fingers gently pressed over my hand, "You are a young man, Brant. You're only thirty. It's not too late to start over. You could go somewhere else where nobody knows what they did to you. Maybe there's a chance you like girls. If you started so young making gay videos, you never got a chance to find out. You could get a wife, get married, have some kids."

I couldn't pull my hand away, strapped down as it was. I opened my eyes and matched the brown-eyed stare evenly. "I know what I want. I just got him back and I'm never losing him again."

Don Johnson flipped his hair back off his face. "We aren't going to get anything out of him."

"I said shut it, Conner. Just get out."

"You can't be alone with…"

"Get out. Get a coffee or something. Take a smoke break."

He listened as Conner stomped out of the makeshift hospital room, then I felt a thumb rub at the corner of my eye. I didn't even know I was crying.

Buzz Cut's voice turned soft and wheedling. "Look at you, Bran-flake. Look at what those men have done to you."

Bran-flake? Oh, Emily...

Well, that explained it. My stomach started acting up again with a roiling wave of agony.

"Yes, Bran-flake. Your sister told us what Wilber and Constantine did to you. What they've done to you since you were just a little kid. Sixteen years old, for fuck's sake, that's just sickening. HQ made us watch your video, Williams. We can't identify the boys who did that to you, there're too many of them and the copies we have are too digitally degraded to retrieve ID but you know who did it, don't you?"

Soft and gently finger tips brushed my bangs back off my face. "You know who it was that took your virginity. Even if you can't give us Constantine we can go after the man who took your innocence. They should be made to pay for what they did to the little kid you once were."

Kenny? He was the same age as I was and he got knifed turning tricks in an alley when I was twenty.

217

Brush Cut's voice was soft and low, whispering right into my heart. "You saved your sisters, Bran-flake. You saved them from a dreadful life. Watching all those horrible things they did to you your first time… If that had happened to those little girls… well you know that it would have broken your little sisters. You offered up your body to defend them because they were too young to defend themselves. Now, it's their turn to save you. Let them save you, Bran-flake. Let your sisters show you how much they appreciate your sacrifice."

The pain in my stomach began to creep up my esophagus. I winced and forced back a grimace.

"Bran-flake, even your body is telling you to get the hell away from those people. You owe Constantine nothing. You don't even owe him loyalty. You were forced into prostitution. You told me yourself, you're just that sadistic fucker's sex slave who also happens to know how to file. You don't have to stay with him. Help us take him down."

"No." I shook my head.

"Look at what staying with him is doing to you. You coughed up blood, Williams."

"Leave me alone."

"People disappear around Constantine."

Too many people just vanish if Constantine gets annoyed.

Buzz Cut was talking about Guy. He just disappeared. If he had been running, why didn't he take the collection monies? Constantine knew Guy was my bodyguard and only friend. He knew that his sudden mysterious disappearance would cow me quickly and he'd been right. A single finger on my breakfast tray just once, and I never tested Constantine openly again. I didn't know whose it was at the time. The big fear was that I thought it was Wilber's. It hadn't made it any easier learning that it was Guy's.

You don't challenge Constantine – ever. He finds your weaknesses and has no qualms about exploiting them. He does it in a way that only needs to be done once. He was quite effective in his methods.

My stomach gave me another sharp stab, and my heart seemed to catch fire. I tried to curl in on myself but I was strapped down too tightly, and I ended up just jerking hard on my confined wrists. I cried out in pain that blocked all possibility of comprehension of the words the man was saying out and for that, I was thankful. I didn't have to listen to his questions while suffering. I knew in the corner of the back of my mind that pain was something I relied on to make it through each day and that was not a good thing.

****

I refused to help the Feds bring charges against Augustus Constantine, II. So, they tossed my ass to the sharks in lock up. It took six weeks to get a trial date set. Once the judge had found out that I was a wealthy fuck toy, I had been denied bail as a potential flight risk. I found that absolutely hilarious. As if I was going to run. If I was going to flee, I would have run decades ago. Maybe they thought now that Constantine had a new boy toy, the obsolete model would be left twisting in the wind and dying for revenge.

After I got sent to jail I fully expected a bullet in the back of my head. People everywhere owed the Organization something. The cost of a single bullet could wipe out six months of payments on a loan and a bullet would ensure that someone with dubious ties to the head man wouldn't have the chance to betray him. Half of the time, I'd been the one sealing the deal on someone's destruction. Constantine might have killed physically, but I'd been just as bad. I murdered with the enter key and send button. I extended his terrible presence.

I hadn't expected Constantine to show up at my trial and I wasn't disappointed. I didn't even rate making the local news. In the world of crime, I was currently an unattached cog in the Organization machine. The fact that Constantine sent me his personal team of lawyers was amazing. I could only assume that Mrs. Constantine might have had some influence in his decision. The few times we had met, she had treated me rather well for being her husband's male mistress. I had even received Christmas presents from her and the children.

When the sentence was handed down, I received eighteen months in the Federal pen for obstruction. There was no mention of the kidnapping by the Federal authorities, or the use of drugs to try and force a confession or plea bargain out of me.

The guilty verdict was rather fitting, so I thought.

What I'd be walking into was just as bad as a brothel, or perhaps even worse. The clock had struck midnight, and Cinderella was forcibly escorted out of the ball. I had my client face on, along with my grey pinstripe suit, dark grey tie, with custom designed tie tack and cuff links, with the *"Breitling Chronomat"* watch, given by Mrs. Constantine last Christmas, on my wrist. I didn't look the part of a poor fucked over kid. I didn't fit the mold of a forced prostitute who needed mercy and pity from society. I deliberately cultivated the look of a high-level mobster the day of my trial. The jury found it hard to feel sympathetic for someone who had so obliviously benefited from human misery.

Dad, Emily, Sarah, Tanya and Erris were in the court house to hear the verdict. Emily broke down and wailed as I was handcuffed. She rushed forward and wrapped her arms around me.

"I didn't mean for this to happen to you, Bran-flake. I wanted you free from them. I wanted you to come back home."

I leaned in, pressing the side of my head up against hers. "Don't you ever repeat that in public *anywhere*. If they think that you are in any way involved in this, *they will kill you*. They might kill Madison. I know you mean well, Em, but don't try and help me again. You're only making things worse."

I kissed the top of her forehead the same way I used to when I tucked her in at night when she was so small and scared of the dark. I stood up straight looking down at Dad, "Keep everyone safe. Don't let all my sacrifices be in vain."

Dad dragged her back off me before the bailiffs could get to her. I heard her openly crying as they began to lead me away. Tanya and Erris were staring with confusion and pain in their eyes. They really didn't know me. I'd been out working on my back when they were going through their formative years. It might have been easier to let them believe that I had just run away when I was a kid. They might have hated me, or at least felt indifference towards a brother who had simply vanished from their lives but Emily and Dad had insisted on telling them the truth. Whoever said, 'the truth shall set you free' never had to consider the teary blue eyes of little girls who didn't know how they should feel about their brother who had sold his ass to save them from prostitution, to keep a roof over their heads and to send them to good schools. Even now I was selling my freedom to keep all of us alive. Erris opened her mouth to say something, but I turned on my heel. I didn't want my last memories of my sisters to have tear-filled eyes. I started this whole mess so they wouldn't have to live in perpetual misery.

I didn't look back into the courtroom as I was led out. Wilber never came to my trial. I'd sat in jail for those first weeks waiting for my trial date, and the only one who'd visited beside the lawyers was Loretta. The lawyers mentioned that the Feds had barred my family from coming to see me, thinking that they could break me through extended isolation. It was a healing balm to my confused heart and soul as well as my body. I had asked Loretta once if Wilber knew what was happening to me. She just pressed her hand to the thick Plexiglas window for what seemed like an epoch then nodded yes, he knew.

He just didn't care.

The agony in my heart had been worse than the pains that lingered in my stomach. They'd given me doctor's prescription, so I'd taken my meds, sat in my cell all by myself and done nothing as I waited for the trial to start.

I don't think the Feds had planned on keep me in isolation the entire time.

At first, they had tried to scare me into squealing on Constantine by releasing me into the general population. It didn't take long for word to get around that the infamous "Cinderella" was in the block and never got any visits from the Master, showing that my status had fallen and that I was up for grabs. Or so they thought. I had said, I wasn't a victim and no one was going to make me be one again.

After I started working as a loans officer, I was threatened when I had to turn down an applicant. Guy and Loretta had to save my ass that time. It was then that Wilber had someone teach me to shoot. Later, Constantine had me trained in martial arts after I got kicked in the face on a business trip in Singapore. It was after working hours but it didn't look good to have the executive PA attend the meeting with a split lip and two black eyes. Randal had taught me knife fighting because he and the other guys agreed that I was too damned pretty to be defenseless.

I remembered those lessons and only had to defend myself once. Once. This was one thing that Wilber and Constantine had agreed on in philosophy. You teach a lesson once and only once. The lesson? I was nobody's bitch.

That first night in jail had been everything I would expect it to be -- and not. I'd fully expected to get jumped. My cell that night had another newbie, a nineteen-year-old who would end up as chopped liver soon enough because he was pulling that music gangster rap attitude. He was all bravado and blow. You could smell the fear on him. Those who are truly dangerous don't need to advertise. I'd ignored his rants and had gone to sleep on the top bunk.

Four days had passed before someone had finally gotten the nerve or else the order was given to do it. To do me. To take me out of the picture. The scary part was that I'd looked forward to it. The waiting was finally over. Snake-Face Tattoo wanted a little something, something before breakfast. He'd surprised me with a punch in the face, knocking me backwards into the metal bars of an adjacent cell. If he'd had help, his accomplice could have pinned me against the bars and that would have been the end of my resistance. But he didn't and I wasn't about to allow this opportunity to get away. I'd retaliated hard and fast, just like I'd been taught. He'd looked so damned surprised when I double fisted him high in the chest, rocking him back on his heels, and followed it up with a roundhouse kick to the head. I was tall enough that I'd kicked him right in the tattoo on his face. I honestly thought I'd heard a crack in his cheek when my heel connected. He'd gone down hard in a tangle of limbs.

I hadn't kidded myself into thinking it was over, and I'd been right. Snake-Face had gotten back up with something sharp and yellow in his fist. I'd twisted my torso so the stab whooshed by, brought my elbow up connecting with his temple on the same side where my kick had broken his orbital and zygomatic bones. With my other hand, I'd wrenched his wrist, bending it down with enough force that he'd drop his weapon –the flash of yellow had been a sharpened toothbrush. Once he'd been disarmed, I'd thrown him to the cement floor, but he didn't give up. From the floor, he'd lashed out at me with his feet. He had no training to speak of, so I'd easily danced out of his reach.

His hand swept the floor to collect the toothbrush. Then he'd rushed at me like a linebacker with his arms wide and his mouth opened in a scream of rage… which had briefly turned into the absolute silence of those who are too surprised to comprehend what had happened. Use your opponent's energy against him. He thrashed on the linoleum floor clutching at the yellow handle sticking out of his eye while Snake-Face's cried in agony. The cafeteria had been quiet.

I'd thought the whole attack had been long enough to call the whole prison guard down on us, but there hadn't been even time for taunting or cheering. It was more like a two hit fight: Snake-Face had attacked; I had put him down.

Suddenly I became more than just a pretty face. End of story.

My cell mate, Blowhard, had wanted to be my bitch in exchange for protection. I'd found that absolutely hysterical. I'd pushed him off my bunk then maniacally laughed my head off. I wasn't throwing myself up as a shield for this prison boy. I had learned from my mistake with Nicholas. I had taught a lesson. I couldn't back down now. I had more at stake than just an attitude problem in this place. However, my worries were unfounded because I was moved to isolation immediately after that. I'd heard through the grapevine that Blowhard ended up as everybody's blowup doll.

Isolation gives you lots of time to reflect on your life. The choices you made. The regrets you had. After all the horror and madness and ruthlessness, I had no regrets.

I had a beautiful niece and another on the way. Ironically when I showed up at Easter after the Christmas fiasco, Roger, Emily's husband, had brought his gay hard core bondage watching brother as my surprise date. It was an experience to be fangirled all evening that ended up with a herd of chocolate bunnies wrapped in gold foil with little red bells on them. Forty-Two to be exact and twelve of them were minus the ears as promised. I could see the hopefulness in Emily's eyes as she watched over her me and her brother-in-law. I guess that was Roger's way of trying to smooth things over between us. He hadn't needed to make the effort. He had only spoken the truth.

After her talk with Wilber, Sarah had pulled up her boot straps and got down to studying. She did well enough to announce that she had earned a partial scholarship for the next semester. After dinner was done, as I got ready to leave she pulled me aside to the front hall closet. She dragged out a two-foot-tall solid chocolate rabbit to go with the ridiculous amount of baby bunnies being shoved into a laundry basket so I could take them.

"I guess we should have coordinated our efforts a little better. This one is special. Share it with Wilber." It felt good to get hugged by her. Actually, it felt damned good to get to see all of them. Since then Sarah messaged me once a week to complain about her classes and about this guy she liked in one of her lectures.

Modern technology was wonderful. All my sisters texted or sent me little videos at regular intervals now. Tanya had gotten a full scholarship starting next year and now had a part-time job at the library because she was trying to save up to buy a used car. Erris was on track to getting a basketball scholarship if she kept her academics up. She had a major growth spurt and was almost as tall as Poppy, our grandfather.

I did the right thing sixteen years ago. I did the right things now, with what I had control over. I had nothing to regret.

Suddenly I became popular with the legislative set. Constantine's lawyers dried up as soon as the gavel came down so this next batch of suits that came at me was a surprise. Sitting down in the visitor's room in the mandatory prisoner conspicuous orange jumpsuit, I watched dumbfounded as the legal counsel laid down the facts. As the sole heir and beneficiary of the Rodriguez Estate, a trust fund which had been set up by my paternal grandparents after their son passed away. Because my mother moved us right after Poppy died and married David changing our last names to Williams, leaving the Barstow maiden name moniker behind, the lawyers couldn't find us. No, not us. Mom still wasn't good enough for their deceased son. The legalese came down to providing a DNA sample for testing; and, changing my last name to Rodriquez. Only then, the trust fund would be mine.

The Rodriquez lawyers didn't know what exactly my situation was or they would have known that I wasn't going to jump at the chance to stick a cotton swab in my mouth. I already had more money than I knew what to do with. Money, even if it was earned flat on my back, was earned by my blood, sweat and tears.

"Thank you for your visit, however, I'm not the one you're looking for."

"You are the spitting image of your father, Brandon Rodriquez." One suit started.

"My Father is David Williams. Before that, my father figure was Ellis "Poppy" Barstow. Brandon Rodriquez was nothing more than a sperm donor for all the influence he had over my life."

The suit's partner started up. "Mr. Williams, you don't seem to realize that this is a substantial sum for a man in your position."

225

Eyes flicked to my orange jumpsuit.

"Describe substantial."

"$120,000." It was presented like a windfall.

I stared to laugh.

The partner suit sat up put out at my humor. "I fail to see the humor in this situation."

"My annual salary exceeds that inheritance. You want me to deny my mother for a pittance. What makes you think that I would do that? What makes you think I need an inheritance from a family that called my mother a white trash whore and her son a bastard?"

"I am sure that if Mr. Rodriquez could have located you when you were younger, your upbringing..."

I let the Iceman cometh. "We're done."

"Mr. Williams."

"Get out."

"All you have to do..."

"What part of *get out* do you not understand?"

"I can see that this may not be the appropriate time to broach the subject of inheritance. We will be back at a later date." Those suits gathered their briefcases and departed then I was shuffled back to my own cell.

My stomach began aching again. Just because Mom wasn't the doting stereotypical mother with me, doesn't mean she was horrible. That boy who bore my face tore out her heart. I don't think she ever recovered but she did love Dad in her own way and she was the hearts and cookies mother to my sisters. Money doesn't solve all the problems in the world. The Rodriguez's tried to buy me once when I was a child and tried it again from the grave.

I knew who I was. I knew what I was and I knew what I was capable of.

~~~~~~~~~

"Mr. Williams!" I glanced up and saw Constantine's prime lawyer standing at the cell door with a guard. It had been eight weeks since the arrest and I had seen neither hide nor hair of him. I thought today I was supposed to be transferred to prison.

"We're filing for a retrial. The tox screen that was mysteriously lost these past six weeks was found and shows high levels of sodium pentothal in your blood stream. That's a violation of your civil rights. Bail has been granted. You're free to go."

I just stood there and stared at him.

What?

"Mr. Williams?"

I'd been in jail for over two months. I'd just been convicted and was supposed to be transferred down to the state penitentiary later today... and now I'm free?

"Mr. Constantine has a car waiting to bring you home."

I couldn't shift gears quickly enough to keep up with the lawyer. I frowned. "I don't have a home. I sold the penthouse..."

"To take you to Mr. Brawden's."

"I can't go there." I shook my head. Out of all of this, the only thing that truly hurt me was the fact that Wilber hadn't bothered to come to visit.

"Mr. Brawden will be glad to see you. He was released from the hospital yesterday but was..."

My client face shattered. "WHAT? Hospital?"

The lawyer looked at me funny. "Mr. Brawden had a heart attack six weeks ago. He was in a coma for three weeks. Once he woke up and stabilized, he had to undergo quadruple bypass surgery. Surely, someone told you."

Coma? Wilber had been on his deathbed and no one had told me?

"No... this is the first I've heard of it."

"He's been asking for you, Mr. Williams."

And I had forsaken him. Oh, my God! I had forsaken the love of my life. All this time, I'd cut him out of my heart, and he had his own chest broken open.

"Get me out of here!"

It took hours. I had prepared myself for eighteen months of hell, but these two hours of processing to get the hell out of the legal system were pure torture. My stomach pain started up again. I hadn't eaten anything today and the peptic ulcers were getting worse. The prison doctors had given me the great news. I had this searing stomach pain, because I'd regularly used pain-killers. It had inflamed my stomach lining. So, that Fed had been partly right. Constantine had given me bleeding ulcers. Stress just aggravated it.

I hadn't known Wilber was in the hospital. Did he even know I was in jail?

Mentally, I shook my head. *Not if he is asking for me. He's probably wondering where I've been in his hour of need. Son of a bitch.*

I couldn't get out of the station fast enough. I had to sign everywhere. Sign this. Sign that. I grabbed the manila envelope and clattered down the steps of the courthouse, pausing as I noticed the black, nondescript sedan parked at the curb. Randal was loitering against a no-parking sign as he took a drag on his smoke.

He snapped to attention when he spied me and opened the back door.

"Mr. Williams."

"Enough of that, Randy," I slipped into the back.

"Nice to see you out, Brant."

"Thanks. Take me home. Please." He closed the door behind me. I ripped open the envelope and pulled out my personal effects. Money was missing out of my wallet, but my credit cards and other ID were there. I pulled out my cell phone, but the battery was long dead but there was a charger in the car. I was still scrounging through the envelope when I felt the car do a u-turn in the middle of the road and merge with westbound traffic.

"Sorry, Randy. I meant Mr. Brawden's."

I caught Randy's gaze as he flicked his eyes up into the rear-view mirror. "Mr. Constantine gave me strict instructions to bring you to the office, Brant."

The privacy partition slid closed before I could get to it. Damn it. I grabbed at the door handles. They were locked. Sonofabitch. I let out a roar and slammed my fist into the partition. It rattled, but that was it.

I was done playing Top Bitch.

I'd stabbed a man's eye out in jail for daring to touch me. Cinderella might have left the ball, but I wasn't going back to my hovel by the hearth to be treated like ashes and dirt.

My name was Brant Ellis Williams. You couldn't make the word whore out of my name because I wasn't going to let you.

Not anymore. I leaned back on the leather seat and looked out at the buildings that passed by. Not anymore.

Chapter Eleven: Unchained

Righteous anger

I had thought it was just pious mutterings to justify doing something obscene. Now that I was experiencing it, I knew it wasn't just a phrase. How dare Constantine do this? He knew. He knew that Wilber is in my heart. I may have been his mistress, but he never had my love. I didn't have to say it aloud but he knew. I damn well made sure of it.

Fuck!

Anger surged through me again. No one told me about Wilber's coma, not even Loretta. Maybe she didn't know? No, of course she would have known. Wilber ran the District. Wilber was the District. The District answered to Constantine and the only way Loretta would have withheld that piece of information was because Constantine ordered it. Therefore, Constantine fucked me over yet again.

Was he still in the hospital? No, the lawyer had said that he had been released. Wilber was at home, and he was asking for me. He was waiting for me on his sick bed.

And Constantine was standing in my way, again.

Lucas and Anthony, Constantine's personal guards, were waiting for the sedan to pull up in front of the Moda Monde Logistics building.

Why was he sending his personal security down to meet the car? Something was going on. I didn't rollover on him at court, so now he was going to make sure that I couldn't? Why would he do it here? If he were going to have me killed, it would have been easier and more plausible to have it done in jail. Just because I'd defended myself from one attacker, didn't mean that could've held my own if several ganged up on me and that would have been a nice and neat solution.

I narrowed my gaze. The only explanation I could come up with was that Constantine didn't want this pretty face fucked over by strangers. He was more of a "hands on" kind of guy and wanted to do it himself.

Lucas opened the door. Anthony gestured me forward with his arms wide as if to corral me. Internally, I sneered at them; if I were going to run, I would have taken off long before I ever heard of Augustus Constantine, II. My life had never been days of wine and roses prior to meeting the Top Man. Wilber had been a total bastard that had me shaking like a tea cup poodle when I was just a kid. He was the Master of my wellbeing until I got big enough and strong enough to stand up on my own. I wish I could say that I'd done that in my teenage years but truthfully, I'd been almost twenty six years old before I could. Wilber showed me long ago just how strong he was and that he could use that strength against me when it was needed, to defend me if required, to protect me if necessary and to love me. And that he did. He loved me.

Wilber. Cassius. Brawden.

I stalked forward heading right for the double doors of Moda Monde Logistics leaving Constantine's guards to follow. I might have had the brass balls to come to Wilber, to make myself into the fabled Cinderella of the whoring world, but if not for his guidance and care, I wouldn't have survived. Cinderella was a stupid name and a coveted title. From what I understood, that was the goal of the ambitious and desperate, to find a strong and connected patron to get your sorry ass out of the brothel circulation. Being Constantine's Cinderella wasn't all it was cracked up to be.

I had been an attitude problem on the fast track to nowhere in particular, most likely with the final destination being the local landfill. Wilber saw more than that in me. Mom had undermined everything I had ever done even if it wasn't done intentionally. I had no goals and coming to Wilber was my way of throwing away my future. I was tired of hurting and I wanted it to go away. Mom had died. Everyone was lost in their own grief and I couldn't even pretend. Wilber made it his mission to unlock the potential within me. He tempered my core so I could withstand anything the world would throw at me; even someone like Constantine. Wilber had always said that I was strong but the best part was that he made me see that I was. That was his gift to me.

Now, he was lying alone.

He was at the mercy of his enemies, and where was I? When my love needed me, where was I? In jail, then when I got out of jail and could come to him, where was I going?

I was going to see Constantine. I'd spent too much of my life at the beck and call of Constantine.

I bypassed the security checkpoint without incident. They said nothing, not because of my look of determination or my quickness of step. As far as security knew, I was the right hand of their God.

A mantra was running through my head. *Whatever Constantine wanted, Constantine got.*

I stabbed at the elevator button, but by then Lucas had caught up to me and motioned me forward toward the private elevator off to the right of the main banks of lifts.

What the hell is going on? This would take me right into Constantine's office.

I had never been allowed to enter his office directly and I only knew of a few who had that privilege.

I couldn't stand the suspense any more. "What's going on?"

"We are not at liberty to discuss this, Mr. Williams."

Shit. I was going to get a bullet between my big grey eyes.

Lucas gently, then not so gently, urged me forward into the elevator car when I balked for a moment. I staggered forward, and the elevator doors closed. I was alone. As the elevator accelerated, I felt the familiar feeling of losing your stomach. The only destination for this private car was the top floor. While I never used this elevator before, I'd seen a few men in Constantine's domain who'd never passed by my desk.

I watched the lights on the floor indicator flicker, one after the other in sequence, as the elevator lifted me higher and higher. My thoughts still raced around in my mind.

The elevator dinged me out of my thoughts and the doors opened to a carefully poised and obvious display of Familial power. Each District Head, except the one I desperately wanted to see, was there in Constantine's office, lined up on both sides starting where Constantine sat at his desk and flaring outward toward the elevator entrance like a funnel's lip. Constantine looked up and motioned me forward. I stepped out, aware that every eye was on me. I had met all the District Heads at one point or another. Most of the time, it had been behind Wilber; a few times, behind Constantine. I could read their faces easily.

Eye Candy.

Whore.

What is going on? I thought as I walked forward and gave Constantine the slight bow of the head that he so adored.

Everyone assembled was immaculately dressed. I fit in with them so seamlessly in my designer suit that I had worn for court. I had lost some weight due to my ulcers and two-month incarceration, so my clothes wasn't as fitted as perfectly as before. I needed a haircut, and desperately needed a shave because my hands were shaking with worry when I was trying to get dressed and out of count lockup.

Constantine stood up from his desk and walked around to the apex of the 'V', subtly showing that he was the power within the room as well as the hinge point of the Organization. Constantine did know how to stage things for the best effect. I doubt that I was the only one who saw this. However, I probably was the only one in the room who knew how smoothly he could arrange people without them knowing that they had been positioned. This left me face-to-face with the Head of the Organization, so I stayed behind my client face.

"Gentlemen, you have heard my opinion on this matter. The only fact here that is under scrutiny is that Mr. Williams as worked his way up through the ranks, and I mean that literally. He has cleared his family's debt through service. He has worked under Mr. Brawden's authority on the front lines, much to Mr. Ghiarbaldi's nephew's chagrin after all the ruckus he had kicked up, unfortunately for him

Mr. Williams has showed himself to be a very competent loans officer. These past few years Mr. Williams has come to work for me as a very integral part of the Organization. The fact that he has proven to be intelligent, trustworthy, and extremely loyal, even under duress has to be taken into consideration."

Constantine deliberately turned his back to me -- unprotected.

If the District Heads didn't get the apex analogy, they'd have to be idiots to miss this message. Constantine had just showed them his confidence that I had his back. Former eye candy had more trust than most of the District. I wanted to thank and curse Constantine; in simply giving me his back, I'd inherited all of Constantine's enemies to add to the ones I already had. This was a fact that couldn't have been lost on Constantine.

Bastard.

My cold eyes looked out at the five men lined up around me. Wilber was missing but that was to be expected considering how ill he was.

I could feel their gazes on me, silently re-evaluating me. I returned their cool looks with no hint of self-consciousness. I knew that Wilber had run into minor conflict over me with each of them when I'd become a loans officer.

Eye Candy doesn't get promoted. In fact, it tends to get disposed of.

My eye caught Constantine as he walked a few paces closer to the others before pushing my head further into the noose. "Loyalty in this day and age, gentlemen, is a rare and valuable commodity. Loyalty is more valuable to me than gold, and even more precious. Mr. Williams's loyalty has been tested in a court of law and he has NOT been found wanting."

I had no idea what he was up to, but it felt a whole lot like his ramming a proposal down someone's throat.

Constantine paced slowly in front of the five District Heads pausing before each of them, giving them the benefits of his wintry cat green-eyed gaze. "Each of you has been tested in different manners in your day and you have provided excellent leadership to your District and this Family. Mr. Brawden has been a solid asset to the Organization over the years and the Family takes care of our own when they are unable to care for themselves. We all know that Mr. Brawden has shunned the company of women and therefore lacks a blood heir to take over his territory. However, he has found, educated, and developed one of our brightest minds in Mr. Williams. Mr. Brawden lacks an heir in name only."

Constantine turned smartly on his heel. "So, Mr. Williams stands before you now, ready to face the final test."

I tensed. *Final Test? What the hell is going on? What is Constantine doing?*

Constantine strode toward me, caught me around the back of the neck and dragged me forward until my chest bounced off his. He brought his mouth to my ear. "Do you love Brawden, Brant?"

I tried to jerk backwards. Constantine's hold tightened, "Answer me, Brant."

"Yes. You know that I do."

"Brawden has fallen. His District is up for grabs. The wolves here have gathered. They came here today to force me into a decision. They want to slice it up between them. They don't want another District Head. No matter what happens, there will be chaos and bloodshed when they leave my office. So, the question before you now, Brant, is can you protect Brawden now that he is weak? It's do-or-die time. Can you step up and take his place? Can you protect what he has created? You know he has enemies who want his ass on a spit. To give him some time to recover in the hospital, I strongly requested a truce for the interim, but that period ends today. Can you be Brawden's successor? Or are you truly just a fuck toy?"

Constantine let me go and gestured off behind me. "Mr. Williams, now is the time to show everyone what you are made of. Family is important to the Organization. Family shares a common bond. That bond is blood."

I heard struggles and squeaks, sounds of someone being dragged up behind me.

I was glad my client face was on. *Sonofabitch.*

I turned on my heel as a man was dragged forward by Lucas and Anthony. Whoever it was, his hands were tied behind his back, and a black pillow case was over his head. His squeaks and squeals were muffled, so I could only assume that he was gagged. His clothing was ripped, showing bruising and dried blood. He was obviously behind and in collection.

"Blood binds us as a band of brothers, Mr. Williams."

I felt my insides get cold. My stomach clenched tight. The burning started once again. Finally, it clicked.

If I kill this man, and I would be protecting Wilber and the rest of his household... and myself. I'd be protecting Loretta and the rest of the staff down at the loans offices. I would also be protecting my family who had, in their desperation to save me, tried to take Constantine down.

Five years ago, I had watched a hostile takeover while standing in Wilber's shadow. Everyone with a link to that department head was swept away. There was no such thing as job security if the District Head fell. I looked up into Constantine's cat green eyes and he smirked. He knew I understood what he wanted of me.

Damn him.

I decided to play it cool, "How is Nicholas working out?"

"More work than I had expected, but then again you were the best, Mr. Williams. I will leave his training in your hands."

"Is he here?"

"Out in the antechamber."

I took a deep breath. "Call him in."

Constantine caught my eye for a moment then nodded to one of his personal guards at the door.

There were voices of protest behind both of us.

Constantine's cat eyes narrowed on me, "Explanation, Mr. Williams."

A gave him a cold smile of deliberation. "You know how I like to multitask and Nicholas is more of a straight forward sort of fellow. Like it or not, Nicholas is in the shadows and even when his debt is paid, he won't get to walk back in the light. Lay it out for him and you'll get better results."

Constantine lifted a sculpted eyebrow. "True, you seem to know what works best."

Sexual innuendo aside, I did work best when I was multitasking.

"Lucas, bring Nicholas in. You'll have to hold him, he's a little skittish."

At the signal, Anthony ripped the pillowcase off the bound man's head. He was severely beaten. His face was black and blue, and one eye was swollen shut, but the disfigurement of his face didn't fool me at all. I knew he who he was - Mr. Dulett, my first life insurance security applicant.

Mr. Dulett's eye widened and he looked around wildly as his attempts to speak grew in volume. His terror was real. His one good eye locked onto me and widened even more in fear.

The outer door opened from the front of the office, and Lucas dragged Nicholas inside. As soon as he saw everyone in the room, he stilled.

At least the little punk had the good sense to keep his mouth shut.

Lucas pulled Nicholas up beside Mr. Dulett but made sure the big boss's new mistress was facing sideways so he could see both me and Mr. Dulett.

"Mr. Williams," Constantine softly said causing my attention to turn back to him. In his hand, he held out a snub nose .38 special. "Claim your place within the Family."

I felt nothing as I took the revolver. I wasn't lying. I wasn't feeling anything at that moment. I was uncomfortably numb. I walked back towards Dulett and squatted before him. "Do you remember me, Mr. Dulett?"

He nodded. His lips were swollen and cut. Blood seeped out of the vertical slits in his lip. "I told you what would happen if you couldn't keep up with the payments. Did you at least take out your own life insurance policy?"

He nodded. He began to cry. He began to mutter something through the gag. Constantine must have made a motion behind me because Anthony wrenched the gag out of his mouth. "Thank you... thank you... my wife is..."

"I'd told you, I never wanted to see you again." The revolver was like an ingot of lead in my hand as I stood.

He nodded, shaking and leaking tears, "Everyone is healthy. Thank you for your help, Mr. Williams. I tried but I just couldn't keep up..."

His voice was cut off as I joined the Organization.

I told you, you wouldn't be able to keep them up in the first place.

Constantine returned to his position as head of the Organization in the rapid blink of an eye. "Blood has been split, gentlemen. You have heard my view on the retention of the status quo. Peace among the siblings is preferred; it's more lucrative that way and more importantly, it makes me happy. As you know, anything that makes me happy makes the Family more profitable, and that in turn makes you more profitable. Vote now: Does Mr. Williams succeed Mr. Brawden?"

One by one, they voted until there were four ayes and one nay.

"Welcome to the Family..." Constantine removed a gold and diamond ring from his finger and gestured me forward. Steadily, I held out my hand. He turned my palm over and slipped the ring on my pointer finger, just like an engagement ring, "...little brother."

I narrowed my gaze. Realizing I still had something of his in my other hand, I handed the gun back to him.

"I know how well you treat members of your family thus I know that we are in good hands." That seemed to be a dismissal for the others but Constantine's gaze ordered me to remain.

Nicholas stood frozen like a rabbit in the presence of a fox. Some blood spray had landed on his face but he wasn't aware of it, yet. It contrasted so brilliantly with his ashen face – marked by

Constantine's own personal brand. His eyes were wide and locked onto what used to be the father of Richard, Jacob, and Clarisse. His eyes snapped up from the freshly-made corpse, and he backed into Lucas trying to get away from me as I reached out and caught him by the back of the hair. His pupils were dilated with fear and terror. He had witnessed a murder.

"The glass slipper is now in your hands, Nicholas. Together, we can make it fit… or you can join Mr. Dulett."

"Please…" Nicky's voice broke with panic and fear.

I wasn't going to be swayed by his terror. He had played me once. Never again. I whispered into his ear.

"It's now or never, Nicholas. No more attitude. No more manipulation. You know what is expected of you. Are you the next Cinderella? Yes or no."

"Yes." He shook as realization of his position truly began crystallizing in his pretty brown eyes.

"Position," I ordered, softly.

Lucas let go, and Nicholas dropped down in an inelegant slump facing Constantine. His whole frame shook, but he pulled himself up, straightening his shoulders. I crossed behind him and set my body behind him. It was a better attempt. I adjusted his head then looked over at Constantine.

"I have always said you multitask well, Mr. Williams." He glanced down at Nicky's trembling shoulders but seem satisfied with it.

Once the others had filed out speaking whatever parting words they needed to both me and Constantine, Constantine asked, "Care for a drink?"

"Thank you but no. I have someplace I'd rather be as you well know." I said as I watched as Nicky bring Constantine his scotch on the rocks without being asked.

The young man's hands trembled leaving the twenty-year-old liquid millimeters away from soaking into the carpet. No doubt to save his carpet and his drink, Constantine placed his hand over

Nicky's and pulled him in close. After taking the glass, he wrapped an arm around the youth's shoulders.

"I'll send Nicholas to your house in the morning. Wilber could, undoubtedly, use something to do during the day and I'm sure that he can improve this guy's lackluster bedside manner. Wilber mastered you and look at how well you turned out. He will make a good trainer. You will be too busy securing your District to take my Nicholas in hand the way I'd hoped. Good night, Mr. Williams. Give Wilber my get well wishes."

Nicky winced slightly as Constantine gave him a hard squeeze. "Good night, Mr. Williams."

"There, see, manners are not so difficult, Nicholas. Practice makes perfect. As I said, Nicholas, Brant is the ideal. I doubt you can reach his level of expertise, but I want you to try."

I was dismissed.

Christ.

I gave Constantine his little bow then turned and headed out of the office. I should be falling apart. I should be shaking or throwing up. My ulcers are stabbing me in the stomach. Inside at the core, I was cold. I was numb. When the elevator spilled me out to the lobby, I saw Terry and Rick standing there. Their faces lit up for a moment then they saw my expressionless face and the glint of gold on my finger. They shared a glance between them that spoke volumes, even though they said nothing at all.

"Sir." Terry held the glass door open for me as I exited Moda Monde Logistics.

"I need to see Wilber."

"Yes, sir."

Shut it down. Shut everything down. You can't fall apart. Don't think of what you just did. Don't think of it. I just kept speaking to myself in a loop until the car slid to a stop outside of Wilber's house. Terry opened the car door and Mikey opened the door to the house. I don't remember mounting the stairs, but I must have climbed them because I saw Wilber up on the second floor in his master bedroom.

240

My eyes just drank him in. He looked old and frail… and so still. The only time I'd seen him so still was when he was stupidly drunk. I don't ever remember him looking so old. My last memories of him were of us together on my birthday. He was so vital and strong that he made me feel safe. He'd lost weight. He had always been a big man but he didn't run to fat and maybe that's what made him look so frail. His pallor was sallow. I just stood at the end of the bed staring at him.

Wilber has never been weak.

He was my rock.

He was my strength.

The numbness that had carried me through the meeting began to break inside me. I could feel the tears welling at the corner of my eyes. I couldn't find him during my trial because he was in the hospital… like this… alone. After all the times, he was there for me, the one time he truly needed me with him, I couldn't be there.

I lifted a hand to cover my eyes. I didn't have the right to cry and my hand had no right to shake… not after all I'd done. My throat tightened, and my nose began to run. My legs felt weak, and I lurched, shifting the bed slightly.

"Goth Boy." The whispery sound of his voice broke open the floodgates.

I just wilted to the floor at the foot of his bed and began to sob as realization seeped into my mind shredding the last vestiges of the numbness. I had shot a father of three in the head and he thanked me for it! How fucked up is that?

"Brant. Get up. Get over here." I bit my lip and sat up, brushing at my tears with the back of my hand. The fading light of day caught the gold ring as it flashed on my hand.

"Brant…" Was that a sign of disappointment in his voice or… no, it was resignation.

"You knew Constantine was going to do this?"

Wilber lay back and patted the mattress at his side. "I missed you." I stretched out on the bed carefully, trying not to shake it or rock him. He lifted his arm and draped it across my shoulders. "You have no idea how much I miss you when you are not around."

"I didn't even know you were sick. Nobody told me," I admitted with a voice that was broken and cracked with stress.

"Constantine told everyone to keep it from you. I know you realize that all this has been to test your mettle. He needed to see how you'd react if you thought everyone had abandoned you."

Smiling, he shook his head, maybe at Constantine, "He had you all those years, and he never really knew you, did he?"

I couldn't help smiling at Wilber through my tears as he lifted my hand and looked at the gold and diamond ring. "And you passed his test. You now run my District."

"I killed…"

"So, have I. So, has Constantine. So, has the Organization that you are now a part of. You have made yourself into something greater than I could have ever hoped. Even though you weep, know that I am proud of you, Brant." Wilber groaned as he twisted toward me.

"Give me a kiss then let me rest a bit. I am getting stronger, but my stamina is low."

I didn't know if he should be moving like that. I leaned over and looked Wilber in the eyes. Blinking, I met him gaze for gaze.

His body might be weak, but what did they say about the eyes? The eyes were the windows to the soul. His spirit still burned hot. Just because he was down at this moment, didn't mean that he was down forever. His thumb brushed my tears out of the corner of my right eye.

Swallowing hard as I carefully brushed his hair away from his face, I whispered, "I thought I couldn't feel anymore. Everything just got cold in my core."

I don't think I have ever seen his hair this shaggy.

"That's called the zone. Sometimes, it's called the killing zone. I'd hoped you wouldn't have it, but to survive in my world, I knew that you'd need it if you were going to take over for me." Wilber lifted his hand to my cheek.

I turned my head and leaned into it. I missed his touch. I missed his scent. I was here now. So was he.

"Brant."

I opened my eyes. "Wilber?"

"I miss your hair."

I gave him a weepy smile. I didn't need tailored suits. I didn't need a penthouse with a view. Wilber had shown me through actions that he held me dear in his heart. "I miss it, too. I'm going to grow it out again."

"Not just for me, I hope."

"For me, too. It's easier to hide in it when I get emotional. This client face is numbing me." I leaned forward and pressed my lips to his. I could see the desire for more burning in his eyes, but the flesh was weak. "I've missed you, Wilber Cassius Brawden."

His eyes were slowly closing, but opened wide at his middle name. "Where the hell did you hear that?" he growled with some of his old testiness.

"The Feds." I slid to the edge, stood up and then smoothed the covers where I had been laying. "What kind of nickname did you have as a kid? I can't see you as a Willy or a Cassie."

Wilber's lips curved up at the corners. "I'll let you get away with that because I'm tired. Those who dared to called me Brawn."

"I like it. It suits you. I'm going to stay with you here," I pulled up a wingback chair and set it beside the bed, "so you can sleep, Brawn."

His lips snarled but then curled up at the edges as he nestled back down under his covers. Healing sleep gathered him quickly. Now that the shock of seeing Wilber sick had passed, I could see some color in his cheeks. I looked at his hands. I knew they were oversized mitts. His knuckles were big and looked like they had been broken. I noticed the pale strip on his pointer finger where the match to this golden monstrosity on my hand used to sit. The torch had been passed on. I reached out and gathered his hand in my own. It tightened around my palm. I glanced up. He was sound asleep.

I held his hand as the last of the day was replaced with darkness of night.

Mikey knocked lightly and poked his head in. "Would you like dinner brought up here, sir?"

I tried to pull my hand free. Wilber's hand tightened around mine. I got the hint. I nodded to Mikey whose eyes studied Wilber's prone form. "He's calm now. Since you've been gone, he's been restless. I'm glad to have you home, Mr. Williams." The door shut quietly behind him.

I lifted Wilber's hand and pressed a kiss to the back of it.

"Don't leave me, Brant."

I looked up into his face. He appeared to be sound asleep.

"I'm not going anywhere, Brawn."

"I love you, Brant." I stilled. No, he wasn't faking. He was sleeping.

"I love you, too, Wilber."

I held his hand and rested my head against the wing of the chair. I watched him sleep with the innocence on his face that he had lost so long ago. I would pick up the slack and take over this District and even though I had been voted in, it wasn't unanimous; so, the wolves would be circling. If they thought they could carve off sections of my District to be absorbed into their own, they had another think coming. I'd had two extraordinary teachers.

Constantine showed me the ruthlessness to get what I wanted and Wilber showed me how to keep, cherish, and nurture it. I will protect what Wilber had built. I will protect Wilber.

My Wilber.

I smiled down at our clasped hands.

Why?

That's what lovers do.

Chapter Twelve: One Year Later

I carried our lunch order out to the cafe tables, nodding my thanks to Terry as he held the doors open for me. I kept from rolling my eyes as I noticed the large patio umbrella had been angled to a ridiculous slant keep the sun off my pale skin. I set the tray down, then reached up and shifted the umbrella back to upright. I really didn't need the ghostly pallor contrasting with my growing hair. I turned back to get our tray and found Wilber with it setting our places with food. I watched rather impressed as he set his vegetarian spinach wrap and vegetable soup in front of him then set the delicate china teapot down with the tiny teacup. I found it endearing to see those big hands of his handle something so precious.

"I'm not a rabbit." He caught me looking at him and groused at me.

"You're a rabbit until the doctor says your cholesterol is good," I retorted, giving him a serious frown while he set my food on the table.

Wilber snagged a fry off my plate. I stabbed him lightly in the hand with the fork I'd just picked up. The fry went flying, and a rodent with a furry tail ran up and snagged it. "What did I tell you?"

"I can't resist temptation." Wilber had a little twinkle in his eye, even as he rubbed at the four parallel wounds just above his knuckles.

Right now, we were just like a fairy tale. Jack Spratt could eat no fat; the wife could eat no lean. Wilber had high cholesterol, and with his pre-existing heart condition, I made sure he was nibbling healthily. Here I was, sitting beside him with a big bloody steak on a ciabatta bun, because I was anemic. The fries were just because.

"Brant." Wilber's voice was soft, and I looked over at him. "You are so damned beautiful."

Crap. My whole face flared beat red at the compliment. He caught my hand and raised it to his lips. He kissed my knuckles like I was a princess, ignoring the other cafe patrons. No matter how hard-assed the District viewed me, I was putty in Wilber's hands. I ducked my head and my shoulder length hair swung forward covering my cheeks.

"You know men can't be beautiful," I softly said after clearing my throat.

"Says who? Besides, who made the cover of that magazine?"

"Gus was on it, too."

Wilber's knees brushed against my own then the side of my calf. I sat up straight in surprise. Wilber nonchalantly picked at his greens. "Really? I never noticed him. Still, I got the better deal."

A woman's voice floated over to our table, "Oh, I beg to differ on that, Mr. Brawden."

Both of us turned to see the Constantines standing on the other side of the wrought-iron railing dividing the cafe from the sidewalk. Gus and Carmilla, with Lucas and Anthony in tow, were out enjoying the lingering warmth of fall. Even though this petite, raven-haired beauty handpicked me to be her husband's stress relief, I ended up liking the woman. Gus might crack the whip in the Organization, but it was amusing to see him dancing to his wife's tune.

There was movement behind them, and I saw Nicholas and own his two bodyguards approaching carrying shopping bags. He had come a long way from the brothel punk he was just a short year ago. Since the multitasking incident, Nicholas has straightened up and flies right for Wilber. He wasn't stupid. He had already gotten back up to a grade eleven level where he should have been at if the Organization had never entered in his life. There had been talk of post-secondary education if he kept it up. If Wilber had just judged a book by the cover, Nicky might have been left languishing in the brothel. Looking at this now told a story of an intern with a respectable international business. Today, he was in casual clothes, but they were quality. I looked like a slob compared to him in my jeans, white tee, and old brown sweater.

"Good afternoon, Mrs. Constantine," I said as I stood at the same time Wilber did.

"How many times have I asked you to call me Carmilla, Brant?" Her face turned up to me and her brown eyes sparkled.

"Carmilla. … Gus." Constantine gave me a little eyebrow arch. I was the only one who got away with calling him that at the office and within the Organization. To everyone else he was Mr. Constantine. "Nicholas."

"Mr. Williams. Mr. Brawden." Nicky returned quickly with proper manners.

"Honey, I'm going in to grab a latte. You want something?"

"A coffee would be good." I watched as Gus leaned over and kissed his wife.

This should be so strange: current lover, ex-lover and a wife. Gus waited until Carmilla was inside cafe before he turned back into his ass-ish self, "Brawden looks good on you."

"Don't be a dink. It's been a nice day," I sighed, shaking my head at his antics.

"It's been a nice year for you, Brant." Gus leaned over the railing.

"Annual reports are finalized?" Wilber asked as a fry disappeared into his mouth. I took my plate and pushed it to one side, far away from grubby thick fingers.

"How'd Brant do?"

"Better than you, Wilber," Gus teased. I noticed that if someone wasn't in business or working Family, Gus used his first name. It was all about respect with Constantine. If you were current part of his Family, you were a Mister. If not, you were just a working Joe.

"I actually expected your District to dip in profits mainly because of Ghiarbaldi's attempted hostile takeover. I didn't expect you to head hunt his best people, Brant."

It seems I was the exception in Constantine's world view.

Then again, I just picked up that Mr. Ghiarbaldi had dropped in status.

Interesting.

I'm sure that a few of the other District Heads were savvy but I had the 'privilege' of getting to know Constantine personally. I knew more about the bastard than I think he realized. Knowledge is power and I'd make sure he never knew I had this type of understanding of him.

I picked up my green bottle of imported water. "Treat people how you like to be treated. Apparently Ghiarbaldi didn't know the concept of respect." Constantine's eyes flashed briefly and a corner of his lip turned up. Very interesting. I now had permission to do some more expansion of my own if I wanted to. "The flip side of the coin is that they were lacking loyalty," he said.

"There can be no loyalty without respect."

"So, you respect me, Brant?" Gus leaned over the railing casually as if leaning toward a lover.

I shoved a fry in my mouth. He laughed and straightened back up. He reached up touched his hair then did a quick sweep with his eyes. "You're upsetting the status quo, Brant. The other District Heads are grumbling about the amount of territory you took from Ghiarbaldi."

"My record stands on its own merit."

"True."

"Ghiarbaldi started this. If I crumbled under his attack, would the rest of the Heads be rallying under my banner? No. We both know they would just laugh at the eye candy who'd slept his way to the top. My District has expanded because Ghiarbaldi lost the battle... it will stay expanded."

Constantine gave me a real smile. "I should have promoted you sooner. You, Brant are going to make me a very rich man."

"Share some of it with Nicholas."

"Orders, Brant?"

"A gentle suggestion. I had Wilber waiting for me. Nicholas has nothing." I shifted my gaze to look directly into his eyes, "How shall I put this delicately? ... You can be an overbearing asshole."

Constantine's face darkened, but I didn't back down. "You can break him. You have him working in your office but we both know what that means. He's just a kid. He's working with the hand the

249

world dealt him. Respect him, and I think you'd be surprised at the results."

"You are pushing it, little brother."

"I had good teachers." Wilber pressed his leg up against mine under the round cafe table in support.

Constantine glanced into the cafe. "Carmilla won't take no for an answer this year for the Christmas party. You got out of it last year because Wilber was still recovering. Trust me, you don't want to get on her bad side."

The little woman came back carrying a cardboard tray with enough coffees for everyone but she brought me tea. Constantine looked over at her, and his green eyes just seemed to soften. He truly loved his woman and his children. He just had an overly sadistic sex drive. He took the tray from her and handed her the tall cup with its corrugated sleeve. Carmilla smiled at her husband, then looked over at Wilber's healthy lunch. "Wilber, did you get the painting I sent?"

"Yes, I did. It was very beautiful. Thank you."

"Brant..." Constantine started up again.

"Augustus, we have bothered them enough. Their food will be getting cold. Nice to see you up and about, Wilber. I see that Brant is taking good care of you."

"Yes, he is."

"My office. Monday morning. My PA will call Loretta with the particulars."

As Constantine and his wife wandered off, I gave Nicholas a wave as he passed by. He nodded at me. He didn't seem to be wilting under Constantine's sexual demands even though I suspected that they were nothing like mine were when I was with him. I caught Wilber snatching another freshly cut fry. I brandished my fork in his direction but he extended his hand until the crispy fry was lightly stroking my bottom lip. The sun was warm on my flesh, but its light was nothing compared to the expression of warmth in my Wilber's eyes. I opened my mouth, and he slowly slid the fry inside. I bit down on it, closing my lips around his thick fingers. A fire burned inside

250

Wilber that burned only for me. I licked at the fingers in my mouth. Instant conflagration flared up in both of us.

The actions I've taken over this past year are things I'd never thought I was capable of, but I could lay those events at Constantine's feet like a cat bringing back its kill. He had shown me how to get what I wanted come hell or high water. Wilber showed me how to live with the consequences. I didn't need the sun to bring the light back to my eyes.

"Brant..." Wilber pulled his hand back and cupped the side of my face.

"My Love..." I felt him shift. "You touch another one of my fries I'm going to shove this fork through your hand right into the table. Eat your spinach."

Wilber grunted at me, but his hand swept over my ear before he settled back in his own chair. He scowled as he picked up his spinach wrap, but he grudgingly bit into it.

I didn't need the sun to bring me to life, I had Wilber. I would do whatever I had to keep him healthy and by my side, even if it meant getting physical. I watched his massive and scarred hands reach out and pour green tea into the small tea cup. Looking at him, you would never think that he was refined or capable of being so gentle. Not that he was a marshmallow, but with just a little bit of heat, you could make a yummy treat.

Just as he took a swallow of his tea, I rubbed his calf with the side of my leg.

I don't mind being smushed and gooey under the right circumstances, I thought while I listened to him choke on his tea.

Smiling, I picked up my steak sandwich and took a big bloody bite. He narrowed his eyes and wiped the tea from his chin. "You're going to pay for that, Goth Boy."

"I'm sure I will," I said.

In fact, I was looking forward to it.

www.ingramcontent.com/pod-product-compliance
Lightning Source LLC
Chambersburg PA
CBHW050507260626
47157CB00004B/1221